THE HOPEFUL HEARTS SERIES ◇ BOOK TWO

PERFECTLY PLACED

LIANA GEORGE

Scrivenings
PRESS
Quench your thirst for story.
www.ScriveningsPress.com

For Kayley and Abbey, my favorite daughters

Published by Scrivenings Press LLC
15 Lucky Lane
Morrilton, Arkansas 72110
https://ScriveningsPress.com

Printed in the United States of America

Paperback ISBN 978-1-64917-218-1

eBook ISBN 978-1-64917-219-8

Editors: Shannon Taylor Vannatter and K. Banks

Cover by Linda Fulkerson, www.bookmarketinggraphics.com.

ACKNOWLEDGMENTS

I thought writing a second novel would be easier than the first, but I was wrong. Very wrong. My sophomore book journey was just as exciting as my debut novel adventure, but equally as challenging. Thankfully, I had a wonderful group of people surrounding me; without them, this book would have never seen the light of day.

To my publisher, Scrivenings Press, and the fantastic team who make this story come to life: Linda Fulkerson for her beautiful cover design, Shannon Vannatter for her wise developmental edits, and last but not least, Kaci Banks for her sharp eye to correct my grammatical errors (of which there are many). Thank you, ladies! You are a dream to work with, and I am so very grateful to have your love and support.

To my mighty prayer warriors: Lisa, Lisa, Teresa, and Melanie. Knowing you have my back in the heavenly realms makes it easier to keep going on the rough days. I'm blessed by your friendship and faithfulness to me and the task.

To my hardworking launch team: Word of mouth is the best way to let others know about a book, and you all rocked it! Your efforts reached more people than I could have done alone, and my heart overflows with gratitude for each of you.

To my fantastic friends who encourage me every step of the way: Jon and Regina for reading early drafts and offering me an oceanfront view to channel my creative energy; Danielle, my laugh-o-meter, for listening to my crazy stories, so I know whether to include them in the book or not; and Kathy, for continuously checking on me and listening to me babble on about books, writing, and life.

To my right-hand woman: Erika, you have been a true gift to me, and I am blessed beyond measure for all your help and creativity to get this book out into the world!

To my writing coach: Sandra, your wisdom and guidance are invaluable, and I appreciate all you have done to make me a better writer. Our partnership has lasted across the years and miles, and I pray it continues for many more! Not only am I fortunate enough to have someone like you in my corner, but I'm also blessed to call you my friend.

To my three loves: Clint, Kayley, and Abbey, your unwavering belief in me keeps me going. Thank you for giving me the time and space I needed to write, even if it meant placing my role as wife and mother on pause at times. Although I'm a wordsmith, there are no words that can truly convey the depth of my love for each of you.

To the One who created me and called me to this amazing life and job where I get to make up stories in my head and pen words that can touch other people's hearts. May You continue to use me as a vessel to share the comments and ideas You place within me. And may You and You alone receive the glory!

1

Opportunity only knocks once.
~ Chinese Proverb

I'm not an expert on Asian culture, but here's what I know about the Chinese New Year celebrations: it's their most important holiday; each year is symbolized by an animal; it's nothing like our Western Christmas; and decorations are a must.

That last detail would explain why the lobby at New Hope Orphanage reminds me of a colorful carnival of sorts when I step back inside after being gone for six weeks. Red and gold cutouts adorn the windows, rooster posters and large banners with Chinese writing cover the peeling white paint on the walls, and globe-like lanterns spin from the ceiling. Every square inch of the usually-bland room has been transformed to pay tribute to this annual fete.

And it's a beautiful sight to behold, so much so that I'm lost in admiration when the receptionist greets me from her spot at the information desk.

"Miss Mayfield, so nice to see you."

I pull my eyes from the festive décor toward the voice

addressing me. "Thanks, I'm glad to be back." Which I am. I had been counting down the days until my return, excited by the possibilities in store for me, and this place, in the months to come. "I hope it's okay I'm here. I came straight from the airport."

"Of course. How can I help you?"

"Is Director Wu available?"

"I'm sorry." She wrinkles her nose. "Director Wu won't be back until Monday, February thirteenth, when the Chinese New Year holiday is over."

"Oh." My shoulders droop with disappointment. "What's today?" Between the long-haul travel, jetlag, and the time difference, I've lost track.

"It's Tuesday, the seventh." She peers down at her desk as if checking her calendar. "Was she expecting you?"

"No, I wasn't supposed to arrive for a few more weeks, but I took an earlier flight." I glance over my shoulder and point at the red and gold trimmings splashed across the room. "I wanted to get a glimpse of the celebrations before they ended." I turn back toward her. "And I need to start working."

"Well, Assistant Director Chang is here. Would you like to speak with her?"

While I'd be more comfortable meeting with Director Wu, I don't want to waste any time. "That would be great."

"Have a seat, and I'll see if she's available." She bows and then scurries off behind the doors that serve as a safety net from the outside world.

I retreat to the waiting area and the same rusty chairs where Ms. O'Connor and I had sat during our first visit two months ago. Little did we know then how much New Hope would change our lives. For the better.

As I plop down onto the cold metal, my stomach growls loudly. I scavenge through my bag for anything that might temporarily appease the beast within and let out a huge sigh of relief when I find a lone fortune cookie. Success! When I break the hard shell in two, crumbs dust my jeans, and a slip of paper flitters onto my lap. I toss one half of the treat into my mouth and then read the tiny blue words staring back up at me.

Opportunity knocks only once.

Although I tend to trust in Biblical proverbs more than random sayings tucked into cookies, this particular adage tugs at my heart. The truth is I only have one shot.

To restore order at New Hope.

To guarantee continued funding for the heart center and the children who live here.

To reconnect with the little girl who stole my heart.

All while the clock is ticking.

"Miss Mayfield?" The receptionist calls out, interrupting my thoughts.

I swallow the pointy pieces lodged in my throat. "Sorry, I was hungry." Standing, I tuck the other half of the cookie and its fortuitous message in my coat pocket. "Can I see the AD now?"

"I'm sorry." Frown lines crease the corners of her mouth. "The AD is occupied at the moment. You can wait for her here. I could bring you a snack if you'd like."

Tempted by her offer of food, I lower myself back onto the chair. "That would be great."

She bows and strides back toward her desk.

"Wait!" I jump back up.

Pivoting, she gives me a quizzical look.

"Could I go back to the toddler room and wait for the AD there?" I rush over to her. "I'd like to see Lei Ming for a few minutes ... if that's possible."

The young woman bites her lip and glances over her shoulder in the direction of the children's rooms. "I'm not sure if you're allowed to go back there. The AD—"

3

"Oh, it's all right. She's let me tend to the kids before, and technically I'm an employee here, so it's really not a problem."

Like the gatekeeper she is, she sizes me up as if debating whether I should be granted entry or not. Finally, her face lights up. "I guess it will be okay. Let me get you a nametag."

She promptly returns and hands me my pass.

"Thank you." I beam my gratitude, then drape the lanyard over my hair, which must resemble a bird's nest after my lengthy travels.

I waste no time crossing the dingy white tile to a second set of doors guarding the children against the outside world. As I do, a shiver of excitement courses through me. It seems like a lifetime has passed since I'd last seen Lei Ming or held her in my arms. Now I was only moments away from doing so again.

Inching closer to the toddler room, however, my heart cools. What if she'd forgotten who I was? What if she no longer wanted me to hold her or read to her? Maybe someone else had taken my place. *Please, Lord, don't let that be the case.*

I gently push open the top of the Dutch door leading to her room and peek inside. The normally busy room is dimly lit and quiet. Naptime. With bated breath, I lean against the bottom half of the door in an effort to spot Lei Ming from my long-distance position. Sensing my struggle, one of the workers rushes toward me. She taps her finger against her lips and invites me inside. I imitate her gesture and tiptoe into the room.

Anxious for a glimpse of my sleeping beauty, I snake through the rows, searching for Lei Ming. All the small bodies look identical in the dark, with their locks of black hair poking up from underneath tightly wrapped blankets. But it only takes me a few minutes to locate her.

With her long eyelashes curled over her eyelids, her thumb hanging from the edge of her mouth, and her cheeks rosy from the warm cocoon she's wrapped in, she looks exactly how I remembered. I reach down and brush my fingers over her free hand, careful not to wake her.

I'm not sure how long I hover over her crib, but I don't care either. I could spend all day here just watching her. Eventually, a tap on my shoulder indicates my time is up. I blow Lei Ming a kiss goodbye and turn to acknowledge the caretaker's dismissal. But it's not one of the workers. It's Assistant Director Chang. She points to the door and heads in the direction of the hallway.

I sneak one last look at Lei Ming before following the AD. "*Nǐ hǎo*, Ms. Chang." I survey her no-nonsense attire, the same as in our previous encounters. Dark blazer, white blouse, charcoal slacks, and flats. Her cropped hair, every strand perfectly in place, ages her more than she probably is.

"I'm surprised to see you here, Miss Mayfield." She shuts the toddler room door behind me.

"Please, call me Nicki." My eyes dart between her and the sealed-off room. "Didn't Director Wu tell you I would be returning to do some work here?"

"Yes, I heard." She purses her lips. "Only we weren't expecting you for a few more weeks."

"I was able to obtain all my paperwork faster than expected, so I took an earlier flight. I'm ready to start working."

"Then why are you *here*?" She cocks her head towards the closed door.

"I wanted to check on Lei Ming first."

"Ah, yes, the two of you formed quite a bond during your last visit, correct?"

The word *bond* grabs my attention and causes my stomach to flip. Until recently, I'd been an organizer who saw children as a nemesis to an orderly life. The last thing I'd expected was to form an attachment with one. Now I was curious to see if my and Lei Ming's bond still ran strong while I was gone.

"We did, and I was hoping to spend a few minutes with her before I started working." I reach for the door handle.

"Oh, I don't think that's a good idea." AD Chang places her hand on my arm. "Naptime can last a while, and once everyone is awake, the caretakers will have to attend to all their needs. It can get chaotic in there, so it's probably best if you try again another time ... when it's less inconvenient."

I shrink back. "O ... kay." While I don't want to interfere with the workers' care, it's probably best if I leave now anyway. I should start working on Ms. O'Connor's list, and had I stayed in there much longer, they'd need a bulldozer to get me out.

The AD offers me a faint smile. "Why don't we go to my office, and you can tell me what you'll be doing here at New Hope."

I glance back at the door, longing for another look at Lei Ming. Sensing the older woman's steely gaze on me and the fact that I don't have any power over or responsibility for this sweet child, I succumb to the AD's wishes. "Sure, that will be fine."

The quick trek to her office doesn't give me much time to think about how I will answer the questions she's bound to ask. I know my assignment. I'm just not sure yet how I'm going to execute it. That's why I came to New Hope first. I couldn't formulate a solid plan of action until arriving and completing an overall assessment of the orphanage. Once I do, I have to get to work. Three months isn't a lot of time to accomplish such a lofty —and critical—mission.

"So," the AD says as we both take a seat in her tidy office. "What exactly do you intend to do here at New Hope as Ms. O'Connor's representative?"

I pull my purse into my lap and retrieve my phone, where I've stored the long list of instructions I was given before I left the States. Scrolling through the document, I debate how much to share with the AD. It would be better, and more professional, if I spoke with Director Wu first and then let the information trickle down as needed. But it seems she's not here, so I have no choice but to fill the AD in.

"It's a detailed list, but basically, Ms. O'Connor would like me to organize all the rooms so they function more efficiently, and she'd like me to check that all the systems within the orphanage are clear and running well."

Stopping to catch my breath, I cut my eyes toward the AD, whose face is unmoved, so I continue reading. "Lastly, she'd like me to declutter, scan, and digitize all the paperwork at the orphanage for the last five years and bring it into the Twenty-first Century for easier access. The O'Connor Foundation, which we hope will oversee the funding from now on, will prefer to receive all the records in a digital format."

The AD holds out her hand. "May I see that?"

I clutch my phone against my chest. "I'd prefer to give the list to Director Wu first, and then she can fill you in as she feels necessary. I've provided the overall scope. That should be enough until the director returns."

"When you say 'paperwork' ..." Her eyes narrow. "What exactly are you referring to?"

"The documentation required for adoptions and for the treatments the children receive from the heart center, as well as just the papers to keep a place like this running—"

"So, you'd need to see all of it?"

"Yes," I say, surprised by her line of questioning. "Is that a problem?"

"No," she snaps. "I mean, we just have to take into consideration that there is a lot of private information in the paperwork, and we can't just let anyone have access to it."

"I understand that, but you have to know that if I can't do the job I was asked to do, then the orphanage, as well as the heart center, will lose its funding. I'm part of the organization now, so nothing is off-limits to me. I promise I will keep personal information strictly confidential."

"I'm fully aware that the continuation of our organization depends on us pleasing you." She folds her arms on her desk. "Of course, you'll have whatever you need."

"I appreciate that."

"Well, it sounds like you have been charged with a large task. I'd be happy to help you make speedy progress. How long do you expect it will take you to finish everything?"

"I think I can get it done fairly quickly if I have the proper support," I say. "But my deadline is the first week of May. Ms. O'Connor will submit the necessary documents to the Foundation for their meeting sometime later that month. I plan to return home after that."

"And you wanted to start today?" The AD blinks rapidly.

"I thought I'd use the time to go through all the rooms and do some needs assessments so I can get them and the storage closets in order first." I rise from my chair as proof I'm ready to work. "It shouldn't take me too long to do that."

"Why the rush?" AD Chang matches my stance.

"As I said, I'm on a tight deadline. Ms. O'Connor expects me to get started right away, and I don't want to disappoint her." I pause. "In any way."

"You are aware, Miss Mayfield, that we are still observing Chinese New Year, correct?"

My ears perk up at the mention of the well-known holiday. "Of course, the decorations are amazing."

"Then you'll understand why I must request you return once it's over to start working."

"I'm sorry, but why do I need to wait?"

"You may not realize it," she says, a hint of irritation lacing her voice. "But our country honors these fifteen days by not working unless absolutely necessary. That's why Director Wu is not here. And it seems that for you to accomplish what you've been sent here to do, you'll need her assistance with your ... long list of actions. Unfortunately, she won't be available to discuss anything until the new year celebrations are finished, which is still a few days away."

She steps closer to me, and I can make out the taut lines around her face.

"Plus," she continues, "that will give the Director and me time to discuss how we can best help you. Given Ms. O'Connor's demands and timeline, we'll need to prepare a few things before you start. I'm sure you won't mind giving us some time to ... how do you say? Get our ducks in a row?"

I consider her request. I'd hoped to hit the ground running, but as I did show up unannounced, the least I can do is give them time to prepare for my unexpected intrusion into their space.

"If you think that's best, then sure." I try to hide my disappointment.

"It is." The AD sprints toward the office door.

If I didn't know better, I'd say the woman didn't want me around any longer. I shake my head. No, I'm sure that's just brain fog and jet lag toying with my mind again. She knows I have to complete my job for her to retain hers.

A yawn escapes from my mouth as I follow her. "Oh, excuse me." I clamp my hands over my lips. "I guess I'm more tired than I realized."

"You've had quite the day, Miss Mayfield." She places her hand on my shoulder and guides me into the hallway and toward the exit. "Use the next few days to rest and recover from your long journey so you can be sharp when you return. Travel can take a lot out of you, and you'll need to be at your best for the work ahead." She pushes the glass door open for me.

"That's true." I strut back outside. "I'll look forward to seeing you and the Director Monday morn—"

"Goodbye then." She shuts the door behind me with swift precision and without further discussion.

I stare at the doors and question my quick exit. Why was the AD so anxious to have me leave? Had I offended her by keeping the task list from her? Or is there more to it?

As my driver speeds away from the orphanage, I take one last look over my shoulder at New Hope. I'm not sure what, if anything, is going on there, but I refuse to be sidetracked from fulfilling Ms. O'Connor's directives. Even by the AD. As my fortune cookie message so aptly reminded me earlier, opportunity only knocks once.

And I intend to make the most of it.

2

An old broom has its value.
~ *Chinese Proverb*

After fourteen hours of solid rest and some much-needed nourishment in my system, I decide to get my own ducks in a row. I unpack and organize all my clothes, set up my workspace, and place my mom's Bible on the bedroom dresser next to a picture of my dad. A few simple touches to make the suite Ms. O'Connor had arranged for me seem more like a true home away from home. Once I've finished all my housekeeping tasks, I call my mom.

"Nicki," she says, answering after the first ring. "Everything okay?"

I plop onto the living room couch. "I'm fine. I just finished putting my things away and getting settled in my room. Why? Are you worried?"

"Somewhat. I know you're an adult and can take care of yourself, but a mother never stops worrying about her child. You'll understand that one day when you're a parent."

"Mom." I shake my head. "You and I both know that's a long time off. Don't get your hopes up."

"Never underestimate God's plans for you, Nicki. You didn't think you'd end up in China again, but there you are." She chuckles. "Speaking of which, what are you up to today? Any excursions or activities on your agenda? You really should take advantage while you're there to absorb as much of the culture as you can."

"Yeah, I should." My eyes fall on Ms. O'Connor's list of directives lying on the coffee table. Unfortunately, my time in China isn't a personal vacation. I'm here to do a job and do it well. Nothing can fall between the cracks. For the sake of the orphanage, those kids, and my boss, I have to get it right.

"But I don't have anything lined up at the moment," I continue, "So I think I'll just take it easy and go over Ms. O'Connor's notes again to be ready to start working as soon as the holiday finishes."

"Well, that doesn't sound like much fun. You should be taking in the sights, meeting people—"

"Mom," I growl. "I didn't come halfway around the world to meet a guy and get married, I came here to ensure the future and well-being of New Hope."

"Fine," she huffs. "You can't blame me for trying." She pauses. "So, what's your plan of attack for New Hope? There's no doubt in my mind you have one."

"I do."

Warmth floods my heart at my mom's belief in me and what I'm doing, but then again, don't most parents think their child hung the moon? Knowing she'll want all the details, I spend the next thirty minutes outlining my ideas for when I return to the orphanage on Monday.

"You can do most of that organizing blindfolded, Nic. I can't imagine it will take that long, then maybe you could connect with some other expats—"

"I appreciate your confidence in me, but it's not as easy as it sounds." I push down the fear that's been festering in my stomach since I took off from LaGuardia.

"Why do I sense you're not telling me something?" she asks with the intuition only a mother could have.

I bite my lip and take a deep breath before confessing my concern. "For the most part, organizing the rooms and storage closets will be a breeze ... but the other parts—the policy and procedures, as well as the sorting, organizing, and scanning the paperwork—will prove to be more difficult." I pinch the bridge of my nose.

"Especially since I haven't heard from Julia about helping me translate it all. Ms. O'Connor had addressed her concerns about this before I left, but I assured her I had it all under control. Obviously, I don't."

"Is it strange you haven't heard from her yet?"

"It is, which worries me for several reasons." I push the negative thoughts that have been swirling through my head since I first reached out to her a few weeks ago back to the recesses of my mind. She's fine, just busy. That's all.

"I'm sure you'll hear from her soon." My mother yawns. A subtle reminder of the twelve-hour time difference between us.

"It's late, Mom. You should go to bed. We can talk later."

"Okay, dear, but don't forget what I said about meeting people. You never know what might come of it."

Shaking my head, I hang up the phone. My mother will be sorely disappointed when I come home in a few months with nothing to report.

I set my phone on the coffee table and traipse over to the large window offering an amazing view of the street below. Even though the sun is barely poking through the thick gray smog shrouding the city, the sidewalks are crammed with people milling around, and the roads are crowded with cars, bicycles, and buses.

Not what I'd expected during their holiday season. I'd assumed it would be more like the States, where a long break often offered empty streets as everyone kept their celebrations closer to home.

The familiar ding of an incoming text draws me away from my lookout. Julia? Excited at the possibility my fears might be erased soon, I race back to the living room and open my phone. Surprisingly, it's not a message from my young friend but from Zhou Longchen, the liaison from my first trip to Beijing with Ms. O'Connor. I had emailed him about my return to his motherland this week and hoped I'd be able to see him at some point over the next few months.

Glad to have you back in China. Up for an afternoon adventure? I can pick you up at 3.

Today? I should go over my game plan again but heeding my mother's advice to take advantage of my temporary downtime and socialize might be a better idea. I can always work later. Plus, opportunity only knocks once, right?

Determined to relax and enjoy myself a bit, I type out an affirmative reply. The last time I was here, Longchen introduced me to authentic Chinese cuisine, ignited my interest in Asian culture, and connected me to Julia. I can't wait to see what he has in store for me today.

I head to the lobby a few hours later, checking my phone messages as the elevator whisks me down. Still no word from Julia. While I desperately want to reach out and make sure she's okay, I know that she'll contact me when she's able. I just hope for both our sakes it's sooner rather than later.

When the doors open, Longchen stands guard in front of them, waiting to greet me.

"*Huānyíng huí dào zhōngguó*, Nicki!" He opens his arms wide, his face beaming.

I hug him. "Oh, Longchen, it's so good to see you, but I have no clue what you just said."

Pulling out of our friendly embrace, he holds me at arm's length. "It's good to see you, too, but we'll have to work on your Mandarin while you're here."

We both chuckle at the implausibility of me becoming fluent in such a short amount of time.

"I was simply welcoming you back to China." He turns and offers his arm to escort me out to the car waiting outside. "Are you ready to go?"

"Lead the way." I slip my arm into his.

During the thirty-minute journey, I badger Longchen with questions about this mysterious outing, but he kindly diverts the conversation to other topics, including Ms. O'Connor, New Hope, and what I'll be doing while I'm here. I'm flustered by his refusal to offer me any insights but catching up with him is a joy.

"Ah, we're here," he says as the Buick stops in front of a tall building, clustered among others with the same height and facade.

I exit the car and study my surroundings. It's definitely not a tourist attraction. "Where are we?" I wrap my coat around me and join Longchen on the sidewalk.

"Welcome to my home, Nicki."

"You live here?" I point to the shiny skyscraper in front of us, my eyes bulging at the sheer size of it.

"Well, my family and I occupy one of the apartments here." He winks at me. "Not the whole thing."

I laugh at my gaffe. "That's what I meant, sorry." I gaze up at the complex once more. "I just thought you were taking me to a famous site, not your home."

Longchen leads me inside through a revolving door. "I thought you might enjoy partaking in the Chinese New Year celebration with my family. You seemed so fascinated by it when we discussed it the last time you visited."

Touched by his recollection, I put my hands over my heart. "You remembered?"

"I did." His eyes sparkle as he leads me up the stairs.

The minute I step into the hallway of his floor, my senses go into overdrive. The smells of food, incense, and lingering cigarette smoke bombard my nose. My ears pick up the cacophony of voices and music blaring from each apartment. And, like everywhere else I'd seen since arriving back in China, red and gold decorations occupy every flat surface of the hall while lanterns sway from the ceilings like tiny piñatas.

He stops at a wooden door with a poster of a chunky golden cat holding up one arm in the air. "Here we are." When Longchen opens the door, an entirely new set of people, aromas, and noises explode on the scene, this time much more up close and personal.

"*Gōngxǐ fācái!*" A stream of voices greets me as we enter the apartment.

"*Nǐ hǎo.*" I wave at the mix of old and young alike before shooting a glance toward Longchen for translation.

"They are wishing you well for the new year." Longchen guides me inside his cramped home. "Come this way, Nicki."

I scan the apartment, which is sparsely furnished but overflowing with people and happiness.

Longchen whistles, and the room grows still as he introduces me to everyone in Mandarin. Thirty sets of eyes fall on me. Like a lab specimen under a microscope, I fidget under their stares and somehow eke out a tiny grin. But the joy on their faces replaces any fears or discomfort I might have. I am welcome here.

"Let me have your coat, and then I'll show you around." Longchen takes my jacket as I walk into the living room, where most of the action has resumed.

Petite, white-haired ladies lounge in chairs. Men of varying ages huddle around a card table in the corner. Younger children race around the room in jumpers while the older children carry red envelopes around, flashing crisp Chinese yuan at one another.

"So, what do you think?" Longchen asks as he passes me a warm drink.

I take the cup and sip the green tea within. "Delightful!" I look out at the crowd in front of me. "Are all these people related to you?"

"Most of them are. There's my mother on the chair next to the TV." He points at her and waves. "And I believe my son is somewhere over by the mahjong table." He cranes his neck in the direction of the men clustered together in the corner.

Even from across the room, I can see the similar features between the father and son.

"My wife is in the kitchen cooking," Longchen continues, pulling my attention back to him. "I'd take you to meet her, but no wise or right-minded person would dare go in there at the moment. Those women take their task seriously and don't like to be interrupted for anything." He chuckles. "Then there are a few neighbors, co-workers, and friends who couldn't be with their families at this time, so we have them join us. Our New Year's celebration should never be spent alone."

His words offer me the perfect opportunity to inquire about my unresponsive friend. "Speaking of friends and coworkers, did you invite Julia today too? I'm anxious to talk with her."

"I did. And Ben Carrington as well."

"Ben?" My cheeks burn at the mention of his name.

"Yes, the nice young man I introduced you to at the coffee house the last time you were here."

"I remember him."

How could I forget? Green eyes. Blond hair. Texas drawl. Oh, and a good listener too. I'd kept the email he sent me after I returned to the States on the off chance our paths might cross again during my stay here. I'd just never thought I'd be seeing him again so soon.

"I think you'll enjoy visiting with him today. Sadly, most of my family doesn't speak English, so at least you'll have someone to talk to other than me."

"And Julia," I add. "She and I have a lot of catching up to do. Between the two of them, I should be good."

"I'm afraid Julia won't be joining us today, Nicki." Longchen grimaces. "Her sister has been sick for some time and was taken to the hospital earlier this week."

Visions of Julia's twin sister, Mingyu, who has Down Syndrome, pepper my mind. "I hope it's nothing serious."

"The director of their orphanage didn't give me much information. We can only hope she'll be okay. Otherwise, Julia will be devastated."

My heart aches. Not only for Julia and her sister but for my situation as well. How could I possibly ask Julia to translate for me while she's dealing with this type of family emergency?

I couldn't possibly request her help now. Which means I'm in serious trouble.

How will I get the work done without a translator?

My scrunched-up forehead must signal to Longchen that something's wrong.

"I'm sorry, Nicki, I didn't mean to upset you. This is supposed to be a joyous occasion."

"Oh, no, Longchen, I'm okay." I plaster on the best smile I can. "I was thinking about something I needed to discuss with Julia, but it can wait." Just not long.

"Okay, good." Relief washes over his face. "I want to show you the heart of our celebration then."

We amble over to a large table where a feast fit for a king has been spread.

"Wow," I gasp. "I can't remember seeing so much food in one setting."

"Behind spending time with friends and family, Chinese New Year is all about the food." He hands me a plate and a pair of chopsticks. "Please, help yourself."

Rice, noodles, dumplings, buns, vegetables, meats, soups, and fruit cover every flat surface of the table. I set down my tea and peruse all the options. Where do I even start?

As if sensing my hesitancy, Longchen points to a platter of fluffy round balls. "Here, try this." He scoops up one and drops it onto my plate.

"What is it?" I poke at it with a chopstick.

"It's called *Tang yuan*. In English it would be translated as sticky rice ball." He pops one in his mouth. "There are all kinds of rice balls, but these are my favorites because they have a filling on the inside—either peanut butter, sesame, or red beans. Try one."

I carefully raise the ball to my mouth and take a small bite. Peanut butter flavors explode on my tongue. Not at all what I was expecting but definitely a sweet treat I could eat more of. "I like it," I tell him after swallowing it. I hungrily load six on my plate, then, realizing my mother would take just as many or more, I return three of them to the platter.

Once I've decided on a suitable amount of food to sample, I settle into a cozy spot on the couch. Various people sidle up next to me, but as Longchen predicted, the language barriers keep our chats short. I'm disappointed I can't converse with them as I'd like, but I am grateful to have been included in their festivities.

"Enjoying yourself?" Longchen joins me on the sofa after fulfilling his duty as host.

"Yes, thank you so much for inviting me." I survey the crowded space. "It's just my mom and me when there's a holiday, so it's nice to see your family having fun all together."

Longchen scans the room full of his loved ones. "I'm a blessed man, Nicki."

"You are." Pangs of jealousy stab my chest. I'm too ashamed to tell him the true reason why we don't hold fun gatherings like this at my mother's house.

Before I can elaborate, his phone dings. "Excuse me a moment." He flips open his phone and squints at the small screen. "Ben has arrived." He stands. "I'll be right back."

"Sure." I immediately primp my hair and check my breath. Since there were a lot of onions and garlic in the dishes I just ate, I dig for a breath mint and chomp on it as fast as I can.

"*Gōngxǐ fācái!*" The room erupts in prosperous greeting once more.

I look back toward the entrance, and there, towering over Longchen, is Ben. I try not to swoon over his handsome physique. He looks as good as he did a few weeks ago when I'd first laid eyes on him. Except now he's dressed in an amethyst sweater, a perfect complement to his emerald eyes, and black slacks. Not quite the boy-next-door look from the coffee house, but swoon-worthy.

If a girl were looking for a guy to swoon over, which I'm not.

I rise from my spot on the sofa and walk toward him and Longchen. "Hi, Ben. It's good to see you again."

"Hey, Nicki." He flashes a row of pearly whites at me. "I'm glad you made it back."

Goosebumps grow on my arms at the sound of his Texas drawl. I'm a sucker for a guy with an accent. "Yeah, I just arrived."

"Well, your timing's perfect. Experiencing Chinese New Year should be on everyone's bucket list. Right, Longchen?"

"I couldn't agree more." Longchen pats Ben on the back. "That's one reason why I invited her here today."

"Oh, I thought it was to see me." Ben laughs. "Regardless of the reason, I'm glad you did." His eyes fall back on me.

Taken aback by the tenderness of his stare, I shift my gaze away.

"Why don't the two of you catch up, and I'll check in with you later." Longchen bolts off, leaving us alone.

"Let me grab some food, then we can talk."

Carefully balancing his plate, Ben sits down next to me a few minutes later. "So, Nicki, as I recall, you were on an expedition last time you were in China. Did you find what you were looking for?"

"Expedition?" I furrow my eyebrows.

"Yeah, you said you were searching for something. Did you find it?" He digs into the food.

My mind drifts back to our short conversation at the coffee house when I was desperate to discover something that would keep Ms. O'Connor from shutting down the orphanage. "I guess you could say that."

He takes a bite of dumpling and swallows. "So then, what's on the agenda this visit?"

"I'm here on a new mission."

"New mission, uh? Now you've caught my interest." He taps his chopsticks together. "Please, do tell."

While Ben wolfs down the rest of his food, I share with him what Ms. O'Connor and I discovered at the orphanage and my reasons for returning.

"That's awesome." He drags a napkin across his mouth, then sets it on his lap. "Your boss and the kids at New Hope are lucky to have you."

"We'll see, but enough about me. What's going on with you?"

"I just got in myself." He sets his wiped-clean plate onto the coffee table. "I was looking for a place to live when I return home for good this summer. Can't live with my parents, you know?"

Boy, do I ever.

"You're leaving China then?"

"My teaching contract here expires in July when classes end, so it's time for me to stop running and go home."

I'm puzzled by his comment, but since I don't know him all that well, I don't pursue it. "That's right," I say instead, "you teach English at the school where Longchen volunteers."

"Yep, for the past five years."

"Five years?" My jaw drops open. "No wonder you're so good at Mandarin."

"I wouldn't go that far, but I get by." He takes a sip of water. "I can converse with my students without any problems, but I wouldn't say I'm an expert. Reading and writing have been a challenge for me."

"You're probably way better than you give yourself credit for."

His long blond bangs shake from side to side over his

forehead. "Not really, but I can get myself out of trouble if I need to."

"That's only because he's always finding ways to get into it." Longchen rejoins us and sits on the armrest. "Ben is drawn to mischief like a nail to a magnet."

"I'm completely innocent." Ben throws both his hands up in the air.

"Don't let his charm fool you, Nicki." Longchen grins. "He's a prankster, but his heart is in the right place."

My eyes dart between the two men as they continue their banter, and I can't help but admire the deep respect they have for one another.

"Nicki," Longchen says once their jesting ends, "you mentioned that you had something you needed to talk to Julia about. Is anything wrong?"

"Um, well, sort of."

"Can I be of help?" Longchen's brown eyes are filled with worry.

"I'd be happy to help too," Ben chimes in.

I smile at their concern and willingness to bail me out. "I need a translator to help me at New Hope with some of the work I have to do. I can organize easily, but I don't read Mandarin, so that's an issue." I sigh. "I planned on asking Julia if she might be available, but that's no longer a possibility. Yet it doesn't change the fact that I need help right away."

"Oh, that is a problem." Longchen ponders my words.

"Would either of you happen to be available to help me out?" While I'm not normally so direct, desperate times call for desperate measures. "Please?"

Both men look at each other and then back at me.

Longchen speaks up first. "I'm sorry, Nicki, but I'm busy facilitating tours for the next several weeks."

"School starts on Monday for me," Ben adds. "Between my day and night classes, I'm afraid I'm unavailable too."

"That's okay." I twist my mouth. It was a long shot, but at least I'd tried. "I'll figure something out."

We remain silent until Longchen's mother rises from her chair. The room grows still, and everyone turns their eyes in her direction. She spurts out some type of instruction that causes everyone to quickly gather their belongings. Clearly, when she talks, people listen.

Once the commotion dies down, Longchen fills me in on the details. "It's time for the Lion Dance, and Mother wants everyone to go, including the two of you." Like everyone else, he hustles to fulfill his mother's command.

Ben jumps off the couch, ready to bust a move. "Alright, let's go." He holds out his hand to me.

"Um, I don't think that's a good idea." I sink back in my seat.

"Sure, it is." He shakes his hips. "It's easy, and I promise I won't embarrass you."

"I see that." I chuckle at his antics. "But really, it's not you, it's me." He keeps moving, but his efforts to persuade me are useless. I don't dance. Not. At. All.

"Nice moves, son, but it's not that kind of entertainment." Longchen sidesteps Ben and hands me my coat. "We watch the professional performers dance."

I take my coat from him. "I'm sorry, Longchen I will have to pass on the Lion Dance. I need to get back to the hotel." A long yawn escapes from my lips. "Jet lag is setting back in."

Ben stops his frolicking. "You're not serious, are you?"

"I am," Longchen confirms, a twinkle in his eye.

"Me too." I quickly shift my gaze away from Ben to avoid cracking up. "Thank you for today, Longchen. This has been great, but I should get some rest and see what I can do about finding a translator."

The elderly man does his best to hide his crestfallen look, but I can see his spirits have waned. "I'm the one who should be apologizing, my dear. I should have considered you'd be tired still." He holds out his arm to escort me. "Let me take you to your car."

"No worries, Longchen." Ben steps forward, cutting him off. "I'll walk the lady out." He takes my arm and leads me toward the door.

When we get downstairs, Ben opens the car door for me like a true gentleman.

I slide inside and peek back at him. "It was nice seeing you again, Ben."

"The pleasure was all mine, Nicki." He leans against the door. "If there's anything other than reading or writing Mandarin that I can help you with, let me know." One corner of his mouth lifts in a smile. "And if you're interested in getting a behind-the-scenes glimpse of China, I'd be happy to show you around before we both head back to the States."

Touched by his kindness, I nod. "I appreciate the offer, but I'm not sure how much free time I'll have. If I can fit it in, I'd definitely take you up on that."

"Great, I'll text you." He shuts the door.

As the car swerves in and out of traffic, I lean back against the headrest and replay the day's events. Despite having to leave early, I'd enjoyed every minute of the festivities. Even spending time with Ben. He's quite the character. Plus, it's nice to have someone from back home close by. Just in case.

My joy evaporates, however, when I reflect on the predicament I now find myself in with Julia being unavailable to assist me. Not only can I not reach out to her, but I failed to recruit any help as well. It seems I'm out of options.

Which means there's only one thing left for me to do.

Please, Lord, send help soon!

3

Better to be too skeptical than to be too trusting.
~ Chinese Proverb

I arrive at New Hope on Monday morning promptly at eight. Although my prayer for help hadn't been answered yet, I decide to do what I can at the orphanage on my own. I'll just have to start with the tasks that don't require translating.

But first, to reconnect with Lei Ming.

I quickly sign in, then slip past the offices and head straight for her room. Hopefully, nothing, and no one, should stand in my way of spending quality time with her.

From the open Dutch door, I wave down one of the workers scuttling around the room. "*Zǎoshang hǎo.*" I share the good morning greeting I'd practiced all weekend.

She beams her gratitude. "*Xièxiè, nǐ yě yīyàng.*" Without another word, she shuffles off to tend to a crying child.

Taking that as my cue that it's okay for me to enter, I let myself in.

The room buzzes with activity. Several children munch on a late breakfast in highchairs while others zip around the toy area, picking things up and dropping them whenever their interest subsides. From the cribs, wails of dissatisfaction float across the room as one or two toddlers demand freedom from their temporary holding stations and the pungent odors filling their diapers.

I scan the room for the familiar face, the one whose features I had memorized by studying her photo on my phone every night for the past six weeks. Those huge chocolate brown eyes, chubby cheeks, porcelain skin, and jet-black hair are ingrained in my mind. When I spot Lei Ming by the tiny kitchenette in the corner of the room, my heart races. While every part of me wants to run and pull her into my arms, I have to be careful not to startle her. We will need a proper re-introduction before picking up where we left off.

I repeat my Chinese greeting once more, then trot over to her. She's busy "cooking" something on the stove, and while I don't want to interrupt her imaginative playtime, I can't wait any longer to reconnect with her.

My breath hitches as I stoop to her level. "Lei Ming?"

At the sound of my voice, she turns her head in my direction.

"Hi!" I wave and offer her a friendly smile. "Do you remember me?"

Her lips remain firmly shut as her big eyes size me up. I pray that her steely gaze means her brain is busy making a connection to me. A positive one.

"Hey there, sweetheart." I inch closer to her until we're almost nose to nose and stroke her hair. "Are you having fun in the kitchen?"

She stands frozen in place, her gaze laser-focused on me. I clap my hands and hold out my arms, hoping she'll fall into them, but like a statue, she doesn't move.

I make one more attempt to draw her closer before a loud cry erupts and pierces my eardrums. I wince at the shrieks her small body emits. As the crocodile tears flow down her face, a lump grows in my throat. She doesn't remember me.

Before someone can whisk her away or her cries start a chain reaction that will make me the disdain of all the workers, I pull Lei Ming into my arms.

"Shhh," I murmur into her ear while patting her back. "It's okay, sweetheart. It's just me."

She struggles to escape my embrace, so I shift to a bouncing motion like I'd seen others do to restrain and calm her down. Yet nothing seems to work. Clearly, I'm not cut out for motherhood.

Flustered, I roam around the room with her. "*Zǎoshang hǎo,*" I repeat like a broken record before reverting to my native tongue. "I'm the one who read *Spot the Dog* to you."

Since she can't understand a word I'm saying, her wails continue. For another five minutes.

When one of the workers heads in my direction, shivers nip my spine. My eyes plead with her for a little more time. She stops short of us and purses her lips before finally conceding.

"It's okay," I tell Lei Ming in a soothing tone once the threat of having her taken from me is gone. "It's been a while, but I'm sure it will all come back to you in a bit."

I cradle her hand in mine and press my lips against her forehead. Her breathing slows, and she relaxes in my arms. I exhale and pray that she's remembering who I am and not preparing to share her breakfast all over me like last time.

"See, I'm not so bad." I crane my neck back and rub my nose against hers. "I just wanted to see you and let you know that I'm back."

She hiccups and rests her head on my shoulder. With her settled in my arms, I tighten my grip around her frame, which seems lighter than the last time I held her, and nuzzle my head against her neck. The sweet smells of cereal and milk linger on her skin and clothes, perfuming the space between us. I inhale deeply as my heart fills with joy that we somehow managed to connect.

Although I need to get to work on my real purpose for being here, I twirl her around and cherish this precious bonding time.

"We're going to be together a lot, and maybe someday soon I'll even get a smile from you."

She tugs on one of my curls, and I take that as a yes.

Setting Lei Ming back on the floor, I pass her a plastic apple, which she plucks from my hands and pulls towards her mouth. I jump to remove it from her slobbery lips just as Director Wu sidles up next to me.

"I thought I'd find you in here," she says.

My gaze veers from Lei Ming to the heart and soul of the orphanage. "Director Wu, it's so good to see you!" Without asking I carefully embrace the elderly woman. Like my grandmother had, she smells like mentholatum and peppermint.

"So, when did you get back to my beloved *Zhōngguó*?" When she pulls out of our hug, her whole face lights up at the sight of me.

"Didn't AD Chang tell you I was here last week?" I knit my eyebrows together.

"No, she didn't." Her joyfulness diminishes, and the color drains from her face. "Or maybe she mentioned it, and I just forgot. My memory isn't what it used to be."

Although we laugh it off, an unsettled feeling forms in my gut. AD Chang had said she'd discuss my work projects with the director before I returned today. If she hadn't, why not? If she had, should I be concerned with the director's mental capacities? Either way, I need to find out—not just for my sake but for the future of New Hope as well. After all, I am responsible for determining if the funding should go forward.

"Shall we go to my office and talk?" Director Wu peers over my shoulder. "Or are you still busy in the kitchen?"

I spin around and watch Lei Ming. She's chatting away to herself while simultaneously banging pots on the stove. As much as I'd love to stay, I need to get busy.

"I think my sous chef can handle things for a bit."

We exit the toddler room without much fanfare and walk to her office, catching up with each other's activities since we last saw one another. She fills me in on her New Year celebrations with her family, and I share my experience at Longchen's last week.

"It was wonderful and one of the many reasons I wanted to return," I say. "I'm not sure how often I'll make it back to China after this, so I want to make the most of my opportunities before leaving."

Within minutes we arrive in her office.

"Let's hope you are blessed with many more visits." Opening the door, she gestures for me to enter.

When I do, I can't help but gasp. Her office is even more cluttered than the last time I was here. I try not to gawk while I scan the cramped space. Piles of paper cover every flat surface, and mounds of folders line the walls as if they were the only things keeping the building erect.

"Have a seat." She points to one of the two wooden chairs across from her desk before closing the door behind us. "Would you care for something to drink? Coffee? Tea? Water?"

"No, thank you." I set my purse on the floor and remove my jacket. "I'm anxious to get to work on Ms. O'Connor's list. I'm already behind schedule."

Director Wu takes a seat behind her desk. "List?"

"Yes, her contingencies for the O'Connor Foundation to continue funding, which I believe she mentioned on her previous visit." I pull my phone from my purse and scroll to the sacred text. "Didn't the AD tell you about it?"

Director Wu's eyes grow dark. "No, but I'll discuss it with her later."

"Okay." While I want to dig more into the lack of communication between the two women, I let it slide and concentrate on what I do have control over. I continue, "Please know that Ms. O'Connor appreciates all the hard work and effort you and your staff have done with the orphanage and heart center. However, she has some significant concerns she would like addressed."

I pause to let my positive words sink in before I drag in the sledgehammer of negativity. "She'd like me to target three specific areas while I'm here. One, the overall organization of the children's room. I need to ensure they are functioning properly and up to safety and modern standards. Two, update the policies and procedures for the well-being of staff and the children to avoid any liability complications."

Stopping to catch my breath, I assess her reaction to my words so far. Since she's unfazed, I proceed. "Finally, she asked that we declutter and digitize all the paperwork for the last five years, especially the financials the Foundation will need. If they continue funding New Hope, they'll require everything in a digital, easy-to-read, and readily trackable format. Ms. O'Connor wants me to handle that as well."

"That's quite the list, Nicki." Director Wu pushes back in her chair. "I think building the Great Wall was a simpler task." She chuckles and shakes her head.

"You're probably right. Believe me, I know firsthand how Ms. O'Connor's requests can be a bit overwhelming. But as a professional organizer, I'm certain I have a plan that will meet her expectations in the timeframe she's set."

"How quickly does she want the work done?" the Director asks.

"By the first of May, so roughly three months."

"Hmm, that's not much time. And with the holidays finishing, I may need a few days to get things in order before you start."

Next week? "That's kind of you, but not necessary," I tell her. "I was hoping to start right—"

The office door bursts open, and AD Chang rushes in, red-faced and out-of-breath.

"I didn't realize we were meeting this morning." She takes a seat next to me. Uninvited.

The director squints at the AD and frowns. "I assumed since you were already informed about Ms. O'Connor's requests and instructions for Nicki to complete, your presence wasn't necessary."

My eyes dart between the two women, who stare at each other with such intensity I squirm. While I don't particularly want the AD intruding in our conversation, I need to convince Director Wu to let me start working immediately, and this stand-off is only prolonging the process.

"It's not a problem, Director." I offer up a truce. "The AD is welcome to stay for our discussion." I cut a sideways glance at the AD. "As I was saying, I thought I'd start right away with an overall organization of the rooms first. There isn't much that needs to be done in them except for a few tweaks. It's the policies and procedures, as well as all the paperwork, that will take more time."

"That sounds fine, Nicki," the director chimes in. "We'll be happy to help you any way we can to ensure that you are successful and Ms. O'Connor is satisfied."

"Great, so it's okay if I start today?"

"Excuse me," AD Chang interrupts. Again. "There are a few things I'd like to say."

My head snaps in her direction. Seriously? My patience with this woman is growing thin, and it's only my first day at work. However, as a guest in this country, it's best if I keep my mouth shut. Pouring out my frustrations won't do any good.

"Is it important?" Director Wu sighs, obviously as weary as I am by the AD's obtrusion.

"Yes." The AD opens the folder that's been sitting atop her lap. "After Miss Mayfield mentioned her plans to me last week, I took it upon myself to address some of Ms. O'Connor's concerns. I've typed up a list of the organizational changes I've implemented and had the staff work on these past few days, so all Miss Mayfield needs to do is approve them."

She passes both of us a small stack of papers and continues, "As for the policy and procedures, I have each department working to update their handbooks and should have them in the next five to seven days. I'll have them translated into English so she can read and sign off on those as well."

I study her notes with consternation. It's a meticulous checklist of the tasks I envisioned myself completing over the next few weeks. As well as some I hadn't considered.

"This is impressive. I can't recall the last time you finished something in such a timely manner," Director Wu says.

AD Chang beams and bows her head. "I think Ms. O'Connor will be pleased."

"But how did you do all this?" I drop the papers into my lap.

"We Chinese are quite adept at doing what is necessary." She narrows her eyes. "Is there a problem, Miss Mayfield?"

"Yes, no ... I mean, I don't understand." I raise my voice an appropriate level without coming across as too irate. "You told me there was no working during the holidays, so how did you manage to get all of this done?"

"You must have misunderstood, and I apologize if I caused you any confusion. Perhaps my English isn't as good as I thought."

"Your English is just fine," I say sharply.

"Good." She turns her gaze back toward the Director. "With the majority of the work completed, it won't be necessary for Miss Mayfield to stay as long as she planned. Perhaps we could arrange some sightseeing activities for her? There are so many wonderful attractions here in Beijing."

I grip the edges of the papers causing them to crinkle under my tight hold. "I appreciate the AD's efforts to assist me with this project. It looks like she did a thorough job. However—"

"It wasn't a problem." The AD dismisses me with a wave of her hand. "I was happy to help. With the first two requests already underway, she and I can start on the paperwork. I've already purchased a scanner. It should be here soon."

"Wait." I hold up my hand. "When did this become a team project?"

AD Chang huffs. "I was only trying to be helpful." She looks to Director Wu with a pained expression.

"Don't get me wrong. I appreciate what you've done." I perch on the edge of my chair to stave off my growing irritation and keep myself from blurting out something I'll regret. "But it wasn't your job to do all this. Ms. O'Connor requested that *I* do it."

"Yes, but now it's done, and you can be finished here sooner rather than later," she says coyly. "You do have a deadline, don't you?"

I ignore the AD's remark and focus my attention solely on the director. "If Ms. O'Connor had wanted you and your staff to handle her agenda, she never would have sent me back here or stipulated that I was the one who was to do the job."

"I would think it wouldn't matter who does the work at this point as long as it gets done," AD Chang says. "Wouldn't you agree, Director?"

The director remains silent.

"Unfortunately, it's not up to the Director to agree or not. It's up to Ms. O'Connor," I remind them, even though the AD is right.

Considering I'm already behind, I should be grateful for her help. I'm just being territorial. What's done is done, and I need to let her have her moment to shine. Plus, her efforts will allow me to focus on the more important and most troublesome of Ms. O'Connor's tasks—the paperwork. It can be very time-consuming to deal with, and twelve weeks may not even be enough for me to get through it all. Especially if I don't hear from Julia soon.

Yet it might be in my best interests if I removed AD Chang from the equation altogether. Between Director Wu's comments and the AD's unusual behavior, something in my gut tells me not to trust her. Does she think I'm incapable? I mean, why else would she do my job for me ... unless she has something to hide.

Whatever her reasons, she's been entirely too eager to get rid of me from the moment I arrived.

"Director Wu." I break the quiet that has settled over the room. "I'm fine with the AD's assistance. Once I evaluate what she's done and find it suitable, I'll be happy to sign off on it. Going forward, however, I won't need her help."

The AD bolts from her seat. "How do you plan to translate all the documents to know how to properly organize them?"

"Yes." Director Wu leans on her desk. "How were you going to handle that?"

While I have someone in mind, Julia's not locked in to help me just yet. But I'm not going to admit that to them.

"I've arranged for a translator, so I won't need your assistance," I say to the AD. The fiery look in her eyes screams her unhappiness with my declaration. "Plus, for the O'Connor Foundation to consider New Hope as a financial recipient, the paperwork should be handled independently and not from within the organization."

"Of course, I hadn't considered that." Director Wu fingers one of the pearls on her necklace. "We'll leave the paperwork and translation in your hands then. You have full access and freedom to do what you need. Don't you agree, AD Chang?"

The AD glowers at me before addressing the director. "Fine."

"Good." The director rises from her chair, a skeptical look coloring her face. "She can start with the paperwork in your office then, and you can translate for her until her help arrives."

"What? No!" The AD steps toward the director. "I—I need some time to get things tidied up in my office. Since I was busy organizing things for her these past few days, I have neglected the space, and it's not conducive for that type of work right now." She walks backward toward the doorway. "I'll let you know when it's a good time for you to come in."

Without further discussion, she leaves, slamming the door behind her.

"I'm sorry, Nicki." Director Wu saunters around her desk,

shaking her head. "I don't know what is going on with her, but I'll look into it. She's never acted like this before."

Unsettled by Chang's reaction and hearing that it's out of character, I attempt to tamp down my worries. "I know she was just trying to help, but Ms. O'Connor was clear about her instructions. We both know how much is riding on this." A picture of Lei Ming in her kitchen flashes through my mind.

"I do," Director Wu agrees, "and I have complete confidence that you'll do a wonderful job and ensure that the children here at New Hope are well taken care of for years to come."

Standing, I blush at her words. "I appreciate that." I grab my jacket and purse. "But I should probably get busy. I'm just not sure exactly where to start now that my plans have changed." And without someone here to translate for me, there's not much I can do.

"Well, you may not be interested in my opinion, but perhaps you could begin here in my office?"

"Here?" I scan the crowded room.

"Yes, it might be a good idea to do some decluttering in here." She surveys the room. "That way, it will be easier for you and your assistant to sort and organize everything."

My stomach sags with dread. There's no doubt the Director's office is the cog in the wheelhouse of the orphanage's paperwork, but I'm not sure this is a room I want to handle right away.

From the looks of the leaning towers of yellowed manila file folders that are about to tumble, the musty smell of old paper wafting through the air, and the documents jutting out of the file cabinets looking for escape, my organizing gut tells me this room will need extra attention. In my professional opinion, it would rank on the hoarding scale; I'm just not sure to what extent.

It's also eerily reminiscent of another space I'm all too familiar with—my mom's house.

I shiver at the memory of attempting, unsuccessfully, to remove the stacks of clutter that had overtaken my childhood home. I couldn't do anything to help my mother then, nor could I now. What if working with the director yielded the same results? Disappointment like that would only hinder me from what I was sent here to do.

As I rack my brain for an excuse to offer the director, my eyes land on a collage of photos tucked in the far back corner of the room. The cheerful faces of children who had passed through here on their way to a better life returned my gaze. That's when it hits—none of this is about me.

It's about the heart center and the hope it offers.

It's about the children who, for whatever reason, have been left behind.

It's for Ms. O'Connor and the legacy she can leave one day by funding this place.

And after holding her in my arms this morning, I know it's about Lei Ming too.

Whatever personal fears I may carry are insignificant compared to New Hope's success.

I tear my watery eyes from the collage and focus on Director Wu. "I think that's a great idea." I push up the sleeves of my sweater. "Are you ready to start now?"

The elderly woman's face glows. Always a good sign.

"Let me just double-check my schedule. I don't think my first meeting is until ten." She sidesteps a box of Chinese New Year decorations and meanders back to her desk.

I cast a sideways glance over my shoulder and assess the possibilities of where we could work in that short amount of time. "We could probably knock out a few of the bookshelves and newspaper piles. What do you think, Director?"

"That sounds like a—"

Turning around to glean her thoughts, I watch in horror as she trips over a stack of file folders and crashes to the ground.

4

To be as uncomfortable as sitting on a rug of needles.
~ Chinese Proverb

Two hours. That's how long it's been since AD Chang left with the Director, and there's still no word on her condition. I pray she's okay.

While I wait and try not to worry, I've managed to stay busy. I organized some office supplies and removed the out-of-date newspapers and magazines that were hidden in every nook and cranny of the room. It hasn't made a dent in the overall chaos, but at least it's something.

If only I could read Chinese. Since AD Chang made remarkable progress on the other organizing projects, the paperwork is all that's left for me to deal with now. Without someone to decipher it, however, I'm at a standstill. I have to remedy the situation.

With trembling fingers, I tap on Ms. O'Connor's number in my list of contacts.

She answers on the first ring. "Nicki, what's wrong?"

Why does everyone keep asking me that when I call? "What makes you think something's wrong?"

"Because it's eleven o'clock at night, and we weren't scheduled to talk for another week." She breathes heavily into the phone. "Has something happened?"

I sink into the director's chair. "Director Wu had an accident."

"Is she okay? Is it serious?"

"I don't know. They took her out of here about two hours ago, and I haven't heard anything yet."

An eerie silence fills the phone line.

Finally, Ms. O'Connor speaks up. "So now what?"

"I'm not sure." I sigh. "But that's not the only thing you need to know."

"I'm listening."

I quickly share what AD Chang did behind my back, trying hard not to let the bitterness in my heart creep into my voice. "So that only leaves me with the paperwork to deal with."

"I see." She pauses. "Well, that wasn't my intent, but I guess it's probably for the best."

"What?"

"I know you're the professional organizer, Nicki, but the rooms and policy and procedures weren't my main concern. Yes, they needed to be done, but what matters most is that I have all the documentation in perfect order to submit to the board before their May meeting. Now that you don't have to worry about the other tasks, you can concentrate on the paperwork and guarantee that we have everything on time."

I rub my forehead. "I don't understand. They could easily upload the documents you want without my assistance."

"I was planning to tell you," she clears her throat, "on our call next week, but I've recently learned from the ministry that has been handling the money between my father and the orphanage that no monthly reports have been submitted by New Hope for the past six months."

"That long? How is that possible?"

"I can only assume that since my father was the sole benefactor, no one addressed it when he took ill."

"So, what does that mean?"

"I'm not certain, but it does cause me concern on many levels. Was it simply an oversight or something more nefarious? That's what I need to know."

Her words bring AD Chang to mind, but without any definitive proof, I shrug them off.

"Furthermore, The Foundation will expect those reports to be included in my submission in May. They'd be none too pleased to see missing documentation, which would not be unfavorable for the orphanage, but it could ..."

"Jeopardize their chances for continued funding." I wince at the implications this situation creates.

"Nicki," she says firmly, "we need those papers organized and to figure out where the missing reports are. Like I said, I don't know if it was just an oversight or something else, but the problem needs to be fixed." She clears her throat again. "And I don't want anyone else handling this. Only you. You're the only one I trust."

"Of course, I'll get started right away," I say.

"Good. You did find someone to assist you with the paperwork, correct?"

I consider whether to divulge my difficulty curating a translator to my boss. If I let her know that it is now a major obstacle to what she wants done, I'm not so sure she'd be pleased with me. No, I have to keep my promise. I'll figure something out. I will not admit defeat.

"I've got it under control." I hope the fear in my voice doesn't betray me.

She emits a sigh of relief. "Thank you, Nicki. I know you won't let me down."

"I won't." I squeeze my eyes shut. "I'll get working on things as soon as possible and let you know on our call next week how things are going."

After we say our goodbyes, I place my head on Director Wu's desk. How in the world will I make any progress without someone to translate for me?

I rack my brain for an answer but still end up empty-handed.

"Falling asleep on the job already, Miss Mayfield?" AD Chang's voice booms through the room from the doorway.

I pop my head up. "Of course not." I stand and trot over to her. "How's the Director?"

"Come to my office, and I'll fill you in." She peeks inside the director's cluttered space and scowls. "I avoid being in here as much as possible."

I quickly gather my things and speed off after her.

"Shut the door." She doesn't bother to look up from her work.

I do as she says, then saunter over to a wooden chair. Unlike the last time I was here, I take a few moments and assess the AD's space in more depth. Like the director's office, it suffers from the same bland décor that graces all of New Hope. However, unlike Director Wu, AD Chang keeps her office immaculate. Everything in its place and not a single dust bunny to be seen. I'm impressed.

But also confused.

"I thought you said earlier that your office was too messy for me to work in."

Her head snaps up. "What? Oh, yes, well, while I was at the hospital with the director, I called and had my secretary tidy up for me. I despise a disorganized workspace."

"I get that," I chuckle.

Scanning the room one last time, I can't help but admire her desire for order. It's a stark contrast to Director Wu's way of handling things. Is it possible the AD and I are more alike than I realize, and we just got off on the wrong foot today?

It would be beneficial for both of us if we could work amicably for these three months rather than bicker the entire time. We are adults, after all. Not that we'd need to be BFFs, but at least we could try and get along. I'd even be willing to take the first step.

From the corner of my eye, I spy a large picture frame perched on the corner of her desk. In it, a young man who resembles the AD sits in front of a lush garden backdrop.

"Is that your son?" I nod in the direction of the photo.

AD Chang shifts her attention from me to the smiling face. "Yes."

Watching her gaze upon her child, I notice the hardness in her eyes soften. Deep down, I think she does have a heart for children, especially her own, despite her rough exterior.

Maybe a compliment might be the sandpaper I need to break through it. "He's cute."

"A little young for you, though, don't you think Miss Mayfield?" She arches her eyebrow. "Or is that how marriage works in America?"

"What?" I blink. "No, I was only trying to be ..."

She tilts her head and glares at me.

"I mean, he's a nice-looking guy and all ..." I take a deep breath. "But I'm not interested in dating or getting married for that matter, right now. I have a job to do. I was just trying to make—"

"Miss Mayfield, I'm not sure you're the right type of girl for my son. He's going to become a doctor, and I doubt you'd meet his—or my—standards."

My eyes widen at her statement. So much for peace and a friendly working relationship.

Before I say something I might regret later, I change the subject. "So, the director ... was her fall serious?"

"Thankfully, no." The AD turns the photo away from my line of vision. "But it does look like she has broken a few ribs."

"Is she going to be in the hospital long?"

"They sent her home since there's not much they can do for her." She settles into her chair as if it were her throne. "However, recovery from that type of injury is slow. To make sure she doesn't overexert herself, and because of her advanced age, they put her on bed rest."

I fall back against the chair spindles, which dig into my shoulder blades, and contemplate the options this information holds. However, I can only come up with one that seems the most logical. And the least favorable. "So, she won't be returning to New Hope?"

"Not any time soon." AD Chang tents her fingers. "Which means, Miss Mayfield, I'm in charge now."

"Oh." My voice drips with disappointment at her confirmation.

"Do you have an issue with that?" She gives me a death stare.

While honesty is the best policy, in this situation, I don't think it will make much of a difference. Instead, I smile and shake my head. "Not really. I have a job to do, and I don't see how your position changes anything for me."

The muscles in her jaw flinches. "You may have a wide field to do as you please, but don't think I will allow you to have free run of the place."

"I never thought I would."

"Well, as Acting Director, I'm implementing a few rules I'll need you to follow."

"I'm sure that won't be a problem," I say through gritted teeth. While I don't like the way she's lording her new role over me, I remind myself that I am a guest in this country and need to be respectful, even if I don't feel like it. Once again, I hold my tongue.

"I'm glad you're willing to cooperate." She releases her fingers and leans against her desk. "The first rule I need you to agree to is that you will not work in my office."

I shudder. Her first rule? This isn't a military operation. But maybe that's just her style. A necessary counterbalance to Director Wu's more laid-back leadership approach. Although I'm not a fan, she has her reasons, and I'm willing to play along with her power trip. For now.

"Nor will you touch any of the paperwork in it unless I have given you permission and am present," she continues.

"I'll stay out of your office. For now." I offer her weak smile. "Once I finish in the director's office, however, I'll need access to the papers at some point. Preferably sooner than later." And especially if she is hiding something.

"I'll make sure to get you what you need."

"I appreciate that." I squirm in my seat, anxious for this conversation to be done. "Was there more?"

Her eyes narrow. "Yes, I'd also like regular updates on the work you're doing. It doesn't need to be every day but at least weekly."

"I don't answer to you. I work for Ms. O'Connor."

The AD straightens her back. "It's no secret that the Director's management style has caused a few things to slip through the cracks, resulting in your needing to return and straighten things up. But I don't run things like she does, and if you want to keep things tidy and orderly, then I need to know everything going on in this place."

I slowly process her directives, implausible as they may be.

"As a professional organizer, I would assume you could agree with me on that." She tilts her head. "Plus, we both know what the consequences could be if things become neglected again."

Unfortunately, she's right. We can't afford to let anything jeopardize the funding. Even Ms. O'Connor would agree. No matter how much I dislike and differ with her on this rule, if it ensures our work has a solid foundation moving forward, I'm willing to give her a brief update each day.

"Fine." I force the word out of my mouth.

"Good, I'm glad we see eye-to-eye on these things."

"I wouldn't go that far."

"You may not understand why I need to implement these edicts, but I can assure you it's what's best for all of us." She offers me a fake smile.

"Is that it?" A dull throb pounds in my head.

"For the time being."

I rise from the chair and head for the door. Before I try to make heads or tails of Director Wu's office and a game plan for attacking it on my own, I want to check in on Lei Ming once more, hoping that will lift my spirits. Thanks to AD Chang, they're as deflated as an old tire.

"Oh, Miss Mayfield," she says, a lilt in her voice.

I remove my hand from the door handle and close my eyes. "Yes?" I don't bother to turn around and address her directly.

"There is one more thing." She exaggerates her words on purpose. "Since you were sent here as an organizer and not as a caretaker, I'm going to insist that you refrain from going back to the children's rooms while you're here."

I spin around. "What?" I feel the heat of my anger burning in my cheeks. "Why?"

"The caretakers are complaining that your unannounced and unscheduled visits are disrupting the children's routines and upsetting them, therefore making their jobs more difficult."

"They never said anything to me or seemed bothered before."

"Of course, they wouldn't. That would be rude." She snaps. "That's why they asked me to talk to you."

"But what about Lei Ming?"

"What about her?"

"How will I be able to see her?" My heart aches at the thought of not having any contact with her on a regular basis.

"You can make arrangements with me, and I will let you know when you can visit her."

"You can't be serious." My voice rises a notch.

"As acting director, it's my job to ensure the well-being and safety of the children." She smirks. "As such, I believe it's best that you follow the protocols we have in place for outside visitors."

"But I'm not a visitor. I work here."

"True, but your responsibilities do not include being with the children."

"A mere technicality, and you know it." I narrow my eyes.

"I'm sorry, Miss Mayfield, but those are my rules. And if I remember correctly, you agreed to follow them."

My nostrils flare. How dare she throw my willingness to follow the rules in my face? I push down the fury boiling within me. I highly doubt any of the workers complained. She's just being spiteful.

If I thought the two of us were alike earlier, I was clearly mistaken. We are on opposite ends of the personality spectrum. I'm no Snow White, but she's acting like the Wicked Queen right now. And giving me more reasons not to trust her.

Considering her demand, I weigh my options. There aren't many. Although I could completely disregard her request and continue to see Lei Ming at my will, it would be wrong. Neither my faith nor my boss would allow for that. If following her instructions means time with Lei Ming then I'll do as she says. Just until Director Wu returns.

"Fine." I grind my teeth. "I'll ask for permission before going to see Lei Ming."

The curves of her mouth tilt upward. "I'm glad you're seeing things my way."

"But," I continue, "I'd like to visit Lei Ming now for a few minutes before starting my work in Director Wu's office."

She squints her eyes and squares her shoulders. I lift my chin and match her steely gaze. I may have surrendered some of my authority to her ridiculous rules, but I wasn't backing down on this. Not one bit.

She blinks. "You have five minutes."

"Twenty." I don't flinch.

"Fifteen and not one minute more."

Satisfied with my small victory, I head straight for Lei Ming.

WHEN I ARRIVE at the toddler room, the workers are busy preparing lunch. I let myself in and drop my bag at the door.

"Nǐ hǎo," the caretakers chime in unison, along with hand waves and sincere smiles.

I blush at their warm greeting, which is unexpected after AD Chang's claims about their changed attitudes toward me. Maybe she wasn't being completely honest with me.

"Nǐ hǎo."

Fei Hung, the main caretaker for this age, marches up to me and points in the direction of the cribs. I follow her guiding hand, which leads me straight to Lei Ming. I nod in appreciation.

Most of the children scurry around the play area, occupied by the toys on hand. Those confined to their cribs dawdle in their small matchbox of a bed, waiting for freedom. Lei Ming, however, just lies in hers motionless. Afraid of waking her, I tiptoe up to her bed. I peer over the edge and study her tiny frame. She looks so sweet, so fragile.

When I caress her soft, black locks, she twitches and turns in my direction.

"Hey, sweetie. Did I wake you?" I bend over the railing and pick her up.

This time she doesn't object, and I'm able to snuggle her body against mine without any fuss. Either she's remembering me, or I'm getting better at snuggling. Maybe it's a bit of both.

Warmth floods my chest as I begin to gently sway back and forth. "Did you finish working in the kitchen? It smells like you baked an apple pie for me." I chuckle, but she remains silent. I guess I still have some work to do when it comes to kid talk.

"Are you ready for lunch, then?" I whisper in her ear. "I don't think you're getting enough to eat. You seem lighter than when I was here last month."

Sensing her body go limp in my arms, I quickly pull back to see what's wrong. That's when I notice her normally sparkly eyes are dull. Almost lifeless. I tickle her tummy in an effort to arouse her, but she doesn't respond.

"Lei Ming, are you okay? You're not acting like yourself." I place my hand against her forehead like my mother used to do with me. She doesn't feel warm, but then again, I'm probably not the best person to assess a child's well-being.

Frantic, I wave at one of the caretakers, but she doesn't look in my direction.

While I race around the room in search of someone else to help me, Lei Ming lets out a yawn.

"Are you sleepy? Is that what's wrong?" I press her chest against mine and instinctively begin rocking her again.

The clock on the wall dings loudly, indicating a new hour. If it's correct, I only have seven minutes left with Lei Ming. But I can't leave her now. Not in this condition.

Uncertain of what else to do, I lower the crib and place her back onto her blanket. A light shade of blue colors Lei Ming's lips. My pulse races.

I holler at one of the caretakers, who finally waddles over to me. Unable to communicate my concern, I point to Lei Ming's discolored lips. The caretaker nods and grabs a blanket from the adjoining crib. She shivers, indicating that Lei Ming is cold, then wraps the thick covering over the little girl's body.

She turns back to me and gives me a thumbs-up before waddling off again.

Despite her positivity, my insides quiver. Something's not right. Lei Ming would be crying if she were cold, but she's not acting out at all. I raise the side rail back up and brush my hand over her forehead again. Maybe she's just tired. It's not an uncommon symptom for children with heart conditions, which so many at New Hope have.

I blow a kiss at her and race back out of the room.

I'm breathless when I knock on AD Chang's office door. No answer. I knock again. When I still get no reply, I head toward Director Wu's office to find some paper so I can leave the AD a note about Lei Ming. I don't want to risk missing her while I work in the director's space, and since she won't go in there, I need to make sure she gets the message.

When I push open the heavy wooden door, however, AD Chang is sitting at the director's desk furiously combing through her file folders.

I barge into the room. "What are you doing?"

The AD jumps and clutches her chest. "Miss Mayfield, you scared me."

"Sorry, but this was the last place I expected to find you." I inch closer to the desk. "I thought you said you didn't like being in here."

"I don't." AD Chang stands and tugs on her collar. "I was just looking for something."

"What?" I raise my left eyebrow suspiciously.

"While it's really none of your business, I—I was searching for the director's calendar." Small beads of sweat form along her upper lip. "I need to merge our schedules now that the director will be out for a while."

"You mean this?" I pick up the open planner nestled on the corner of the desk.

"Yes, that's it." She yanks it out of my hand. "With all the clutter in here, I wasn't expecting it to be out in the open." She steps out from behind the desk. "How can I help you?"

"I went to your office to talk to you about Lei Ming, but when you didn't answer, I came in here in search of some paper and a pen to leave you a note."

"Well, here I am." She grips the planner so tight her knuckles turn white. "What's wrong with Lei Ming?"

"I'm not sure, but she didn't seem herself. She was really listless, and her lips were blue."

The AD looks at her watch. "Well, it is nap time. I'm sure she was just tired."

"But fatigue doesn't explain why her lips were blue."

"It's February, Miss Mayfield." She scoots past me. "I'm sure she was cold. I doubt there's anything to worry about."

I spin around. "Can you please have her looked at by the doctor?"

"I don't think that's necessary." AD Chang frowns. "But I'll check on her again this afternoon and see how's she's doing after her nap."

"Thank you," I whisper. While I know we don't see eye to eye on other things, I want to believe that the AD truly cares about the well-being of the children.

"If that's all, I'd be happy to escort you to the exit," she says.

I bet you would.

"That's okay." I push my sweater sleeves up to my elbows. "I want to see if I can make some headway in here. I need to make the most of my time, you know."

"And what do you plan on doing?"

"I'm not sure, but I'll figure something out." I shrug. "You don't need to worry about me."

"I'm not worried, I just don't think you'll be able to do much." She surveys the room. "Until you get a translator, that is."

Knots form in my stomach at the harsh reality staring me in the face. While it wasn't much, I'd done all I could do in here earlier. Without anyone to help me interpret all the symbols on the papers, working at the orphanage is futile.

"I have a translator." I stiffen my back, refusing to accept defeat.

"I'm aware, but until he or she is physically present, I don't think it's necessary for you to return to New Hope. Since I took care of most of the items on Ms. O'Connor's list for you, there's not much else for you to do, so coming out here would be a waste of time for you and a bother for me."

While I hate to admit it, she's right. Again. Without assistance, I'm useless here. But the clock is ticking against me every day I'm not working. I can only hope and pray that a few more days won't upend things too much. "I'll go and come back when my translator is available. But I can assure you I won't be gone long and when I return, I will need full access to this office and Lei Ming."

The AD plasters an unconvincing smile on her face. "Of course."

"Now all I need is the key to this office." I hold out my hand.

"Why?" She jerks back her head.

"To make sure no one enters in here while I'm gone. I'm sure you remember the director agreeing to that earlier."

Fire glitters in her eyes. "Fine," she scoffs. She removes the key from her keyring and passes it to me. "But just remember that I'm in charge."

"How could I possibly forget when you keep reminding me?"

Without a word, she speeds past me, her lavender-infused perfume wafting in the air. I wait until the sound of her flats hitting the tile floor ceases before turning off the lights and locking the door.

When I'm back in the car, I bury my head between my hands and force back the tears. The harsh reality of my situation washes over me like a waterfall. Until I find someone to translate for me, someone I know and trust, I can't come back to New Hope.

Or Lei Ming.

I brush the tears from my cheeks and gulp down a steadying breath. With no other options, I withdraw my phone from my purse and locate the number I need. I can only hope reaching out like this won't make things worse for someone I care about.

Despite the anxiety swirling within me, I press the call button.

5

*You can't judge people by their looks; you can't measure the ocean
by a bushel.*

~ Chinese Proverb

My stomach gurgles, and I'm not sure if it's something I
ate or my nerves at reaching out to Julia, but I ignore it
and listen to the ringtone.

While I don't expect her to answer, leaving a voicemail isn't
an issue. She cares about the orphanage as much as I do, so
maybe once she hears the distress in my voice, she'll call back so
I can explain the situation and beg for her help. If that doesn't
do the trick, I'll have to ask her for recommendations. If Julia
trusts them, I can too.

"*Wéi nǐ hǎo,*" says a familiar voice as she belts out the
customary phone greeting.

"Julia," I squeal. "You answered!"

"Nicki, hi," Julia whispers. "Hold on, let me go into the
hallway."

"Of course."

Julia clears her throat before jumping back on the call. "Hi,

I'm sorry I haven't called you back or replied to your text messages. I've been busy with my sister."

"How is Mingyu? Longchen told me she wasn't well."

"Better," Julia says wearily. "She's back at Mother's Love now. We had to put her in the hospital for special breathing treatments for her asthma."

"Oh, Julia." I clutch my phone tighter. "I'm so sorry."

"Thank you. It didn't look good for a while, but she seems to be improving. I'm sure she'll be fine. At least that's what I keep telling myself." Her voice cracks. "I don't know what I'd do if I lost her. She's the only family I have."

"I may not be a good substitute for Mingyu, but you have me as a sister in the faith."

"I appreciate that." She pauses. "God is good, so I just have to trust that He's going to take care of her."

I'm touched by Julia's faith. I'm not sure I would have the courage or belief to say the same thing. My walk with God isn't that strong.

"So," she continues, "what's going on with you?"

I wrap my hand around the door handle. I don't want to lie to my good friend, but under the circumstances, I also don't want to make this about me. Yet she did ask, and I'm desperate. Without missing a beat, I quickly replay the past week's events and the grim situation I'm facing. When I finish, she's quiet on the other end of the line.

"Julia, are you still there?"

"I am. I just can't believe no reports have been submitted. I know from working at Mother's Love how important that is for financial accounting. Do you think Director Wu forgot, or do you think it's something else?"

"I'm not sure." I fidget in my seat. "That's why I've been so anxious to talk to you. I need your help, and there's just no one else I trust who is available. If there were, I wouldn't be asking you when you have so much going on."

"I'm glad you called. It's a delicate matter."

"Do you think you'll be able to help me?" I bite my lip.

"There isn't anything I wouldn't do for you ..."

Her voice trails off, and my heart pounds at her ominous words. It sounds like they're leading the way to a refusal. I hold my breath as I wait for her to continue.

"But unfortunately, I need to find some work to reimburse the orphanage for my sister's hospital stay. They've covered all the costs, but it's not their responsibility. It's mine. I wish I could help you, Nicki, but I can't. I'm sorry."

"Don't be! I completely understand." I grip the phone tighter. "I should have told you from the start that I'd be paying you to help me. Ms. O'Connor knew I would need translating assistance, so she allocated money for your services. That should solve both our problems."

She relapses back into silence, and I worry she's trying to find a way to turn me down. I give her all the space she needs in hopes she'll change her mind.

"Okay," she finally says. "I'll do it, but—"

"Oh, thank you!"

"Hold on, you didn't let me finish."

"Sorry." I clamp my hand over my mouth to avoid interrupting her again.

"Like I was saying, I'll do it, but I'll need a few days to get Mingyu settled. Maybe we can start at the end of the week?"

Four more days.

I hate to sacrifice more time, but if it means having Julia in my corner, I'm willing to wait.

"Sure, I'll pick you up Friday morning," I tell her.

When we hang up, a lightness overtakes me. Thanks to Julia, I won't have to spend the next few days wearing the carpet thin in my hotel room or chewing my fingernails down to stubs.

No, from this point on, everything will be just fine. It has to be.

AFTER FOUR LONG days of touring the capital city by myself, I wake up Friday morning energized, excited, and equipped to make a dent in Director Wu's office. And to see Lei Ming.

I devour my breakfast then head off to Mother's Love, the orphanage where my sweet friend and her sister with special needs have lived their entire lives. When I arrive, Julia's waiting outside the front doors. Puffs of cold air float around her Harry Potter glasses and up to the cute knit cap that hides her gorgeous black hair. Bundled up in a heavy down jacket and jeans, she looks much younger than her twenty years.

She quickly opens the door and slides in. "Nicki," she squeals.

"I can't believe we're together again." I wrap my arms around her neck and squeeze.

"I'm so happy you're back in China. When you left here last time, I was worried I'd never see you again."

"God works in mysterious ways, my friend."

We settle into our seats, and the driver sets off for New Hope.

"How's Mingyu?" I ask right away, not only out of concern for the young woman's well-being but to let my friend know that her sister is a priority to me.

"Much better, thanks." She removes her mittens and stuffs them in her coat pocket. "She's down to only one breathing treatment a day, so that's good news."

"I'm so glad to hear it."

"Thanks for being patient and understanding. I would much rather work with you than at a greasy-smelling restaurant." She scrunches her nose.

"You're welcome, but you're really the one saving me, you know." I chuckle. "I don't know what I would have done if you couldn't translate for me."

Julia grabs my hand, her fingers still cold from the frigid outdoors. "As I said, there isn't anything I wouldn't do to help you."

I tear up. I'm so blessed to have her as a friend and work partner.

"So," she says, "tell me what you've been up to these past few days while you were waiting for me."

As we cruise out of the concrete jungle of Beijing towards the outskirts of town, I fill Julia in about my sightseeing adventures to Tiananmen Square, Forbidden City, and Summer Palace.

"Wow, that's a lot in a short amount of time. I don't think there's much more I could show you once we're done working."

"Sadly, I'm not sure when or if I'll be able to play the tourist again anytime soon. There's so much to be done, Julia." I blow out my lips. "I'm just praying all the drama is over and we can focus on getting the papers Ms. O'Connor needs without any more problems or distractions."

She cranes her neck over the front seat. "Well, we're here, so I guess we'll find out."

Once we've registered and cleared the lobby, we head straight for Director Wu's office. I slide the key into the lock and open the door. "Feel free to look around. I'm going to find out when I can check on Lei Ming, and then we can get started."

Julia nods and moves into the room. "Oh. My. Goodness." She halts at the entry and takes in the disorganized room.

"Yeah, there's a lot of paper in here for us to deal with." I lean over the doorframe. "Everything needs to be sorted, organized, and digitized by May first. You can't tell, but I even did a little bit of work in here the other day."

Julia gasps. "Do you seriously think we can get all that done and locate the necessary documents for the foundation by the deadline?"

"If it takes us working in here every day until May, I'm willing to do it. Too much is riding on this."

"I'm not sure how ..." She loosens the rainbow-colored scarf fashionably coiled around her neck. "But between your skills, my Mandarin, and God's help, we'll get it done."

My heart bursts with love for this wise and faithful woman. "You're absolutely right, so let me figure out when I can see Lei Ming, and we'll get started."

When I arrive at the AD's office, the dark crack under the door tells me she's not there. I'm anxious to see how Lei Ming is doing, and while I could just trot down there and check in on her, I'd said I didn't want any more issues. If I were to visit outside of AD Chang's approved times, I'd create enough drama for my own Shakespearean tragedy.

Deflated, I retreat to Director Wu's office, where I find Julia knee-deep in papers.

"Nicki, there's a lot of stuff in here." She holds up her hands, full of assorted documents spread out like a fan.

"Tell me something I don't already know." I remove my jacket, pull my curls into a messy bun, and join Julia. We work for three hours straight, looking at each sheet of paper, determining the years and contents, and sorting everything into like groups. Although we only need to present the Foundation with paperwork from the last five years, everything is so intermixed that we don't have any choice but to look through all of it to find what we need.

"Can we take a break?" Julia asks. "My eyes are getting blurry."

I look up from the box I'm rifling through. "Sure. What time is it?"

"One-thirty." She carefully stands up from the mangled mess and wipes the back of her pants. "I'm hungry."

"Your request is my command." I chuckle.

We grab the sandwich boxes I'd brought from the hotel and have lunch. Weary from our work, neither of us is up for chit-chat.

"Nicki." Julia takes a long slurp of her soda before tossing her trash into the bin. "I know earlier I said we'd get this done, but we've been in here for hours and only made it through three boxes."

"I didn't realize these boxes were full of paper too, but I guess it's to be expected." I shiver, thinking about how similar Director Wu and my mom are. "People who suffer from hoarding will use every possible space they can find so they won't have to let go of anything."

"Why do you think she kept all of this?"

"There's a multitude of reasons why a person hoards." I close up my lunch box. "Fear of needing the item someday, not wanting to be wasteful, the security of having the item 'just in case,' or simple attachment. It's hard to pinpoint."

As I rattle off the various explanations my former clients would offer when we attempted to declutter their stuff, I once again consider the eerie similarities the director shares with my mom. Maybe once everything is in order in a few weeks, I can talk with the director more about it. I may not have been able to save my mother, but maybe I can help her.

"That's so sad!" Julia shakes her head. "I guess it doesn't bother you as much since you work in these types of situations all the time."

I tightly twist my napkin around my finger. While I trust Julia completely, I've never shared with her the truth about my business failure or my mother's issues. I will in time but not now. We need to stay focused on the task at hand and not bring up old wounds. That will only hinder our efforts—or at least mine—and I can't let personal issues interfere with my work.

A knock on the door keeps me from having to worry about baring my soul.

"Nǐ hǎo." The receptionist from the front desk stands in the doorway. She makes eye contact with Julia.

I take that as a sign that she wants to speak in Mandarin, not English, so I stay seated and silent.

"Nǐ hǎo." Julia rises to greet her.

The two carry on for a few minutes before Julia stops and turns to me. "She says that the scanner won't be here until the end of next week. Bad weather caused a delay."

I exhale harder and deeper than I intend to. "Okay, well, that doesn't help." I slam down my soda can with a thud. "I thought I could start scanning while you kept sorting. That will definitely slow us down."

"She assures me it will be here next week," Julia confirms. "Is there anything else you want me to ask her?"

"No ... Oh, wait," I jump up from my chair. "Can you ask her where AD Chang is or when she'll be back?"

Julia nods and inquires about the AD's whereabouts. After a few more minutes of chatting, the receptionist leaves, and Julia fills me in. "She said AD Chang was in a meeting then got called out by the doctor."

"Doctor?" My heart races. "Did she say why the doctor wanted to talk with her? Is it Lei Ming?"

"She didn't say, but that doesn't mean anything is wrong with her. There are tons of sick kids here, remember?"

"You're right. I'm sure Lei Ming is fine." Or at least I hope she is.

"Exactly." She clears the last remains of our lunch from the desk. "Let's get back to work. That will help keep your mind off things."

We work for four more hours, and when our brains and bodies can't take anymore, we call it a day. "I need to use the restroom," Julia says as I gather my belongings. "I'll meet you out front in the lobby."

"Sure, I'll text the driver and let him know we're ready." I unearth my phone from my purse for the first time all day and unlock it. Fifteen emails vie for my attention, but I'm only concerned with two—one from Ms. O'Connor and one from *texasbbguy*, also known as Ben.

I debate which one to open first. Both are a surprise, but I click on my boss's email given the current status of our workload.

Nicki,

I know we have a teleconference scheduled for tomorrow, but I wanted to make you aware of a situation so you can be prepared to discuss it on our call.

The Foundation has moved submission deadlines to May 1. They need more time to consider the large number of submissions they're already receiving, so I'll need all the paperwork from you by early April at the latest.

While this is a detriment to our timeline and to me, I have complete confidence that you will manage to find a way to get it done.

I hope this email gives you some time to strategize before we talk.

I switch over to my calendar and count the weeks.

Six.

Half the time I had initially allotted to get the job done. I study the shambled mess in front of me. How are we possibly going to get through all of this and the AD's office in only six weeks? The only answer that comes to mind is a daily commitment to the job until it's done. There's no other solution. I'll just let Ms. O'Connor know that and assure her once more that she can count on me.

With that issue resolved, I tap on Ben's email.

Hey, Nicki,

Sorry I wasn't able to reach out to you earlier. School has been crazy busy this week! Anyway, I was wondering if you might be able to meet me Sunday morning at ten o'clock? I'd like to see you again.

Ben

He wants to hang out? While it would be fun to spend time with him, considering the email I just received about the Foundation's deadline changes, I don't think it's a good idea. Once I've handed off everything to Ms. O'Connor. But not until then.

Firm in my decision, I type out a quick email declining his invitation. Before hitting the send button, however, I read what I wrote and cringe. My short and tactful reply sounds like I'm corresponding with a business associate rather than the adventurous and gracious guy he is.

No, responding by email is a cop-out. I need to meet with him on Sunday and explain the situation face-to-face. It's the least I can do. Once I have, then Julia and I can head over to New Hope and get to work.

I quickly delete everything and re-write my message.

Ben,

Sounds great. I'm looking forward to it. Where should I meet you?

I WAKE up Sunday morning to loud claps of thunder and heavy raindrops pelting my bedroom window. Every part of me wants to stay in bed and snuggle under the covers with a good book until it's time to head to the orphanage, but I'd promised Ben I'd be at the mystery location he'd chosen, and I always keep my word.

Despite the massive downpour and the havoc it wreaks on Beijing traffic, I make it to the address Ben asked me to meet him fifteen minutes early. When the elevator comes to a halt on the eighth floor, I step into a hallway. A mix of fresh coffee and muffled voices float in the air toward me, so I gravitate in their direction.

60

As I round the corner, I spot a large banner that reads *Welcome to International Fellowship Church*. Under it, twenty or so Westerners juggle steaming Styrofoam cups in one hand and Bibles in the other.

I slap my palm to my head. Ben wasn't interested in hanging out with me. He invited me to church!

Chuckling at my woefully wrong assumption, I watch as the cheerful gang of well-wishers trickles through a large set of double doors. A feeling of home floods my spirit, filling my eyes with tears. I'd been so busy worrying about work and all the demands that came with it that I'd completely forgotten to inquire about an English-speaking church I could visit during my stay. I'd read they existed, yet I hadn't taken any measures to locate one.

I scan the hall for Ben's familiar shaggy blond hair and towering frame, but I don't see him. After a few fruitless minutes of searching, I decide to do the next best thing in order to connect with him. I follow the crowd into the worship center, certain they'll lead me to him.

A pretty young blonde with ocean blue eyes greets me at the entrance of the doors. "Hi," she says with an accent that sounds just like Ben's. "Is this your first time at International Fellowship?" She hands me a service bulletin.

I take the paper from her. "Um, yeah, it is."

"Welcome. We're glad you're joining us this morning. My name is Shelby." She clutches the stack of bulletins against her chest. "Are you new to Beijing?"

"I'm Nicki." I shuffle to the side so others can bypass me. "Yes, a little over a week ago."

"Oh, you're a fish," she cackles, causing the few freckles dotting her nose to stand out.

A fish? Like in the soup? Is she joking? Since I don't know what to say about her remark I keep my mouth shut.

"Sorry." She shakes her head, allowing her silky mane to cascade over her shoulders and scent the air with her coconut shampoo. "That's what we called newbies back home in college. It's short for freshman or someone new to campus."

"That's funny," I say, relieved that it describes someone's status and not their looks. "Then yes, I'm definitely a fish."

"So, how did you find us so quickly?" She regains her composure. "It took me a month or so to learn about IFC when I first arrived from the States."

"Ben Carrington invited me."

Her eyebrows rise to the top of her forehead. "You're a friend of Ben's?"

Perhaps "friend" is a little strong for the amount of time I'd actually spent with him. "Acquaintance" might be a more appropriate term to use under the circumstances.

"Well, let me help you find him." She lays the papers down next to the coffee canisters. "We're always together, so I know where he is."

Before I can accept or refuse her offer, she bolts through the doors. I hesitate for a moment, letting my mind noodle on the emphasis Shelby placed on the word together. Was she trying to tell me something about her relationship to Ben, or was I assuming things again? I don't want to create trouble for myself either way, so I chase after her.

She abruptly stops at the end of the long, center aisle. "There he is, Vicki."

Vicki? "Nicki," I correct her before locating Ben huddled with a small group of people praying at the side of the stage. My pulse races at the sight of him in a pair of dark jeans and a button-down polo. While it's not as sharp as the look he donned at Longchen's, he's still just as dashing. And something about his prayer posture gives him an aura of authenticity I've rarely seen before.

Not wanting to intrude on their sacred moment, I take the time to survey my surroundings. The large banquet room has been transformed into a makeshift worship center with a stage upfront and rows of chairs divided into two sections. Westerners mill around the space visiting with one another or searching for places to sit. It isn't much different than church back home except for the wide variety of languages drifting throughout the room. From the lack of Chinese locals, I take it this church only allows foreigners to attend.

"Amen." The prayer group lifts their heads and disbands.

I turn my attention back to Ben and meet his eyes, which crinkle in the corners from the wide smile plastered across his face.

"Ben, Vicki was looking for you." Shelby bats her long eyelashes at him when he joins us.

Nicki, Nicki, Nicki. It really isn't that hard.

"You made it," he says, his eyes shining. "I was worried you might have problems getting here with the bad weather."

I pat my hair at the mention of the damp weather. Curly hair and rain are not a pretty combination. "Traffic wasn't an issue. Thanks for inviting me." I skim the room again. "From your text, I wasn't sure what to expect, but I'm glad to know there's a church I can attend while I'm here for the short term."

"Yeah." He scratches the back of his head. "China and church don't always mix, so I thought I'd keep my text on the vague side."

"So." Shelby steps between us. "How do you two know each other?"

"Longchen introduced us a few weeks ago," Ben says without taking his eyes off me.

"Oh, how nice of him." A hint of sarcasm peppers her words.

I peel my eyes away from Ben and focus on Shelby. "You know Longchen?" I'm surprised by her knowledge of the elderly man.

"Yes, Ben and I teach at the same school." She inches closer to Ben.

"I had no idea." I raise an eyebrow at Ben.

He offers me a sheepish smile, then quickly lowers his head and inspects the floor.

"Well, Vicki—"

"Nicki," Ben and I say in unison.

"Sorry. Nicki," Shelby apologizes as the band starts to play. "Why don't we sit over here?" She points to some empty chairs in the first row. "That way, we can get a good view of Ben while he preaches."

My head snaps back towards Ben. "You're preaching?"

The music crescendos, and the crowd claps along to the beat.

Ben leans in closer to me. "While the church searches for a full-time pastor, some of the congregants are filling in temporarily. The guy scheduled to preach got called in to work, so they asked me to be the sacrificial lamb," he laughs. "You'll be okay down here by yourself, right?"

"No need to worry about me." I inhale his woodsy aftershave. "I'll be fine."

"I have no doubt you can hold your own." He winks at me and then darts off toward the stage.

Like a volcano, a loud chorus of voices erupts without warning, and I take that as my cue to follow Shelby to our seats. Singing along to the familiar songs that I'd heard on the radio back home or sung at my own church, my mind mulls over Ben's announcement that he'd be giving the sermon. I never thought of Ben as a preacher.

Of course, after working with Ms. O'Connor, I discovered you shouldn't make assumptions about people until getting to know them first. Sadly, I'm just not sure how much time I'll be able to spend with Ben so I can learn more about him. I think we'd be good friends, given the chance.

After twenty minutes of praise and worship, the crowd sits, and Ben emerges from the shadows and onto the stage. He jumps right into his sermon on how nothing is impossible with God, dazzling the crowd with fascinating stories and deep theological insights. Based on the laughter and amens radiating through the crowd, I guess I'm not the only one impressed by his natural speaking abilities.

I keep my eyes glued on Ben's every move as he strides back and forth in the pulpit, pouring out his heart for the next half hour. In doing so, a harsh reality creeps in—Ben is on a completely different spiritual plane than me. When he quotes Scripture with such confidence and passion, I want to melt into my seat. Half the verses he recites I've never even heard before.

As if that weren't enough, Shelby has been taking notes and flipping through her Bible as if it were trivia night. I'm way out of my league here.

Finally, Ben closes us in prayer and dismisses the crowd.

"Wasn't that great?" Shelby asks, her voice squeakier than I remembered.

"It was." I wait for lightning to strike me dead for lying in church.

"Do you want to join us for lunch?" She gathers her study materials. "After we clean up, we usually grab something to eat."

We? As in her and Ben, or did others join their party? I bite the inside of my cheek and debate the invitation. Maybe I should wait for Ben to ask me. If it was just the two of them, I certainly didn't want to be a third wheel.

"Nicki." Ben hops off the stage and makes his way toward me.

"That was a great sermon. Are you sure you're not meant to be up there full-time?"

"Thanks, I'm happy to stand in, but that's not my calling." He pulls me towards the stage and away from Shelby's longing gaze. "I'm sorry I caught you off guard earlier. Normally I wouldn't invite someone to church and then abandon her."

"So, I'm not the first girl you've invited to church, then?" I tease him.

He shakes his head.

"All joking aside, Ben, you don't need to explain anything to me. I'm a big girl. Plus, we haven't had much time to talk about the details of our lives beyond what brought us to China. If we had, I'm sure you would've told me you're the next Francis Chan."

"Hardly." He combs his hand through his hair. "But maybe we can fix that. Why don't you join me for lunch so we can get to know one another better?" He grins. "A few of us go out together every Sunday after church, but maybe we can find some time alone to talk."

"That would be great, but—"

From the depths of my purse, my phone rings. I want to ignore it and explain to Ben why lunch isn't an option for me, but I can't. It could be my mom or Ms. O'Connor. If they're always asking what's wrong when I do answer, there's no telling how panic-stricken they'd be if I didn't.

"I'm sorry, I need to see who this is." I open my purse and retrieve my iPhone.

"No problem, I'll go tell the others you'll be joining us." He jots off down the aisle.

The caller ID reads Julia. Worried something might have happened with Mingyu, I quickly answer. "Julia?"

"Nicki," Julia says, relief tainting her words. "I'm so glad you answered."

The sound of her voice causes prickles of unease to nip at the back of my neck. "Is everything okay?" Now I'm the one asking that question.

"I'm not sure." She pauses. "I'm at New Hope. You need to come out here. Now."

6

*No sooner has one pushed a gourd under water than another
pops up.*
~ Chinese Proverb

When I arrive at the orphanage, Julia's waiting at the
front doors for me. I barely have time to remove my
gloves, scarf, and hat before she grabs my arm and pulls me in
the direction of Director Wu's office.

"Julia, slow down." I struggle to keep up with her pace.

She opens the door to the office and flips on the lights. Once
we're inside, she closes the heavy wooden door behind me and
locks it.

"Okay, you're scaring me." I remove my jacket and toss it, as
well as my other winter layers, on top of the cluttered desk.

"I don't mean to, but this is serious."

"Yeah, I can tell. That's why I sped over here. What's
wrong?"

"I know you told me to wait until later to come in, but since
I had the key to the office, I decided to get a head start on
things since we've been slow to make progress." She walks to a
box in the center of the room. There, she picks up three file

folders lying hodge-podge on the lid and holds them out like a deck of cards in front of her chest. "When I started going through this box, I came upon these."

I tilt my head at the crisp new folders. "What about them?"

Julia opens the one on top. It's empty.

"Sorry, Julia, but you're going to have to help me understand the problem." I scratch my head. "Isn't less paperwork a good thing for us?"

She returns two of the folders to their original spots. "This is an employee file." She taps at the small rectangular tab in the upper left-hand corner. "It says that Li Na started working here at New Hope on January twenty-fifth."

"Of this year?" I stiffen my back.

"Yes."

I stride across the room and retrieve the folder, inspecting the neat Chinese symbols and numerical date. "We don't even know if this is the director's handwriting."

"Someone else may have written the information on there and then given it to her."

"Okay, but still, Director Wu was adamant that she hadn't hired any new staff in almost a year." I flash back to the conversation Ms. O'Connor and I had with her just a few weeks earlier. "When Ms. O'Connor brought up the need to hire someone to help get things in order here, she said there'd been no money in the budget for quite some time to pay for additional staff, though they were in desperate need of it. Why would she say that if she'd been hiring?"

Picking up the other two manila folders, I study the dates written on them from last year. December 10. November 2. Clearly Director Wu was mistaken. Or she'd lied to us.

"Nicki," Julia snaps. "While I see how it might be disconcerting, that's not what's troublesome about all of this."

I balk. "If these files are valid that means Director Wu lied to me. And to Ms. O'Connor." An image of the sweet elderly woman flitters through my thoughts. I shake my head. "I can't believe she would be so deceptive."

"Perhaps she wasn't."

"What?" I blink rapidly.

"Maybe she was just confused. She's an old woman, and it's not uncommon for them to get things mixed up." She sighs. "But Nicki, that's—"

"You mean like dementia?" My skin tingles at the thought. If what Julia was saying was true, then I would have to inform Ms. O'Connor, who would likely insist that the director step down for the funding to go through.

"I'm no expert in geriatric illnesses, Julia, but Director Wu never came across as someone who suffered from any mental instability. Sure, she wasn't the best at keeping her office in order, but she never seemed confused about the daily operations of this place. She seemed quite spry and more than capable of fulfilling her job responsibilities."

"But doesn't it seem strange that not only are these files empty, but the reports haven't been submitted either? Is it possible that the director thought she'd turned them into the Coalition of Medical Missions but simply forgot?"

I ponder Julia's suggestions. "It could be the first signs of a larger problem, but ..."

"But, what?"

"Well." I cringe at the words forming on my lips. "If Director Wu is no longer able to handle the day-to-day responsibilities of running the orphanage, then she'd need to be replaced."

"Which would mean AD Chang would be next in line."

While it wasn't a royal accession to the throne, whoever would lead New Hope was still a serious matter. The authoritarian AD was the last person who needed to be in that position—at least, in my opinion.

"Oh, this is a problem." I lean against a stack of boxes. "I'd hate to think what the orphanage would be like under her leadership."

"Nicki, I don't think you fully understand the situation." Julia rubs her hands over her face. "It doesn't matter who's in charge."

"How can you say that? I've told you everything the AD has done and demanded. She's shady and not the best person to run this place."

"Please, for just a moment, can we forget about who's running the show here and discuss the pressing issue that I've been trying to address for the last ten minutes?" Her eyes plead with me.

"I thought that was the pressing issue."

"No, those empty folders are." Julia picks up a thick yellowed folder. "The box I was sorting through earlier contains employee files, mostly from a few years ago. Inside every one of these is a written contract for employment." Like a lawyer, she removes a stapled stack of papers from one of them and holds it up as evidence.

I nod my head to confirm I'm following along. So far.

"According to Chinese law, all employees must have a written contract to start working. If they don't, the employer has one month to get the contract completed, signed, and in the records, or the employee can demand double pay. And if the government finds out the contract was overlooked, they could impose hefty fines or other punishments on the employer."

I glance down at the three empty employee files. Whoever these workers are, it was evident they didn't have a written contract on record and hadn't for several months. This was serious. "So, you're telling me none of these hires have contracts, and without them, New Hope would have to pay financial restitution?"

"Yes. It would be money New Hope shouldn't have to spend and would not look good in an audit."

I press my fingers to my temple. "What—how did this happen?"

"I don't know. I found it unusual that the new employee files were even in the box with the old ones." She drops the papers back into the box. "Even so, the bigger problem is not just what to do about it, but what else might be out of sorts."

A ding echoes from across the room.

"Hold on." I weave my way through the musty paper piles, boxes, and binders scattered around the room and pull my phone out of my coat pocket.

One new notification. A text message from Ben. I click on it.

Missed you at lunch. Hope everything's okay. Let me know if you need help with anything.

I type out a short reply letting him know I'm fine. Even if I'm not at the moment. Right now, I can't afford any distractions, and Ben certainly is one. I stuff my phone back inside my coat and return my attention to the matter at hand. I'll worry about Ben later.

"What do you want to do about this?" Julia asks as I snake back through the messy office.

"I'm not sure." Honestly, there were so many things in play here I was finding it hard to concentrate. But I had to start somewhere. We couldn't afford to waste any more time. With little over a week of February remaining and Ms. O'Connor's new deadline, that only left a little more than six weeks for us to get the work completed.

The consequences were too costly with every delay we had.

"Julia, how much would it cost to backpay the employees?"

She squints her eyes and twists her mouth, and I can tell she's crunching the numbers. "Well, my math may be a little off, but if I were to estimate for just one worker, it would be about twelve thousand, eight hundred yuan. Multiply that by three workers, and it's thirty-eight thousand, four hundred yuan. And that's not including any fines the government might assess."

I quickly convert the yuan into dollars and gasp at the numbers. "That's two thousand dollars for one worker and six thousand dollars for all three."

"Roughly. Like I said, math isn't my strong suit."

"No, it's fine. I just didn't think it would be so much." I gulp. "From what Ms. O'Connor told me, that's about the same amount of money as one heart surgery for a child. About thirty thousand yuan or five thousand dollars."

"Oh." She falls silent.

"And if New Hope had to backpay for each month of their missing contracts, well, that could really add up." A shiver runs down my spine. "Where would the money come from to pay that?"

"New Hope would have to pull from other resources within the budget."

While I know she's right, I hate to think that a simple administrative mistake could endanger the well-being of the children in any capacity. Granted, Director Wu is messy and possibly even a level 1 on the hoarding scale, but I can't imagine she would do anything to put these kids in jeopardy. They mean the world to her. There had to be another reason these files were empty.

"Okay." My mind spins with other possibilities. "What if we're just speculating and the contracts were separated from the files? Then there's no issue and no money lost, right?"

"It's possible." Julia wrings her hands. "But they could be anywhere. And the longer it takes to find them—or not—the more money New Hope might have to pay. We could always ask AD Chang to see if she might know anything about the papers."

"No." I stiffen at the mention of the woman's name. "I don't want to consult her."

Her eyebrows knit together. "Why not?"

"Because this is supposed to be an independent project that doesn't include her input. Plus, I'm already wary of her strange behavior these past few days—first doing my job for me, then demanding that I stay out of her office and insisting I report to her every day. No, I want to make sure nothing is wrong before we have to take drastic measures and secure her help. The less she knows right now, the better."

"Well, if you're leery of her, what about asking Director Wu? It is her office, after all."

I sigh. "True, but she's recovering, and I worry that bringing these issues to light and what they might mean would be too upsetting for someone in her current condition. And I can't ask for her help anyway."

"I know, an independent project," Julia says dryly. "Then what do you suggest we do? Because we have to do something. Doing nothing will only make things worse"—she pauses—"for everyone."

I shift my eyes from her to the board with the kids' pictures. Their sweet smiles and sparkling eyes reach the depths of my soul. Julia's right. We have to act. But we have to do it in a way that doesn't tip off anyone yet. If we can find what we need among all the disarray, there's no need to alarm anyone. But if we don't, I'll have no choice but to get others involved. I'm praying it's the former.

"All right, this is what we're going to do."

Julia leans in closer.

"Before we say anything to anyone about the missing documents, we'll try and find them ourselves. If we're successful, the issue will be resolved without too much drama, and then we can go back to looking for the missing reports and digitalizing everything on time."

"And if we don't?" Julia rubs the back of her neck.

"I'm not sure," I say. "Until then, let's do what we can to avoid that type of catastrophe."

WITH OUR NEW motivation squarely planted at the front of our minds, we get busy combing through as much paperwork as we

LIANA GEORGE

can handle. It's a tedious process as we have to scour every box, some of which are filled with hundreds of sheets of paper.

We're so consumed by the task at hand we don't notice that the sun has vanished and been replaced by the covering of night. The only thing that grabs our attention is a loud tap on the door a few hours later.

We pop our heads up from the dusty floor where we've positioned ourselves and look at one another.

Panic courses through my veins. "What if it's AD Chang?"

"What if it is? So what?" Julia shrugs.

"I just don't want to explain to her what we're doing here so late on a Sunday evening. It's bad enough that I have to give her updates."

The knocking persists more intensely than before.

"Then just ask her what she's doing here," Julia says. "Two can play that game, you know."

"Yeah, I'm sure she'd love that." I pull myself up off the ground and wipe my hands against my thighs.

Slogging through the bulging black trash bags, empty banker's boxes, and paper piles marked with sticky note labels, the dread of conversing with the persnickety woman weighs on me. I grab hold of the doorknob and take a deep breath before unlocking it.

When I crack it ajar, Fei Hung, the primary caretaker for Lei Ming's room, stands in front of me, her face beet red.

She blurts out a slew of Mandarin, none of which I understand.

"Julia, help?" I hold up a finger to Fei Hung, asking her to wait for a moment.

Julia scurries to the door and engages in conversation with the agitated woman. Their voices rise and fall rapidly, making it impossible for me to determine if what is being said is good or bad news. When Julia stops talking and turns back to me, the somber look on her face indicates that Fei Hung wasn't here for a light-hearted discussion.

"What did she want?" My mind percolates with the worst possible scenarios. Why else would Fei Hung have been beating down the door?

She stuffs her hands in the back pocket of her jeans. "She was looking for AD Chang."

"Why? Is something wrong?"

"It's Lei Ming."

"Lei Ming?" I freeze. "What about her?"

Julia's mouth curves downward. "Fei Hung wanted to let the AD know they are transporting Lei Ming to the hospital."

"The hospital?" My teeth rattle. "Why?" Waiting for her response, my anxiety rises another level as I recall the last time I saw the sweet toddler. Blue lips. Clammy skin. Sluggish demeanor. Clear signs something was off.

"According to Fei Hung, she fell asleep in her high-chair at dinner, and they had trouble waking her." Her cheek muscle twitches. "By the time they got her out, she had turned a shade of blue, so they called the doctor and he took her straight to the hospital. I'm sorry to be the one to tell you, Nicki."

I step back, lightheaded. This can't be happening. I skim the room as if the answers to my confusion could be found there. When I don't find any, I flop to the ground.

"Nicki, are you okay?" Julia rushes to my side.

"She has to be fine, Julia." I rock back and forth and take deep breaths. "She just has to be."

"Of course, she will be. It was probably just precautionary, that's all." She gently places her hand on my back.

"Yes, precautionary." I cling to my friend's arm like a lifeline.

"She's a fighter, and I'm sure she'll be back here in no time getting into mischief."

Despite Julia's calm and positive attitude, images of the harsh hospital environment flash through my mind. I shudder at the thought of Lei Ming sitting in the cold, sterile environment with no one to comfort or soothe her. My chest squeezes at the thought of her cries going unattended. I have to go to her.

"I'm going to the hospital." I rise from the floor.

"Are you sure you want to do that? You might just have to sit there and wait. At least here you can work and keep your mind occupied. I'm sure as soon as they have some news, Fei Hung will tell us."

"No, I need to be with her." My voice is firm, as is my determination to be with Lei Ming.

"The New Hope doctor is there. And there are nurses too." She rises, her forehead wrinkled.

"Yes, but their focus will be figuring out what's wrong with her. At least I can comfort her during this scary time."

Straddling boxes like a hurdler, I race towards the desk where I'd left my belongings. "I can't stay here knowing she's possibly all alone." I pluck my purse and jacket off the desk and tuck them under my arm like a football before heading for the door.

"Wait, you can't go alone." Julia chases after me. "You don't even know where you're going."

I turn back towards her. "Text me the address, and I'll show my driver."

"And how are you going to converse with the doctors and nurse?"

"It's a hospital, Julia, certainly someone there speaks some English."

"Okay, you're right." She holds her hands up in defense. "I don't think you should be there alone. Let me go with you."

At her offer, my entire body relaxes. I'm so used to handling things on my own, I often forget that I don't have to be Super Woman all the time. God had placed Julia in my life not only to get me out of translating jams but to support me as well. I need to embrace His gift.

"That would be great." I reach out and put my arm around her shoulder. "Thank you."

"I'm always here for you." She leans into me. "I'll grab my coat and bag, and we can go."

Gulping down the emotions trying to surface, I watch Julia

wade through the mess we've managed to make messier towards her belongings in the far corner of the room. From experience, I know it always gets worse before it gets better, but in this case, it's a complete disaster. Although we made some progress in our efforts to find the employee contracts, there's still so much to do.

Maybe Julia's right. Maybe I should just stay here until we know more. But I doubt I'd be much help. Rather than focus on the work, my mind would constantly drift to Lei Ming and her well-being. I'd be useless. Something we can't afford. Perhaps I should rethink Julia's offer of going to the hospital with me.

"I sent a note to your driver with the address." Julia slides one arm inside her jacket sleeve and advances to the door. "He's waiting for us out front."

I clear my throat. "I think it would be better if you stayed here and kept working while I check on Lei Ming and make sure she's getting the care she needs."

My trusty sidekick stops mid-stride.

"Just look at this place, Julia." We scan the office, which resembles the aftermath of a bomb being detonated. "You would be invaluable to me at the hospital, but I'm not sure we can sacrifice the time. For the sake of the kids and the future of New Hope, we have to uncover the truth about these missing documents, and unlike me, you know what to look for and have the language skills to find them."

"Are you sure that's what you want?" Her eyes register the slightest hint of doubt.

"As much as I'd love for you to be there with me, I can't slow this project down so you can hold my hand. I should go to the hospital by myself."

"If you think it's for the best, then I'll keep working and looking for the contracts, but only if you promise you'll call if you need help."

I nod and force back the tears of worry, failure, and defeat.

"How is it you know me so well after just a few weeks?" I plaster on the best smile I can.

"You're predictable, Nicki Mayfield." Julia shoos me out of the room. "Now go and don't worry about things here. I've got it covered."

I regain my composure and open the door. "Thank you." I take a step out the door and then pivot back towards my friend, who's already removing her coat. "Please pray for Lei Ming. If anything happens to her, I don't know what I'll do."

7

Having to watch the eyebrows and countenance of another.
~ Chinese Proverb

I'M HERE TO SEE LEI MING FROM NEW HOPE.

    I wait for the Google translator to work its magic before flashing my phone screen toward the nurses' faces. When the symbols pop up on the screen, I pass my phone to the two young women dressed in identical crisp white uniforms.

Craning their necks, they lean over the desk to read the converted text. Then they look at each other and back at me. "*Méiyǒu,*" the one with the round face tells me.

Although my Chinese vocabulary is limited, I know that means *don't have.*

"Don't have or don't know?" I blurt out more forcibly than intended.

The tall skinny nurse says something in Mandarin, but of course I'm clueless.

Frustrated, I blow through my lips, pull back my phone, and try again.

A YOUNG GIRL FROM NEW HOPE ORPHANAGE WAS BROUGHT

TO THIS HOSPITAL, AND I NEED TO CHECK ON HER. I AM ON STAFF THERE. CAN YOU TELL ME WHERE SHE IS OR HOW TO FIND HER?

I plunge my phone and my work lanyard back across the desk and pray this will finally do the trick.

After scrutinizing my identification, they read the message on the screen and proceed through the same routine. Eyes darting between each other, unintelligible conversation and then, "*Bù zhīdào.*" *Don't know.*

Forcing back the tears and anger which have been dangling at the edge of my emotions since I left New Hope, I offer them a weak smile and trudge back to the hospital entrance.

Forcing back the tears and anger which have been dangling at the edge of my emotions since I left New Hope, I offer them a weak smile and trudge back to the hospital entrance. I wind my way through the flurry of activity outside to think about what else I can do to locate Lei Ming. I plop down on a cold metal bench next to the door and ignore the medical staff around me as they attend to an unconscious man covered in blood.

If I can't locate Lei Ming, how can I know she's getting the attention she needs? That she isn't scared? That she realizes she's not alone in this world and that someone is looking out for her? My chest tightens at the thought I could be the person who could fill that role. Maybe I could be. If only I could find her.

There's no doubt I'm at the right hospital, which leaves me with only one other choice. Call for backup. My thumb hovers over the call button, and I debate whether or not to push it. Reaching out to Julia will not only affirm her worries I might not be able to handle this on my own, but it will also distract her from the important work only she can do.

No, there has to be something I can do or someone else I can ask for help. Armed with one last idea, I jump from the bench and speed back to the information desk, where the same two nurses stand guard over the hospital's inhabitants. I type on my keyboard.

IS THERE SOMEONE HERE WHO SPEAKS ENGLISH?

Like before, I wait for the translation and then give them my phone. This time their heads bobble in unison then the tall one shuffles out from behind the desk and carts off down the hall.

Five minutes later, she returns with a young man who reminds me of Jackie Chan with his broad shoulders and bulky muscles.

"You speak English?" I ask with trepidation when they arrive at the information desk.

The Jackie look-alike holds up his thumb and index finger with a tiny space between them. "A little bit."

While it's not much, it's better than nothing.

I smile and nod before explaining my purpose for being there. "I work for New Hope Orphanage." I slow down my break-neck speed and speak as clearly as possible. "A little girl from there, Lei Ming, was brought to this hospital for treatment. I'm trying to find her. Can you please help me?" I fold my hands together in a prayerful position.

He digests the information before addressing the nurse. The two jabber back and forth before he finally speaks in a language I can understand.

"I'm sorry, but we need more, more ..." He rakes his hand through his thick black hair, searching for the words. "We need her full name, birth date, and what is the matter with her. Why was she brought here?"

My shoulders sag. I don't have any of that.

"Give me a minute, and I'll get what you need." I hold my finger up and whip out a quick text to Julia, asking her for the information. My pride no longer matters. Struggling or not, this is worth troubling her for.

A prompt reply pops up on my screen.

I'll have to ask and get back to you. Is everything okay? Do I need to come there?

Yes. No. Maybe. I bite my lip and text back.

Thanks.

I add a thumbs-up emoji.

"My friend will send me the info," I inform the duo, only one of whom understands me.

"Would you like to take a seat?" He points to a small area off to the side filled with chairs. The waiting room.

"I'd rather wait here."

Before he can argue with me, my phone dings with Julia's response. I flash the screen at the muscled man and pray that this will be enough to get me to Lei Ming.

"I'm only an assistant, but I will try." He rubs the back of his neck. "Please stay here."

Once again, he points at the chairs.

This time, I acquiesce. Fidgeting in my chair, I watch the clock hands tick at a snail's pace. After thirty minutes pass without a word, I push down my desire to rush back to the nurses and bother them again. When an additional forty-five minutes have gone by without a glimpse of either the male orderly or the nurse, I make my way back to the desk.

But as I open my mouth, I realize it's pointless. No one here can help me. Until I have someone to translate for me, I'll never get to Lei Ming.

Images of her little face, sweaty from crying, make their way into my mind. I can't hold out much longer. I have to find her.

I pivot from the desk and down the hallway. Pulling out my phone, I call the only other person who might be able to help me at a moment's notice. "Ben? Is that offer for help still available?"

Like a knight in shining armor, Ben strolls through the front door of the hospital twenty minutes later.

At the sight of his familiar face, I race toward him. "Thank you so much for coming."

"You said it was urgent." His gentle voice is a soothing salve to my anxious spirit, affirming I made the right choice in reaching out to him.

"It is." I nod and push back the tears brimming in my eyes.

Ben rests his hand on my shoulder and leads me back to a seat in the waiting area. "Start from the beginning, and then we'll figure it all out."

With his arm wrapped around me, I almost forget my momentary troubles. Thanks to his assuring presence, the tension in my shoulders loosens and I'm finally able to relax. I fill him in on the events of the last hour.

"You stay here and let me see what I can do." He lifts my chin so that our eyes meet. "It's going to be okay, Nicki, I promise."

I watch him go and let the tears flow. Tears of frustration. Tears of relief. Tears of hope.

After what seems like a lifetime, Ben returns. From the grim expression on his face, I can tell things aren't as good as I'd hoped.

"What's wrong?" I ask as he sinks into the chair next to me.

"The computers are down so they've had a hard time locating her, but an orderly did manage to track her down."

"And?" I search his face for any trace of good news, but there isn't any.

"She's in intensive care."

The fear in his voice chills my bones. "What? Why?" I clasp my hands together to keep them from shaking.

"They wouldn't give me any details on her condition since I'm not her family or New Hope staff." A pained expression covers his face. "I'm sorry."

I glance back over my shoulder at the nurses huddled

together at the desk. "Did you tell them you were with me? They know I work at the orphanage."

"I did, but they said they had to verify your work status before releasing any information."

"Verify? From whom?"

He rubs his hand over the stubble on his chin that's grown in since I saw him this morning. "I don't know. They said they wouldn't tell me anything else until the director arrived."

"But Director Wu is out with broken ribs."

"No, not her. The Acting Director, I think, some lady named Chong?"

"Chang." I seethe.

"Yeah, her." He snaps his fingers. "She's on her way to the hospital."

"AD Chang is coming here?" My eyes widen.

"That's what they told me." Ben's eyes move past me. "There's a woman walking towards us now. Is that her?"

I turn my head to see AD Chang marching in our direction. "That's her," I moan.

"She doesn't look happy."

"I don't think that word is part of her vocabulary." My stomach fills with dread at the sight of her. I'm not in the mood to deal with her right now.

"Miss Mayfield," AD Chang barks. "Why am I not surprised to see you here?"

Ignoring her snarky remark, I rise. "What's going on with Lei Ming?"

She flops one of her gloves on top of the other. "I can't tell you."

"Why not?" I knew she was sly and unkind, but this was pushing it.

"Because I don't have any information to share. The nurses only said that the doctor will be out shortly with an update."

"But you have to have some idea of what's going on with her."

I take a step closer to her. "What did the doctor say when he checked on her the other day?"

Her body stiffens at my line of questioning. "At the time, he said she was fine, but you can never tell with patients who suffer from heart conditions. It's likely things have taken a turn for the worse." Her voice, as well as her expression, remains neutral. As if she were heartless to the pain and suffering of this little girl.

"So, what does that mean?" I ask.

"I don't know, Miss Mayfield. That's why I'm waiting on the doctor." She scrunches her nose. "I hope it won't be too much longer. The anti-septic smell in here is making me nauseous."

"Please, have a seat," Ben stands and offers her his chair.

She raises an eyebrow. "And you are ..."

Like a shield, I step in between the AD and Ben. "This is a friend of mine from church. He's here to keep me company."

AD Chang peeks around me and gives Ben a once-over. From the corner of my eye, I see him wave at her, but the AD simply disregards him and takes his seat. "So," she says, tucking her gloves into her purse, "I know why you're here, but I don't understand how you found out that Lei Ming had been admitted."

"I was working at New Hope when Fei Hung came looking for you. She told us what happened."

"Us?"

"Yes, Julia and I were working in the director's office." I shift my weight from side to side.

"On a Sunday? I don't recall you requesting to work that day."

"I don't recall needing your permission," I snap back.

She lengthens her neck and narrows her eyes. "And what, exactly, were you working on?"

Tempted by her invitation, I want to inquire about the missing contracts, but I restrain myself. A good poker player never shows his cards too early. Neither will I until I'm certain those papers are nowhere in the director's office.

"We were sorting through all the paperwork." I pause. "However, under the circumstances, I would think your focus would be on Lei Ming's well-being instead of what I've been up to."

Tapping her cherry-red nails against one another, she glares at me. "Of course, I care. I care about all the children—"

"*Zhāng fù zhǔrèn?*" A man's voice interrupts our discussion.

We all turn our attention towards a diminutive figure clothed in faded olive-colored scrubs and a surgical mask wrapped around his neck like a winter scarf. AD Chang greets him, and as the two converse in clipped tones, I surmise he's the doctor we've been waiting for.

"What are they saying?" I scoot toward Ben and catch a whiff of his woodsy aftershave, still strong after a long day.

"He's telling her about Lei Ming and his preliminary findings." His eyes stay locked on the doctor and the AD.

"And what did they discover?"

He turns back toward me. "Sorry, Nicki, but medical terms are out of my realm of understanding."

"Oh, yeah, right."

The quick-paced conversation comes to a halt and the AD swivels back around to me. "This is Doctor Wong, the surgeon in charge of Lei Ming's care."

"I gathered." I offer the doctor a warm smile. "How is Lei Ming? Can I see her? When will she be going back to New Hope?"

"Lei Ming's condition is," the doctor says in English for my benefit. "Delicate."

"Delicate? How so?"

AD Chang clears her throat. "She needs surgery. Immediately."

"It's that serious?" My bottom lip wobbles.

"I'm afraid so," she says.

"But I don't understand." My legs turn to jello. "How did this happen?"

"Lei Ming's heart has a hole in it," Doctor Wong chimes in. "We were aware of the issue but thought we could wait until she was a little older to treat the condition. Unfortunately, it seems to have enlarged faster than we expected and is causing other issues."

A lump forms in my throat at his words, rendering me speechless.

"Will she be okay once she's had the surgery?" Ben asks, stepping in on my behalf.

The doctor shakes his head. "It's a routine procedure, but we can never make any guarantees. However, I've done this operation on several children without any complications."

I exhale, suddenly realizing I'd been holding my breath during the doctor's explanation. "So, you're going to operate now?"

The doctor and AD Chang exchange glances.

"Soon," the doctor says.

A jolt of shock courses through me. "I'm confused. I thought you said she needed it right away."

"Yes," AD Chang speaks up, "but first we have to secure the funding."

I shift my gaze back to her. "But Mr. O'Connor provided plenty of money to cover the costs of these surgeries. Why do you have to secure it?"

"Unfortunately, New Hope doesn't have enough money to pay for the operation right now." She flicks her eyes away. "I'll need some time to raise the funds."

My heart stirs with a dozen emotions, but irritation leads the pack. "There isn't enough? How is that possible?" I moderate my voice to avoid any unwanted attention.

"Not that I am obligated to discuss the situation with you, but we've had quite a few surgeries lately that have drained our funds," she snips.

Instantly my mind flashes back to the recovery unit at New Hope where I'd spent time visiting some of those recuperating patients. Had it just been a few weeks ago that I had cradled Qing Shan in my arms as I sang *Hush Little Baby* and played peek-a-boo with Wang Wei, the young boy who was about to be released? There had been several other children being taken care of in there as well, so it would make sense. But still, there had to be plenty of money.

"I don't understand how something like this happens," I say. "What happened to all the money Mr. O'Connor donated?"

"Are you questioning how we manage the orphanage?"

Fear courses through my body at her refusal to answer my original question. It may not be the time or the place for this conversation, but I can't help but wonder what is going on at New Hope. Missing reports, incomplete employee files, and now this? My gut tells me something isn't right.

Despite my strong need to uncover the truth, it would be inappropriate for me to go to war with the AD here at the hospital about how the orphanage is run. I'll have to wage that battle later. It's important, but it's not my primary concern. Lei Ming's well-being is all that matters right now.

I sidestep the AD's question and address Doctor Wong instead. "Doctor, how long can she wait for us to get the money we need?"

"The sooner the better," he says. "She's in the ICU right now, which already means she's quite critical."

My chest squeezes so tight I'm afraid I might pass out.

"Thank you for your time, Doctor." AD Chang takes charge. "I'll make some calls, and we can hope to have the necessary funds in a few hours."

"Yes, please let me know. We shouldn't wait too long." He bows his head, then like an animal waiting to escape, he races out of the waiting area.

Through blurry eyes, I watch the doctor retreat down the hall. When the first tear drops, a white tissue floats in front of my face.

I take it from the AD's hand. "Thank you." I dab my eyes,

surprised at her small act of kindness toward me. "Now, what do we do?"

"We?" She spits the word out like sour milk. "There is no we in this case, Miss Mayfield. As soon as I return to New Hope this evening, I will make a few calls and see what arrangements can be made."

"And what if you can't get what is needed?"

"Although it's not your concern, I assure you I will find the money for surgery." She pulls her purse higher on her shoulder. "I really must be going."

"Wait." I grab her by the arm. "I can call Ms. O'Connor right now and explain the situation. I'm sure she'd be more than willing to send whatever we needed without hesitation."

The AD flashes a fake smile in my direction, although her eyes convey anything but pleasure. "That's a kind offer but isn't necessary. We Chinese do have our pride, and while Mr. O'Connor's generosity over the past few years has been helpful, we don't need saving. I promise you it will be taken care of." Her tone becomes somber. "You do trust me, don't you?"

Like a burning hot plate, I remove my hand from her arm and study her. I remember what Julia told me about how important saving face is to the Chinese people. While I don't want to offend the AD, I'm not fully confident she'll be able to secure the money in the short window of time Lei Ming has. But what choice do I have?

"Yes," I steady my voice despite the fear and dread shooting through me. "I'll wait to hear from you, but if you haven't been able to secure the funds by the morning, I will."

The corner of her mouth dips before she proceeds to march back out the same way she came in.

Stuck in place like a statue, I stand immovable until I no longer see her figure traipsing down the hallway.

"Nicki?" Ben taps me on the shoulder.

I spin around and face him. "Sorry you had to hear all that."

He stuffs his hands inside his jean pockets. "Obviously, the two of you have issues."

"You could say that." I emit a small chuckle, which helps release some of my built-up tension.

"So now what?"

"I need to make a phone call." I brush past him and pick up my phone.

"Who are you calling?"

"Ms. O'Connor." I thumb through my list of favorites.

"But didn't you tell that Chang woman you wouldn't do that?" His voice holds a thread of warning.

"I told her I wouldn't ask Ms. O'Connor for the money, and I won't. At least not yet. I simply want to apprise her of Lei Ming's situation." I click the call button.

Beads of sweat prickle my hairline when our eyes meet. The intensity of his stare pierces my soul. Not wanting to see the disappointment my decision may cause, I turn away while I wait for the line to connect.

Three rings. Four. Five. No answer. Odd that she wouldn't pick up.

"Any luck?" Ben asks when I drop my phone.

"No, but I'll keep trying." I stuff my phone into the back pocket of my jeans.

Ben sucks in his cheeks. "Nicki, I don't want to cause any more trouble, but I could tell their conversation was pretty heated. I'm concerned things may be worse than what the AD let on."

"What do you mean?" My stomach flip-flops.

"Like I said earlier, I didn't understand all the medical jargon, but there was an urgency to the doctor's words. I'm not sure time is on this little girl's side."

I collapse into the seat under the weight of his words. And the implications.

Lei Ming needs surgery immediately. That is, if the AD can

secure the funds. If she can't, then what? I shudder to think what could happen to Lei Ming if the funds can't be raised in time.

"Hey, are you okay?" He falls into the seat next to me and pulls me from my thoughts.

"Yes." I grip the armrests of the chair. "I'm just considering all the possibilities."

"And?"

"Well, if AD Chang doesn't come through as she promised, and I can't reach out to Ms. O'Connor for assistance, there's only one other thing for me to do."

"Which is?"

I look up and meet his gaze. "Pay for it myself."

8

Dark clouds can't blot out the sun.
~ Chinese Proverb

"You have that kind of money?" Ben's voice rises a notch.

"Not really. But like they say, where there's a will, there's a way."

Ben hunches over and rests his elbows on his knees. "We don't know each other that well, Nicki, but you're aware this kind of surgery isn't cheap, right?"

"It's thirty thousand yuan," I say without flinching.

He lets out a slow whistle. "That's about five thousand dollars."

"I know." My shoulders tighten as I consider my current bank balance, which is far short of that amount, even with the extra money Ms. O'Connor had given me for taking this job.

"So, how do you plan on paying for it?"

"I'll have to apply for a credit card, I guess."

"Oh."

An awkward silence slips between us. For several minutes each of us stays lost in our thoughts.

Finally, Ben speaks up. "I think that's an admirable thing to do, but why are you willing to put yourself in that kind of a financial hole for a kid you just met?"

Before I can answer him, the entry doors fly open and a team of medical personnel rushes through, pushing a gurney loaded with a pregnant woman.

Panicked voices shatter the quiet of the waiting area as they storm past us toward the labor and delivery unit. The wails of this soon-to-be mother send a tingle down my spine. I don't have to speak the same language to know she's writhing in pain.

"Wow, she must be miserable," I say once the excitement diminishes. "I'm sorry, what were you asking me before?"

He swivels his head back in my direction. "I was asking why you'd go into debt for this little girl."

"I'm not even sure I can explain it, really." A lump rises in my throat, threatening to choke off my words. I swallow to push it down. "All I know is it's something I have to do. It's the same as my desire to see her and make sure she's okay."

Ben stares at me like I'm some sort of strange alien.

"What?" Heat spreads up my neck.

"Nothing." He shakes his head. "She must be a special little girl that's all."

"She is." My mouth curves upwards as I remember her cooking at the toy kitchen last week.

"Lei Ming, right?"

I nod, then open the photos on my phone to show Ben the girl at the center of all this attention.

"So, how did you get involved with her?" He looks up from the pictures and back at me.

"That's a long story." I pull the phone back into my lap, noticing the time. "It's getting late, and I don't want to keep you."

"I could never leave a damsel in distress. Let's hear it."

I study his face. The soft lines around his eyes highlight the sincerity in his response. My heart skips a beat at his willingness to be here, not only to translate but to support me as well. "Well, if you're sure."

"I am." He leans back in the chair and places his hand behind his head. "I'm all yours."

I perch on the edge of my seat. "Then I should probably start at the beginning."

For the next thirty minutes, Ben gives me his undivided attention as I detail my early encounters with Lei Ming at New Hope.

"After I removed all the vomit off me, I returned to the toddler room and did what I always do under stress—I began organizing all the toys. When I looked down, she was staring at me with those big brown eyes and holding a book out to me."

"Let me guess. She wanted you to read to her."

"Yes, which made me uncomfortable at first, but when she crawled into my lap, my uneasiness melted away and we somehow connected." My voice cracks as I remember the warmth of her body snuggled in my arms. In that moment, the wall that had been guarding my heart crumbled and this tiny angel cemented her place there.

"Wow, that's quite the story." Ben's eyes double in size.

I arch my back and stretch my arms over my head. "Sorry, I didn't mean to ramble on like that."

Out of the corner of my eye, I notice a pair of young nurses going googly-eyed over Ben, who's oblivious to their admiration. I suppress a chuckle as they return to their hospital duties.

"I'm glad you told me. Now I understand why you're so anxious to see her and adamant that she has money for the operation. I admire your parental instinct." His eyes dart from me to the floor. "I'm not quite ready to have kids, and not sure I ever will be."

My fingers find a loose piece of my hair and tuck it behind my ear. "I understand. Except for Lei Ming, I haven't always been their biggest fan."

"Really?" He jerks back. "I wouldn't have guessed that. From what I've seen of you this evening, you'd make a great mother."

My cheeks heat at his compliment. "I hardly consider myself maternal, but these few weeks have changed my perspective a bit." I flip my phone over in my hands. "I've always believed that getting married and raising a family were not in the cards for me. I'm not interested in a knight in shining armor to sweep me off my feet, and as for kids, well, I saw them as chaos creators and had no desire to add that to my orderly world. But now I sense something's changing."

Ben leans in closer. "About the knight in shining armor or the kids?"

"Just the kids." I snort. "As crazy as my life is right now, romance is not something I have time to think about."

"At one time, I believed in the whole happy ever after scenario too." Tears glimmer in his eyes. "Then things changed."

"Ah, yes." I recall our conversation at the coffee house back in December. "You mentioned something about heartache when Longchen first introduced us to one another. How did you say it?" I rack my brain for the exact words he used when I asked what brought him to China. "A broken heart and a door of opportunity that only God could orchestrate. Wasn't that it?" I poke him in the arm.

"Something like that." Ben's legs jiggle.

"What about Shelby? She seems like she'd be happy to help mend your broken heart." I purse my lips at the slip of her name. My track record with dating isn't that stellar, so the last thing I should be doing is playing matchmaker for Ben.

"We're just co-workers and friends. She's nice, but not exactly my type." He rubs his index finger over his lips. "No, it will take someone very unique to make me change my mind about falling in love again."

Curiosity gets the best of me. "So, what happened that left you so battered and bruised?"

He turns his head toward the vending machines at the far

side of the room and then back at me. "Are you thirsty? I could get us something to drink." He rises and faces the familiar red machine with white lettering. "Or we could walk down to the cafeteria and see what they have to offer."

"Nice try, mister." I wriggle a finger at him. "I shared my story with you, so it's time for you to open the vault and tell me yours."

"You're right, it's only fair I share." He thrusts his hands into his pockets. "But you have to remember, in my story, the prince and the princess don't get their happily ever after."

"I know, but you can't leave a girl hanging."

He tilts his head, and a corner of his mouth lifts into a smile. "Walk with me to the cafeteria, and I'll tell you everything."

I strain my neck and glimpse over at the information desk. "But what if they say I can finally see Lei Ming and I'm not here?"

"Come with me, and when we get back, I'll ask about getting you in to see her. Deal?" He holds out his hand to me.

Excited by the promise of seeing Lei Ming and learning more about Ben, I stand and place my hand in his. "Deal."

"This way."

He leads us down a hallway just off the waiting area. Once we pass a lab technician in a stark white coat carrying a basket of crimson-filled tubes capped off with rainbow-colored stoppers, Ben bares his soul.

"Her name was Katie. We'd been high school sweethearts since tenth grade. When we were both accepted to Baylor for college, there was no doubt in my mind we would get married as soon as we graduated."

"So, what happened?" I glance at him out of the corner of my eye.

The muscle in his jaw twitches. "She died a few months before commencement." He swallows. "A car accident."

I gasp. "I'm so sorry, Ben. That must have been a very difficult time for you." I desperately want to wrap him in my arms right now and offer him the same comfort he gave to me earlier, but since he keeps walking, I let the idea go.

"It was." His Adam's Apple throbs. "Even worse is knowing that if I hadn't been so selfish, Katie would still be alive today."

Hearing the pain in his words, even after all this time, my heart splinters. I know all too well how hard it is to lose someone you love. But I can't imagine the depths of his suffering if he's still carrying the guilt after all this time.

"Whatever happened, you can't blame yourself," I tell him, hoping my words might be a salve to the wound which obviously hasn't healed yet.

When he doesn't respond, I take a few more steps before noticing the shadow of his large frame is no longer overtaking me. Upon pivoting in his direction, I see him leaning against the wall, the harsh fluorescent lighting causing him to look paler than he is.

The normal sparkle in his eyes fades as he slips back in time. "We were supposed to drive home to Kilgore for Easter. I was planning on proposing while we were there with our families. It was going to be this huge event. But right before we left, Coach called us in for a short baseball practice. I knew it was optional, that I didn't have to go, but I couldn't let him think I wasn't a team player. If I wanted to play in the majors, I needed to do everything required of me.

"So, I told Katie not to wait around for me, to drive ahead and I'd meet her there. But she didn't want to leave without me. She begged me to skip just this once, but I wouldn't give in. I couldn't; I was too driven. We fought for a while, but eventually, she gave up and headed home on her own."

Goosebumps pebble on my arms. "But she didn't make it," I say, my voice barely above a stage whisper.

"A storm blew in as she was driving back. Her car skidded off the road and hit a barrier head-on. She was killed instantly." His head droops. "If I hadn't been so concerned about impressing the coach and being the best, Katie would still be alive today.

We'd probably be married and have kids of our own." He raises his head, his eyes brimming with tears. "So, you see, I'm responsible for her death."

I inch closer to him. "It wasn't your fault, Ben. If you had driven home with her that night, you might have died too. It was just a tragedy."

"That's what everyone keeps telling me, and maybe one day I'll finally accept that. But it's been seven years, and I still haven't forgotten what my choices caused." He wipes his face. "After graduation, I drifted for a few years, then I came here. It's been the perfect place for me."

I retrieve the tissue AD Chang had given me and tear off the dirty side before handing it to him. He blows his nose.

"I'm sorry, I shouldn't have pushed you to share something so intimate," I tell him.

"No, I'm the one who's sorry. Sorry that it happened and for depressing you with it. Let's go to the cafeteria and wash down our sorrows with a drink." He manages a tiny grin. "The soda kind, of course."

I nod, and we fall back into step with one another.

While I'm tempted to engage in small talk just to erase the awkward silence that has fallen, I'm at a loss for words. What do you say to someone who just shared their darkest moment with you? Nothing seems appropriate. Despite my desire to know more about the aftermath of Katie's death on his life up until now, I don't want to dwell on the subject. When he wants to share more, he will. Heaven knows there are plenty of things I keep buried.

When we arrive at the cafeteria, it's as dark as the night sky, and a metal gate blocks the entrance.

"Guess we're out of luck." He casts a sorrowful glance at me. "Sorry, Nicki."

"It's okay," I say. "You'll just have to make it up to me another time."

"I will, I promise." He chuckles. "But first, I need to make good on something else."

I furrow my brows.

"Let's get you in to see Lei Ming."

"I'd love for you to ask." A jolt of excitement rushes through me. "That is, if you really don't mind."

"Not at all."

We retreat down the same route we'd just taken, our footsteps lighter and faster without the heavy conversation of earlier.

"I'll go to the information desk and work my magic." He points his thumb back toward the entrance where the same two nurses are busy working. "You have a seat and prepare yourself for a visit with Lei Ming." He darts off.

I pace the waiting area while he's gone, my mind ricocheting between Ben's story and thoughts of holding Lei Ming in my arms again. On my fifth lap around the room, Ben traipses back in.

"I'm ... I'm sorry, Nicki." He grimaces. "But it's a no-go."

"What? Why?" My spirits deflate.

He stuffs his hands into the front pockets of his pants and stares at his shoes.

From his silence, I take it there's more to the story that he's not willing to tell me.

I grip his arm and bend my head to catch his eyes. "Did you remind them that I work at New Hope and the doctor already told me about her surgery?"

"Yes, but they said that AD Chang instructed them not to let you in." He pops his head up. "I'm really sorry."

Rage flows through my veins. "She did what?" I breathe deeply to avoid taking out my boiling anger on the messenger. "Why would she do that?"

"I don't know, but—"

Without thinking, I grab my phone out of my back pocket.

"What are you doing?" Ben places his large hand over mine.

"Calling AD Chang." My voice is firm. "She can't do this."

"Nicki," he whispers. "She can."

"But Lei Ming is so little and all alone. She needs someone familiar to comfort her."

He inches closer and pats my back. "There are nurses and caretakers who are probably doing that. You have to trust she's in good hands."

"Isn't there anything I can do to change their minds?" I look at him with hope and expectation that he can pull off a miracle.

"They felt bad, but I think they're afraid of the AD too." He sighs. "They said if you were her potential adopter or something like that, then they might be able to break the rules and let you see her. Otherwise, you'll have to wait until the AD changes her mind."

I harrumph. "No, I'll just have to find a way to see Lei Ming despite the AD's orders."

"I'm not sure how you're going to do that." He chuckles. "Unless you plan on adopting her yourself."

My head juts back. "That's a brilliant idea!"

"What is?"

"I'll tell them I've decided to adopt her," I squeal. "Then they'll have no choice but to let me in."

"I don't think lying in this situation is a good idea." He pauses. "Or any situation, really."

"What if I'm not lying?" The reality of that type of commitment slowly sinks in. *Could I actually adopt Lei Ming as my own?*

"You can't be serious." Ben's jovial tone turns somber. "That was just a joke. I didn't think you'd take me at face value."

"But what if I am?" I cross my arms over my chest. "If I adopt Lei Ming, I could ensure that she was taken care of throughout the surgery and recovery." My mind drifts toward future possibilities. "And for the rest of her life."

He raises his palms toward me. "Don't take this the wrong way, but you told me you weren't the maternal type a few minutes ago. Now you want to adopt her?"

"I know it seems rash."

"Because it is."

"Well, what else am I supposed to do, Ben? Just sit here and hope I'll get in to see her at some point?" I square my shoulders. "If it means adopting her, then that's what I'm willing to do."

"I understand how much that little girl means to you, but I don't think you realize what you're getting into here." Ben narrows his eyes. "During the past five years, I've heard the stories of what it's like to adopt from China, and let me tell you, it's not that easy. The odds are stacked against you."

His words pierce my heart. Perhaps it wasn't as cut and dry as I'd imagined. But did that mean I should give up so easily?

"Didn't you preach this morning that nothing is impossible for God?"

"Yes."

"So, then you're telling me that it's an impossible dream, is that it? Because if that's the case, you need to revisit your sermon notes."

He doesn't speak or move.

"I'm sorry, Ben." My heart pinches at the tone I'd just used on him. "I shouldn't have been so harsh. I know you're only trying to help."

"No, you're right. I should be the one to apologize. To you and to God." His mouth twitches. "Nothing is impossible for Him, and just because I don't see kids in the cards for me doesn't mean you weren't meant to be with Lei Ming." He scans the room and the hallway. "But maybe you don't need to adopt her to do that." He takes my hand again and leads me to a chair. "Stay here. I'll be right back."

I fall into the seat, curious about what he has in mind. Leaning back, I study the ceiling. *Lord, is adopting Lei Ming such a crazy idea? Could this be the reason You placed me back in China—so that I could give her a forever home?* The pros and cons of doing so swirl through my head, but no clear answer musters its way to the top.

Perhaps Ben was right. Maybe making Lei Ming my daughter would be impossible. To think otherwise might require a leap of faith I'd never taken before.

I'm not sure I'm ready to make a jump like that just yet.

The clock on the wall ticks closer to Monday when Ben returns. Surprisingly, he's not alone.

"I found someone to help us," he says, panting.

"Him?" I point at the orderly I spoke with earlier.

"Yes." Ben's face breaks into a smile as big as Texas. "This is Tao. He's agreed to sneak us into Intensive Care."

"How?" I blurt out.

"Calm down, or you'll give us away." He glances over his shoulder to make sure my loud questioning has not garnered any unwanted attention. "He's going to take us to see Lei Ming in exchange for private English lessons once a week with yours truly as long as I'm here."

My eyes dart between the two husky men in front of me and my heart swells. "You'd—you'd be willing to do that for me?"

Their heads rock in agreement.

"But what if we get caught?"

"We just have to make sure we don't." Ben winks at me. "If we're going to do this, we need to go now. It's almost time for a shift change, and Tao says it will be easier to get in there unnoticed."

Rule-breaking isn't part of my nature, but if this is the only way for me to see Lei Ming, I'll do whatever it takes. "Let's go."

The ICU is as cold as an icebox when Tao ushers us into the unit. Other than my chattering teeth and pounding heart, the only noise I hear is the succinct beeping of the monitors next to each of the patients' beds.

As we tiptoe through the dimly lit room, my eyes adjust to the darkness, searching for Lei Ming's crib. I'm thankful that Tao knows her exact location and leads us straight to her.

When I peek over the edge of her bed and catch a glimpse of

her lifeless frame covered in wires I choke up. Her condition *is* serious.

The two guys exchange a few words in Mandarin, then Ben joins me in front of the crib.

"You only have a few minutes. The new nurses will be making the rounds soon, and we need to leave before they start."

Unable to speak or take my eyes off the sleeping beauty, I simply nod. She's resting peacefully, but her complexion is pale, her breathing labored.

"So, this is Lei Ming." Ben brushes the top of her head. "She's cute. I can see why you'd be smitten with her."

I drop to my knees, reach through the spindles of her crib, and place her tiny hand in mine. She doesn't flinch at my touch.

"Hey, sweetheart," I whisper as close to her ear as possible. "It's me, Nicki. I'm here. You're not alone." I massage her fingers to warm them and to let her sense my presence. "You gave us all a good scare." I chuckle. "That wasn't nice, you know. But if you promise you'll get better, I'll let it slide."

Lei Ming shifts under her blanket. Her eyes flutter for a moment, then still.

"I think she hears you," Ben says softly.

I look up at him, then back at Lei Ming. "I need you to get better, little one. I'm going to make sure you have everything you need. I promise. If you'll do your part, I'll do mine, okay?"

From the corner of my eye, I see Tao tap Ben on the shoulder. Our time is up.

"Nicki ..." Ben's voice trails off.

I hold Lei Ming's hand to my lips and plant a gentle kiss on it. "Stay strong, sweet girl. I'm going to be with you. You are not alone in this world."

I rise from the floor, resolve swelling up inside of me. I curve my body over the side of the crib to get as close as I can to this little girl who has captured my previously guarded heart. I want to make sure she hears my commitment to her. "I'm not going to leave you, Lei Ming." I take a deep breath. "Not now. Not ever."

9

When two tigers tussle, one is bound to get injured.
~ Chinese Proverb

New Hope bustles with activity when I roll in late the next morning. Many things vie for my attention there, but I head straight for AD Chang's office to discuss the idea that kept me up most of the night—starting the process of adopting Lei Ming.

When I'd shared my decision with Ben after leaving the ICU the night before, he cautioned me not to get my hopes up and to wait on God's leading. But after seeing Lei Ming in such a fragile and vulnerable state I don't think I'm supposed to wait. I truly believe this is what I'm supposed to do.

Not only that, but the peace that pervaded my spirit all the way back to the hotel was unlike anything I'd ever experienced before. If that wasn't a sign from God that this was His plan, I don't know what was. He was the one who placed her in my life, after all.

I rub my hands together to dry the sweat from my palms before knocking on the AD's door. When she doesn't answer, I check underneath the door for a light. It's on, so clearly she's in there, and I can hear a muffled voice talking to someone.

Dismayed by the delay, I pivot and scoot toward Director Wu's office. While I'm curious to see if Julia's managed to find the missing contracts, I'm also anxious to share my news with her too. At least that will help quell my disappointment of having to wait on the AD. I have no doubt Julia can give me some insights about officially making Lei Ming my daughter, and having her in my corner makes the task seem less daunting.

"Hey, sleepyhead," Julia says cheerfully as soon as I enter the room. I always forget she's a morning person. "I wasn't sure I'd see you at all today. When I read your text this morning about some big news you wanted to share with me, I noticed you sent it at two a.m. Late night?"

"Yes." I yawn. Sleep eluded me as I stayed up thinking about Lei Ming and how I might get to take her home with me someday.

As if reading my thoughts, she asks, "How's Lei Ming?"

"The same, or at least that's what they told me on the phone when I last checked an hour ago."

"Any word on surgery?"

"Not yet. I stopped by the AD's office to inquire about her progress, among other things." I try my best to suppress the excitement flowing through me. I've never been good at keeping secrets, but I want the moment I spill the beans to be perfect.

"Let's hope she's secured funding. When you mentioned in your text there wasn't any money for the operation, I was shocked." Julia wraps her long, shiny locks into a ponytail. "Have you considered reaching out to Ms. O'Connor? I'm sure she could cover the cost or ask someone at the CMM to look into it."

I frown. "I tried, but she hasn't answered, and she hasn't called me back either." I skim the stacks of papers scattered around the room. "Any luck finding those contracts?"

"Not yet." She picks up a large stack of papers next to her and waves them at me. "There's just so much paper in all these boxes and going through them one by one is taking a long time."

"I know," I chuckle. "Organizing paper is the most time-consuming task, and I'm sorry you've had to do most of the work by yourself. But going to the hospital was the right thing for me to do. I'm sorry I left you to do all the heavy lifting." I drop my personal belongings next to the door. "I promise I'll stay here and help you knock out as much as I can before I have to go back and check on Lei Ming."

"You're going back there again today?" Her tone is sharp and one she's never used with me before.

"Yes, why?"

"There's a lot still left to do here, and we won't meet your deadline if we don't make some real progress soon." She pushes her glasses toward the bridge of her nose.

"Are you sure that's all there is to it?"

"Yes, I mean, no, not really." Her gaze drops to the floor.

I cross my arms over my chest. "Out with it."

She looks back up at me. "Don't get me wrong, Nicki, I'm thrilled that you are worried about her and want to be there to make sure she's okay and receiving the care she needs. I know how scary that can be. But ..."

"But what?"

"I'm worried you're getting too attached to Lei Ming." Her lips press together in a slight grimace. "I talked to some of the staff here last night, and they told me about the kids who didn't get surgeries or whose surgeries failed. There are no guarantees in any of this, and if AD Chang can't secure the money for her surgery or if something happens to her, I'm afraid of what it will do to you."

Julia's sister had just been released from the hospital, so I know there's some deep-seated fear there on her part. But that's not going to be the case with Lei Ming. I'm going to make sure of it. "I appreciate your concern, but she's going to have the surgery and whatever else she needs from now on, I promise." I bounce on the balls of my feet.

"How can you be so sure? You haven't even talked to the AD yet."

"I don't need to," I whisper. Despite no one being able to overhear our conversation, I keep my voice low. "Remember when I texted you that I had big news? Well, I made the decision last night to adopt Lei Ming. That way, I can make sure she's always taken care of."

Her jaw goes slack. "Really?"

"Yes! Can you believe it?" Adrenaline pumps through me. The more I say it to myself and others, the more of a reality it becomes. A joyful one.

"No, I can't." She rubs her temples. "How ... what made you decide to do this?"

I fill her in on all the details from last night and the moment that sealed the deal for me. "When I released her hand from my grip, I knew I never wanted to let it go again. Right then, I decided to adopt her and give her a forever home."

"Wow, Nicki, I don't know what to say." She stares at me. "I'm happy for you."

"Are you?" I take in her sullen eyes and downturned mouth. "Your face tells a different story."

She shuffles around the box she'd been working on, then reaches for her water bottle. She takes a long sip before replacing the lid and meeting my gaze. "As an orphan, I'm the last person to ever discourage someone from adopting, but I don't think you understand what you're getting yourself into. The process may not be as simple as you think."

I cross my arms, remembering Ben's words. "I can't imagine it's all that hard. There are probably a few extra hoops I'll have to jump through as a single person, but I'm willing to do whatever it takes."

"I have no doubt that you would, but in China, you can never be certain."

"That's why it's a leap of faith, Julia." I press my shoes against a stack of binders. "I know my faith isn't as strong as yours, but I believe that maybe this is why God brought me back here. While I wish he'd given me a visible sign, you and I know that doesn't always happen."

"No, He doesn't, so how can you be sure?"

"The only way I can explain it, there was a peace that rushed over me like a waterfall afterward, and I can't help but think that was God confirming my decision. If it was, I have to do whatever it takes to make it happen." I gulp. "And it would be easier to do that if I knew you were on my side."

"I'm sorry. I was just looking out for your best interests, that's all."

I close the gap between us and embrace her in a hug. "Thank you, but I'm more than capable of taking care of myself."

She leans back and looks at me, both her eyebrows lifting her forehead.

"Okay, maybe not when it comes to translating." I laugh. "But I do know what I'm getting myself into. The only thing that will make this difficult for me is not having you with me on the journey."

"Of course, I'm going to be with you," she says. "I'm thrilled by your decision and will support you any way I can."

Seeing the sparkle in her eyes and hearing the joy in her voice, I relax a bit. I was afraid she'd keep fighting me, but now that we're on the same page, I don't have to worry anymore about what could go wrong. From this point on, it should all be smooth sailing.

Suddenly, the door swings open.

"Ah, there you are," AD Chang says. "I was just coming to ask your friend about your whereabouts."

I pivot toward the doorway. "Her name is Julia, and no need

to be concerned, I'm here. In fact, I knocked on your door earlier, but you didn't answer, so I came to see how things were progressing in here."

"Not well from the looks of it." Her eyes dart around the room.

"Things get worse before they get better." I sigh. "Particularly when you're organizing paper."

Of course, we're doing more than just organizing and sorting paper. We're digging for lost treasure. She wouldn't understand that, though. She never lets anything get out of hand. With her, you can be sure all the I's are dotted and all the T's crossed. Despite my concerns about the odd discrepancies going on around here, I doubt anything would be missing under her watchful eye.

"But since you're here, maybe you can fill me on how things are progressing with the money for Lei Ming's surgery," I add.

"Come to my office, and I'll update you. You know I can't stand being in here for too long." She spins and retreats down the hall.

Not wanting to abandon my friend again, I look over at Julia.

"Go," Julia waves me off. "I'll keep working here until you get back."

"It shouldn't take long, but I do want to tell her about my plans to adopt Lei Ming. Maybe once she knows about my intentions, she'll change her mind about letting me in the ICU." I smile. "I'll be back as soon as I can, I promise."

"I'll be praying as I'm sure you'll be needing it."

I give her a thumbs up and then head to the lion's den. The door is open, so I walk right in. I immediately spot the AD hunched over her desk. This time, however, I'm jarred by her vulnerable posture. Sitting like that, she seems less intimidating, more fragile. It's a side of her I've never seen before.

After several seconds of watching her like that, I clear my throat to garner her attention. "You have news to share with me?"

She jumps at the sound of my voice and sits up as straight as a board. "Yes. I wanted to let you know that I was able to secure funds for Lei Ming's surgery. They are set to operate later this afternoon."

"That's such great news." I clasp my hands together.

She puffs out her chest, a smug smile plastered across her face. "I told you I would take care of things."

"You did. Thank you."

"I did it for Lei Ming, not you, Miss Mayfield."

"Right." I take a seat across from her, so we are at eye level with one another. "With that situation under control, there is one more thing I'd like to discuss with you."

She exhales deeply and rolls her eyes. "Now what?"

"I've made a decision."

"Leaving us already?" Her voice drips with sarcasm. I'm sure she can't wait to see me go.

"No." I chuckle before summoning the courage to begin a journey which will undoubtedly be unlike anything I've ever undertaken. "I would like to start the process of adopting Lei Ming."

"Is this some kind of joke?" She scoffs. "If it is, I really don't have time for it."

"I'm serious. I want to adopt her."

Resting her elbows on her desk, she leans so far over I can see the whites of her pupils. "That's quite admirable, but I'm afraid that will be impossible."

Ugh! If one more person tells me that, I might just explode.

I restrain myself as best as I can and choose my words with care. "I understand that the process is difficult, but I'm willing to be patient and do whatever it takes. Complete forms. Provide documentation. Undergo a review or interview." My body trembles. "I'm not sure exactly how much it costs, but I'll find a way to pay for it."

To silence me, the AD holds a finger in the air. "You didn't let me explain."

I purse my lips and give her the space she needs. No matter what excuses she may offer, I'm certain I can overcome them.

"Miss Mayfield, I'm not sure how adoption works in America, but in China, you cannot just march into an orphanage, choose your favorite child, fill out some forms and walk out with a son or daughter to call your own."

"I didn't think that was—"

"No, you didn't think, nor did you do your research." Her face turns a deep shade of red. "In China, we match a child to a potential adopter based on various factors. It's a detailed process that requires the utmost screening and decision-making. We may have a lot of children here, but we don't just pass them out like candy."

"I didn't say you did. I simply wanted to—"

"I know what you want, but the fact that you work for a wealthy woman does not mean you have your 'pick of the litter' or allow you to jump to the head of the line." She rises from her chair like a phoenix. "If you want to adopt, you'll have to go about it the same way everyone else does."

I blink rapidly at her harsh remarks. "I'm willing to do that, but under the circumstances, I'd think you'd be willing to make an exception. I'm happy to go through the entire process like everyone else, but I'd prefer to be matched specifically with Lei Ming, that's all."

"There are no exceptions." She slams her hand down on her desk. "Your adopting Lei Ming is just not possible."

"Why? Because you don't like me? Because you don't want me here?" I spring to my feet. "Don't think I'm unaware of your dislike for me and your efforts to make my job more difficult than it needs to be."

"Despite your accusations, that is not why."

"Then what's the reason?"

"Because Lei Ming has already been matched to another family." She doesn't flinch as she drops her bombshell.

I gasp as if the air had been sucked out of the room. Had I heard her correctly? "Lei Ming is—is going to another family?" I barely manage to get the words out of my mouth before I collapse into my seat and close my eyes. This can't be happening. There must be a mistake. A big one.

"Correct." The AD's voice is softer now.

I open my eyes and gaze back at her. "Why didn't anyone tell me this before?"

"Because it's not our policy to share that information with everyone, and certainly not with someone who is here for a few weeks to get things organized." She pushes back into her chair. "Plus, we only officially matched her yesterday."

"Yesterday?" I swallow to bring my heart down from my throat. "I don't understand. How did you arrange that so quickly?"

She narrows her eyes. "Time was of the essence, Miss Mayfield."

"But why did you match her with potential adopters? She just needed money for surgery right away, not a family."

"She wouldn't have gotten one without the other."

I gather the strength to wrap my mind around the AD's words. "Are you saying that the adoptive family is paying for her surgery?"

"Yes, and you of all people should be pleased about both."

"I'm relieved she's getting the operation she needs to save her life, but I told you I would have handled that." My voice wavers as I internally debate whether I could have arranged for the funds in time. Although my heart was in the right place, my bank account tells a different story.

"I was more than capable of handling the situation on my own." She takes a deep breath and tugs on her blouse collar. "It's my job to ensure that these children get what they need, which is exactly what I did. This family was already in the system when they agreed to pay for the surgery and her future medical costs, so we placed them as the match. It was the only way to get the money in time."

I chew on my lip, still uncertain of what to believe. Could I take her at her word, or had she done this to be spiteful? Either way, it didn't matter. Lei Ming could never be mine. Her forever home was with someone else now. While that was good, it was still hard for me to believe. But my emotions aren't what's important right now. I can deal with those later. The only thing that truly matters is that Lei Ming will get the life-saving surgery she needs—even if it does cost me a future with her.

"So now what?" I brush away a tear.

"Lei Ming will have the operation and return here in a few days for her full recovery period. Once the doctor clears her to travel, her family will come and get her." She licks her lips. "Roughly four weeks from now."

Four weeks? My heart splinters with the information. That's not much time to spend with her, especially with all the work I need to do around here. Perhaps Julia's right. Maybe getting too attached to Lei Ming isn't the best idea, especially if she's going to another family. I stare out the AD's window where dark, ominous clouds have formed. Thunder rumbles and shakes the thin glass barrier. For a moment, I wish I could be whisked away in the storm rather than face the reality of my shattered dream.

"Miss Mayfield? "The AD snaps her fingers to bring me back down to earth. "Is there anything else you wanted to discuss? If not, I need to get back to work."

With my body and mind numb, I turn back to her and shake my head.

"Good, then you can see yourself out." She rearranges the few items out on her immaculate desk.

Unable to form a complete sentence or thought, I leave, sleep-walking my way down the hall. Somehow, I make it back to the director's office.

"Hey, you're back. What did she say?" Julia crosses the room to meet me. "Nicki, what's wrong?"

At my incoherent mumbles, she inches closer.

"Can you repeat that? I didn't understand you."

With a mix of sadness, disappointment, and frustration I share the news that has splintered my world. "Lei Ming already has an adoptive family. They're paying for her surgery and will come and get her in a few weeks." Drained of energy and emotion, I lean against the doorframe for support. I know Julia will want all the details, but I don't have the desire to rehash my discussion with the AD right now.

"I'm so sorry." She rocks back on her feet. "I know that's not what you'd hoped for, but maybe it's for the best. If the circumstances were different, you'd be thrilled by the news, right?"

"Probably." I grimace. "I just thought that I'd be the one caring for Lei Ming, but I guess I misunderstood God's purpose for me here." I slide down the frame and melt into the floor.

"No, what you're doing, getting things in order at New Hope and helping ensure these kids are well-taken care of in the future, is a good thing. That may be God's plan for you here." She drops to her knees and lifts my chin. "Maybe you just misunderstood the idea of adoption. Our emotions can get the best of us, and we assume that because our desire is so strong, it has to be the purpose for our lives. Unfortunately, the heart is deceitful and can't be trusted."

I lower my head and dig my fingernail into the grimy tile grout. "I hear what you're saying, but I don't think I was wrong about adopting Lei Ming. It felt right, Julia. Despite all my doubts and complaints about kids being messy, it all vanished when I held her hand in mine last night and I knew, I just knew God was calling me to take care of her."

"Sometimes He works in ways we just can't understand, and we have to let go of the way we thought it should be." She tucks one of my unruly curls behind my ear. "Are you going to be okay?"

"Don't worry. I'll be fine." Or maybe if I tell myself that enough times, I can make it a reality.

"Do you want to go get something to eat? Or maybe some hot chocolate will make you feel better? I know it does for me."

I slowly stand and brush the dirt from my bottom. "No, since I don't have to go back to the hospital now, we can make some progress in this room and find those missing contracts. I mean, that's the reason I'm here, isn't it? To organize?" And clearly the only reason.

"Are you sure you're up to it?" She eyes me over the top of her glasses.

I nod and walk into the room, looking for a stack of papers to distract me so I don't have to think about Lei Ming and what I lost with her. Or feel it.

Julia scurries back inside and we work on the box she'd been filtering through earlier. When we finish with all its contents, Julia takes a water break. "How are you holding up?" she asks after a large gulp.

"I'm fine." I brush the hair from my sweaty forehead. "Working helps take my mind off of things." *Otherwise, I'd be curled up in a fetal position in my hotel bed.*

"Good, because we have a lot of ground to cover," she says. "By the time we finish in here, you'll be back to your old self again."

"I'm not sure I'll ever be myself again after this, but maybe it will hurt less." I wince at my own words. Am I lying more to my friend or myself? There's no doubt the pain of losing Lei Ming will always be with me. In time it will fade, but there will always be a scar on my heart from what could have been. Until that healing takes place, however, I will just bury myself in work. What else can I do?

I open another box, passing the lid to Julia. "If God brought me here to get things in order so that this place can continue to function, then I'm going to give it my all." I reach down and pull out a handful of papers. "I'm going to find those missing

Perfectly Placed

contracts so no more money is lost, and then I'll submit all the documents so that the O'Connor Foundation will always support this place and ensure that there is plenty of money in the budget for additional staff, surgeries, and whatever else these children need."

"Wow, you're a woman on a mission."

"You bet I am." I pull my damp hair into a bun on top of my head. "No more distractions, just a commitment to do the job I was sent to—"

My phone rings from across the room, interrupting my rant. I turn my head in the direction of the shrill sound but stay glued to my spot.

"Aren't you going to get that?" Julia cocks her head in the direction of the ringing.

A wave of nausea crests in my gut as I glance over at my purse. What if it's Ben calling for an update on Lei Ming? Or Ms. O'Connor returning my call? Or my mom? I don't want to talk with any of them right now because I know that the minute I open my mouth, an avalanche of grief will crash over me. I'm not ready to deal with my emotions just yet. I have a job to do first.

But with that comes my responsibility to communicate with my boss. If it is her and I don't answer, she'll only worry and keep calling back until she reaches me.

I scramble to answer the phone before whoever is on the other end hangs up. From the caller ID, my decision to answer was spot on.

"Ms. O'Connor, hi!" I decide to take the offensive to offset the line of questioning I know is coming after my unexpected call from the hospital. "I apologize for bothering you yesterday. Fortunately, the issue's been resolved." *Even if it wasn't in my favor.*

"Nicki?" The somber voice on the line is familiar, but not that of my boss.

"Heather?" I'm surprised to hear from her.

"Yes."

I relax a bit. "Oh, I assumed it was Ms. O'Connor since her name popped up on my screen." I chuckle. "Is she having you make calls for her from her phone now?"

Heather chokes back a sob. "Nicki, I'm sorry to be the one to tell you this, but Katherine is dead."

10

Exit the door, check the weather; enter the door, check the face.
~ *Chinese Proverb*

My eyelashes flutter, and it takes a moment for my brain to process where I am. The plush king-size bed, rich dark wood furnishings, and the silky linens I've grown accustomed to the past few weeks have been replaced by a twin-size mattress situated next to a stack of freakishly scary porcelain dolls and the lingering odor of a musty resale shop.

I sit up and listen for the cacophony of rumbling buses and honking taxis that have acted as my alarm clock buzzer, but instead hear only the shrill sound of birds chirping outside my windowsill and the sizzle of bacon in a frying pan.

This can only mean one thing. I somehow managed to get on a plane and back home to my mother's house in Connecticut for Ms. O'Connor's funeral.

I flop back on the tiny bed and roll over onto my side. Although the effort removes the dolls from my sight, it also intensifies the dull throbbing in my head. No matter how much sleep I've had over the last two days or how many aspirins I've consumed, the pain of Ms. O'Connor's death is still a fresh, open wound. One I know from experience won't heal quickly.

The red lights on my nightstand alarm clock, as bright as the signs on the Las Vegas strip, glare at me. Nine fifteen. Only two more hours until a car will pick us up and take us to the funeral home.

While I should get up and start getting myself ready for the difficult day ahead, I close my eyes and sink deeper under the covers. Maybe I'm having a bad dream, and when I wake up, nothing will have changed. But when I open them again, I'm back in the one place I said I'd never stay again—my childhood bedroom.

Heather had offered to let me stay at the O'Connor estate in one of the numerous guest rooms available there, but being back in a house that held so many memories of my time with my boss would be too hard. Traipsing through the shoe room I had organized for her or using the bathroom where I first met her and her potty-training cat-child, Princess, would only cause the hurt to intensify, the wound to fester.

No, despite the chaos that engulfs my mother's home and makes me nauseous, it's the lesser of two evils in this case and wouldn't keep me up at night.

Well, maybe the dolls would.

"Knock, knock," my mother's voice squeaks from the other side of the dingy six-panel door. "Time to rise and shine." The door creaks open, and she slinks into the room.

"Hi, Mom." I bring myself back into a sitting position and plaster a fake smile onto my face. No doubt my puffy eyelids and mascara smudges negate my attempts to seem happy to see her. Which I am. If only the circumstances were different.

"Nicki." My mom makes her way over to me. "Did you sleep at all?" She plops down on the bare-thin comforter emblazoned with cats. A thrift shop nightmare she found at the bottom of a bargain bin, I'm sure.

"Some." I twirl a loose thread of the comforter around my

finger until the tip turns a purplish-blue and I can't feel it anymore.

"I'm sorry. Today's not going to be easy for you, but I'm afraid if you don't get up and moving soon, we'll be late for the funeral. Neither you nor Ms. O'Connor would be pleased about that." She stands and brushes her hand through my hair like she did when I was a little girl. "Come on, I have breakfast ready."

I throw back the covers and follow my mom into the kitchen. Not much about the house has changed in the weeks I've been gone. Not that I'm surprised. My mother has a serious problem and refuses help. I tried to clear the clutter from this place in the past, but her attachment to every little thing only caused our relationship to suffer. Since she's all I had left, I had to stop fighting and let her be.

Not an easy thing for a former professional organizer to do.

When I enter the kitchen, my heart sinks as I absorb the fact that my absence has only agitated Mom's hoarding. None of the drawers or cabinet doors can shut properly anymore thanks to all the plastic bags of dollar store and clearance finds she shoves in there for safe-keeping.

I repress the shock and anger that are on the verge of making an entrance and spoiling what little time I have with my mother. While I should probably say something to her about the growing clutter, it would only cause undue stress. That's the last thing I need or want this morning. No, I'll just add it to my ever-growing list of issues to deal with later, along with losing Lei Ming.

"Nicki?"

I pull my eyes away from the mess and focus on my mother. "Yes?"

She sidles up to me with a steaming plate of eggs and bacon in one hand and pulls out a metal chair from underneath the wobbly 1950s Formica table with the other.

"Sit down and get something in your stomach. You've hardly eaten since you arrived and you need some food in your system to get you through the day." She sets the plate on the once-white tabletop. "God's grace is sufficient to get you through the difficulties, but a little protein helps too."

I give her a quick peck on the cheek before sitting down. Although I don't love my mother's house or her hoarding, I adore her.

The split vinyl cushion pinches the back of my legs as I sit down and take a bite of the fluffy scrambled eggs. "Wow, Mom, these are really good." I didn't even know the stove still worked. I'd always thought it was just another flat surface to store more of my mother's fabulous finds.

"Thank you." She falls into the metal chair next to me. "I've been practicing."

"P-practicing?" I almost choke on my food, thinking of the potential fire hazards her culinary endeavors might create.

"Well, with you gone, I didn't want to eat out by myself all the time, so l figured I'd give it a try." She beams. "I like cooking, and when you come back, we can eat here more often."

I cringe at the idea of spending more time in her home than is necessary, but I can't bring myself to diminish the joy radiating from my mother's face. "Sure, that sounds good."

"So, when do you think you'll be coming back?"

"I wish I knew." I break off a piece of juicy fat from the bacon and pop it into my mouth.

"That doesn't make sense, Nic. You're such a wonderful organizer, I figured you'd be almost done by now." Her bottom lip pulls into a pout. "I miss you."

Surprised by her eagerness to have me home, I fight against the piece of bacon lodged in my throat. A sip of orange juice helps it slide down. "I miss you too, Mom, but it's not that simple." I set my glass on the table. "Things are complicated, and I'm not sure if I'm going to be able to fix them in a timely manner. And now that Ms. O'Connor is gone ..."

I reach for a napkin and dab my eyes. "Now that she's gone, I'm not sure what my future is in China. Without Ms. O'Connor to guide me, I don't know how to handle all the unusual issues that keep cropping up." I wipe my dripping nose. "But like everything else, I'll figure out my next steps after the funeral."

"You sound like you're giving up." She leans on the table and studies me intently. "That's not the Nicki I know."

"If you recall, I recently shut down my business. My face should be posted next to the dictionary definition of giving up."

"You're comparing apples to oranges." She waves a hand at me. "You never back down from a fight. Especially not one that's as important as New Hope and those kids' well-being."

"You're right." I exhale deeply. "I don't normally quit, but everything seems to be going against me in China. AD Chang has it out for me, Julia and I can't make progress locating some missing documents, and then there's the whole situation with Lei Ming."

"Lei Ming." She taps her index finger against her lips. "Isn't she the little girl you talked non-stop about after your first visit?"

"Yes."

Her look turns questioning.

Recognizing her all-familiar expression, I release a heavy sigh. "If I tell you the story, will you promise not to make a big deal about it?"

Like a boy scout, she holds up her fingers. "I promise."

I flick both brows up. I know better than to believe her. When it comes to guys, relationships, and kids, she can't contain her emotions. But with no sure path for my future right now, telling her about everything that's happened shouldn't give her any hope. "Okay, but I have to give you the condensed version if we're going to make it to the funeral on time."

She scoots closer and locks her eyes on me before I recount the events that have taken place since I returned to New Hope. The good, the bad, and the ugly.

"When I got the call from Heather about Ms. O'Connor, I asked Julia to continue working and keep tabs on Lei Ming—she's doing fine, by the way—then caught the first plane here." I bend my head. "None of this is going the way it's supposed to, and it makes me wonder if I was even meant to go in the first place."

"Oh my goodness," my mother squeals. "I can't believe what I'm hearing. After all these years of hoping and praying, you're finally considering motherhood." Laugh lines radiate from her blue eyes. "I may be a grandmother yet!"

I crease my forehead. "You did hear me say that Lei Ming was going to another family, right?"

"I heard you." She places her hand on top of mine. "But just because something's hard doesn't mean it wasn't meant to be. God's ways are not your ways, and He may just bring things around differently than how you assumed they would go."

I shake my head at her. Adopting Lei Ming is a dead end. There is no other route.

"The fact that you even considered adopting Lei Ming," she continues, "well, that tells me you're opening your heart to possibilities that before were out of the question. If nothing else, God may have used this time for that reason alone. It may seem wasted to you, but God had a plan for it. Be patient, and He'll show you the rest when the time's right."

She glances at the cuckoo clock mounted on the wall. "Speaking of time, we need to get a move on it. The car will be here soon to take us to the funeral."

Back in my bedroom, I zip up my black dress and ponder my mom's words. Perhaps my time in China wasn't a waste. Maybe it was just intended to break down the heavy walls I'd built around my heart. If that was the case, though, why did losing Lei Ming have to hurt so much? If anything, it only made me want to add more concrete reinforcement to the steel beam structures already in place.

I slip my blazer over my shoulders and tug on the edges of it to get it in place, just like I'd seen Ms. O'Connor do so many times. With shaky fingers, I do my best to button it up but only manage to get one silver clasp in place. I pull harder to close the second one but underestimate my strength and send it flying across the room and into the stack of dolls.

Nope. Retrieving it is not an option.

"Mom?" I yell from my bedroom. "Do you have a sewing kit?" Stupid question. She has everything in this house.

"In the kitchen," she yells from her bedroom.

I head in that direction and quickly begin my scavenger hunt among the drawers. My search is fruitless until I rummage through the fourth one. There I spot a small sewing kit poking out from underneath a stack of bright neon yellow papers. I lift the stack and grab the clear plastic hotel repair kit. When I pick up the papers to put them back in the drawer, the words EVICTION/CONDEMNATION NOTICE catch my attention in bold black lettering.

A lump forms in the pit of my stomach, weighing me down.

Sliding the kit into the pocket of my blazer, I tiptoe back to the hallway and look around the corner to see if my mom is coming this way. With no sign of her anywhere, I race back to the drawer, retrieve one of the notices, and scan the document.

Phrases such as "unsuitable, unhealthy, and unsafe environment" catch my eye. Official Bridgeport city and county seals are stamped along the edge and the letter is dated February 17. A week ago. I browse the other sheets of paper. Except for the dates, they're identical.

"Mom, can you come in here, please?" My heart beats so hard within my chest I think it might explode. "Now?"

She shuffles into the room while simultaneously toying with her clip-on earrings. "What's so urgent, Nicki?" She's wearing the same dress she wore to my dad's funeral ten years ago.

I blink and try not to let that memory paralyze me from the task at hand. "What are these?" I hold up the crumpled yellow papers.

A flicker of shock widens my mother's eyes and panic tightens the lines around her mouth. "Nothing."

"They're eviction notices. For you." Heat rises to my cheeks. "Why didn't you tell me about these?"

"It's nothing serious or anything you need to be concerned about." She marches toward me and plucks them out of my hand. "Junk mail, that's all." She tosses them in the trash bin.

"Mom, it's not junk." I carefully remove one that isn't touching our leftover breakfast from the pile and read it aloud to her. "This is your fifth and final notice ... due to the continuous complaints from neighbors and service personnel as well as the hazardous conditions your property poses, we are notifying you of the intent to evict and condemn your home unless measures are taken to repair said property." I look back up at her. "Sounds pretty serious to me."

"Pssh." She looks out the window above the sink.

I position myself between her and the outside view. "Why didn't you tell me about this?"

Her lips quiver. "Because I thought I could handle it on my own."

So that's where my independent spirit comes from. "But you haven't," I continue. "You kept stuffing them in the drawers. Let me guess, 'Out of sight, out of mind?'"

"Something like that." She turns her gaze back to me. "I didn't take it seriously because I own the house and never imagined they could do that. But it looks like they can." Her shoulders slump. "I can't lose this house, Nic. It's all I have left of your father."

I want to remind her that she still has me. His daughter. But I doubt she'd make the connection. "I understand how you feel, Mom, but this is serious. According to these papers, you are violating several fire and health codes, which the city has the right to enforce either through hefty fines or condemnation. Neither of which you can afford."

"I've tried to do what they asked, but it's too hard." My mother slumps into one of the kitchen chairs. "I can't let go of this stuff. It all means so much to me."

I shake my head and try to reconcile how broken umbrellas, expired food cans, and fabric remnants can hold such an important place in my mother's heart. Sadly, I can't. That's just the way it is with my mom and her prized possessions. And her illness.

While I want to empathize with my mother, the urgency of the situation doesn't allow me the opportunity, so my professional organizer personality takes over. "Have you contacted anyone at City Hall or the Health Department and explained the situation?"

Her dangling gold clip-on earrings jingle as she nods. "I did when the last one arrived. They gave me a thirty-day extension to clean things up a bit, but that's it."

Calculating the time allotted by the city and what work needed to be completed around the house, my brain goes into overdrive on how to best appease the local officials and avoid their threats. The answer was not in her favor.

"Mom, we can't meet that deadline." My stomach gurgles. "I'm sorry, but we need to think about what this means and where we go from here."

"There's no we in this, Nicki. I'll take care of it, and you will go back to China. But right now, we need to get to Ms. O'Connor's funeral."

I glance at the clock. The car will be here in fifteen minutes, and I'm not anywhere near ready. Either physically or mentally. Above all else, I don't want to be late for the service. Not only would it be rude, but it would be a true disrespect to my boss, who valued timeliness as if it were a precious commodity.

"This discussion is not over, Mom. We'll pick it back up later. I promise."

A knock on the door causes us both to jump.

"Our ride is early and you're not ready." She quickly scans from head to toe. "Go get finished and I'll let the driver know it won't be much longer." Since the front door is currently barricaded with newspapers and all sorts of other worthless junk, she has to dash out the back door to meet our escort.

Once we're settled in the town car and racing toward the funeral home, I bring up the topic of the notices again. But this time, I'm not belaboring the point.

"I'm sorry, Mom."

She whips her head in my direction. "For what?"

"For not being here to help you."

"There's nothing you could have done. Really, Nic, let's not talk about it right now. It's not the time or the occasion."

While I know she's right, I can't let it go. If I had been here, I might have seen the notices earlier, or she may have told me about them at one of our weekly dinners at Luigi's over a steaming bowl of pasta. My heart weighs heavily with the burden. I hadn't been there for my mom when she needed me most.

I lean against the door and consider how this could have been avoided.

Maybe if I hadn't given up on helping my mom all those years ago, none of this would be happening. Yet it is, and I have to accept that I am partly to blame. For not being more insistent that she get treatment for this illness, for ignoring the problem to suit my own needs and letting it go unchecked, for leaving to take care of others when I should have taken care of my family. Even if she had encouraged me to go.

My body grows heavier under the weight of guilt and remorse. Not only for how I failed my mother but also for the juxtaposition of our relationship moving forward. I never dreamed I'd have to take over the parenting role so soon, but if that's what I have to do to rectify this situation, I will. Otherwise, my mom will be homeless in fewer than thirty days.

To remain in her home, however, she'll have to start letting go. Unfortunately, I've heard enough stories from other organizers who specialize in hoarding that for someone in her position to do that is akin to hiking Mount Everest. My mother won't be able to climb it alone. With no other family to turn to, I'm my mother's only hope of reaching the summit once and for all.

Except I can't be here because I'm supposed to return to China soon.

"Mom, what if I stayed here with you and helped you resolve this instead of going back to Beijing?" I throw the question out there as bait to see if she'll be willing to finish the discussion.

"Don't be silly, Nicki. There are too many people counting on you to return and finish what you started. I certainly don't want to be responsible for keeping you from that."

"You wouldn't be." I shift in my seat and face her. "I've been thinking about this. Julia could handle the rest of the job on her own without me. Better than anyone, she knows the ins and outs of running an orphanage, and with some cajoling, I could probably convince her to finish the work and supply me with the information the Foundation would need."

Mom's eyes widen as large as saucers. "What about the little girl you've grown attached to and New Hope? Wouldn't you want to go back for her?"

Rubbing my finger against the black leather cushion lining, I force back the tears. "Lei Ming has a family in place. They'll come get her soon and provide her with all the love and care she'll need for a lifetime. She'll be happy with them. That's what matters most." I sigh. "As for New Hope, I can help the orphanage from here just as well, if not better. Plus, AD Chang will be thrilled not to have me return."

A sour taste fills my mouth at the mention of her name. I don't know what games she's playing, but I hope Director Wu will be able to continue and not allow the AD to run New Hope into the ground with her heavy-handed leadership. "The world won't fall apart if I don't go back. And I can't abandon you. Not again."

My mother remains quiet for several moments. "You'd be

129

willing to do that for me?" When she looks up at me, her eyes are filled with relief.

"You and I only have each other, and I can't let you deal with this alone. We're family, and family always stick together." I place my hand on top of hers.

She squeezes my hand. "I'd like that, Nicki, but only if you're certain this is what you want to do."

The car pulls into the funeral home parking lot.

"I am." My heart thumps harder. I'm not sure if it's because I know what's about to come or because of the decision I've made, but either way, I have to stay strong. "We can finish talking about it after the funeral."

"What do you think Heather will say when you tell her you're not going back?"

"I don't know." I open my car door. "We'll find out soon enough."

Mom freezes. "Do you think it's appropriate to discuss something like that at a funeral?"

With one foot out the door, I look back over at my mother. "If I don't do it now, I might change my mind. I can't let that happen."

11

Three humble shoemakers brainstorming will make a great statesman.

~ Chinese Proverb

Ms. O'Connor's Celebration of Life service is anything but a celebration.

With only a handful of people in attendance, it resembles a small business meeting rather than a funeral. And of those suits who did come to offer their condolences, at least half of them sit stoically in the pews glancing at their phones or Rolexes every two minutes. Only Heather, her personal assistant, and I demonstrate any true sense of grief.

It's evident Ms. O'Connor didn't have many friends.

In all, the service lasts less than thirty minutes. As the instrumental sounds of *'Ave Maria'* float through the room, an overwhelming sadness floods my spirit. I never did let Ms. O'Connor know how much she meant to me, either personally or professionally. We didn't always get along, but I adored her. I only wish I'd had the chance to tell her.

When the music finally stops, the sparse crowd rises from

their seats and proceeds to leave. I, however, stay rooted in mine.

"Wait for me in the car," I tell my mother. "I want to speak with Heather privately to make sure she's okay and let her know my decision."

Mom opens her mouth and then closes it. Her pursed lips indicate she wants to question me again about my choice of timing, but she gathers her belongings and glides past me into the aisle instead.

With shaky hands, I blow my nose and wipe my cheeks before walking to the front row where Heather sits. Smaller now than she was the last time I saw her, it's as if half of her petite frame has withered away from the loss of her employer. Hunched over and clutching a handkerchief, she jumps at my presence.

"I didn't mean to startle you." I lower myself onto the seat next to her and notice that even without makeup and with somewhat unkempt hair, she's still a beautiful woman.

She dabs her eyes with a tissue. "Thank you for coming, Nicki."

"I wouldn't have missed it."

"I know it wasn't an easy trip, and you have a lot to do at New Hope, but I'm so happy you're here. Katherine would have been pleased."

Our eyes shift from one another to the bronze urn perched on a single Greek pedestal and flanked between two white rose sprays. Next to it stands a wooden easel holding an oversized, glossy photograph of Ms. O'Connor. Seeing her up-close and personal one last time, my heart squeezes so tightly I can hardly breathe.

"She would have hated to have her face looming over the crowd like that." Heather nods at the portrait. "The funeral director thought it was a nice touch."

"She would have," I whisper, then force myself to look away. "So now what?"

"Well, I'm the executrix of her estate, so I'll handle dismantling everything once the will is probated." She sits up straight. "Then I'll continue her work at the Foundation and ensure her charitable spirit moves on."

"And what about all her shoes? And Princess?"

At the mention of Ms. O'Connor's favorite things, Heather's mouth curves upward in a faint smile. "Princess has been relocated to my house. My girls are delighted to have her, though I think Princess considers it more like prison the way they torture her." She pauses. "As for the shoes, I'll make sure they're added to the inventory for the next Giving Gown event unless you want to take some. I'm sure Katherine would have loved for you to have a few pairs. Heaven knows she had plenty."

The aquamarine Versace heels I'd gawked over the first time I worked for Ms. O'Connor flitter through my mind. We had the same shoe size, so they'd be a perfect fit and a wonderful keepsake to always remember her by, but someone else more deserving should have them. "Thanks, but I'll pass. I'm not nearly ready to fill her shoes." Either figuratively or literally.

Heather nods as tears roll down her cheeks. "Katherine thought the world of you, Nicki. You were able to do what most other people couldn't do for her."

"And what was that?"

"You broke through her tough exterior and helped her to heal."

"Me?" I clutch my hand to my chest.

"Yes, if it weren't for you, she would have never learned the truth about the orphanage or her father's true feelings for her." She daintily wipes her nose. "That healing gave her so much joy. She was a different person the last few months of her life, and that's all because of you."

My face flushes. "I only wish I had been there to see that for myself."

"Katherine would have loved nothing more than to be there

working alongside you in China, but ..." Heather's sad tone turns serious. "It just wasn't possible in her condition."

"What do you mean?" I knit my eyebrows together.

"Katherine had been sick for some time due to the heart issues she developed as a child. When the two of you returned from China in January, the doctor told her she didn't have much time left."

"She knew?" My pulse quickens. "Why didn't she say anything to me?"

"She didn't want to put any pressure on you or let that sway your decision to return to New Hope on her behalf. She wanted you to go because that's what you wanted, not out of pity or as a favor to a dying woman."

I sit back against the pew and try to wrap my head around the fact that Ms. O'Connor had withheld that information from me. Except I couldn't. For whatever reason, she felt it was best I didn't know.

"I ... I wish she would have told me. At least I would have had the chance to tell her how much she meant to me." I gulp. "And to tell her goodbye." I knew from my dad's sudden stroke ten years ago that it's harder to find closure when you can't say goodbye. I'd have to find a way again.

Heather sniffles. "I was sworn to secrecy, otherwise I probably would have. But I'm so glad you went, Nicki. You focusing on New Hope and those kids kept Katherine going these last few weeks, and I think having you there on her behalf gave her a sense of peace and reassurance she wouldn't have had otherwise."

"I haven't done all that much." My stomach lurches, thinking about all the issues facing the orphanage at the moment. And how I've failed to fix them.

"She cared deeply for you, you know." For the first time since I've been with her, she smiles. "You aren't taking enough credit, but I appreciate what you're doing and will continue to do there. Katherine knew she could count on you, and so do I."

"Um, speaking of that." I search for the courage I need to inform Heather of my plans not to return to China. Despite knowing my choice was best for me and my mother, reservation about the decision courses through me.

"Is something wrong?" Her earlier joy dissipates.

"Well, no, I mean, yes." Sweat trickles down my back. Since I don't have all the details on the missing contracts, which might turn out to be a nonissue, I concentrate on what I do know is problematic. "I don't think I'm going to be able to return to New Hope anytime soon."

She blinks rapidly. "I don't understand."

"I'm sorry to have to tell you this here, but I know that if I don't tell you, I'll change my mind. And I can't—I mean, my mom can't—afford that. And the sooner we can make the necessary arrangements, the sooner we'll be able to meet the deadline to submit all the paperwork to the foundation for their consideration—"

"Nicki." Heather holds her hand up to me. "You're babbling. I need you to slow down and start from the beginning."

I take a deep breath and try to stay calm. "I can't go back to New Hope."

"You mean, not in the near future, or not at all?"

"Probably not at all." I lower my eyes to the floor where a service handout has fallen. I shiver at the sight of Ms. O'Connor's name at the top of the paper, a concrete reminder that I'm failing her and the kids. As if I needed one.

"Did something happen that caused you to change your mind?" Heather bends her head to meet my gaze. "If so, I'm sure I can handle whatever it is so that you can focus on finishing up in Beijing."

"No." I peel my eyes off the handout. "It's a personal family issue that I can't ignore any longer, and I'm the only one who can take care of it. I need to stay here for a while."

"I see."

I force down the bile rising to my mouth.

When the tension feels as if it's going to break me in half, I speak up. "I know this is the worst time to drop this in your lap and I'm so sorry, but I needed you to know as soon as possible so that whoever replaces me can get the paperwork submitted in time."

"I appreciate you telling me now rather than later, but I can't say I'm not disappointed." Her shoulders sag. "Are you sure there's nothing I could say or do to persuade you to go back?"

I shake my head.

A heavy exhale escapes from her tiny body. "Well, I guess I'll have to get working on this right away." She tucks her handkerchief into her clutch and rises from the pew.

I stand with her. "Again, Heather, I'm really sorry."

"I know, Nicki." She steps around me. "I'll be in touch soon so we can work over all the details and discuss how to get your things returned here."

When I no longer hear Heather's heels clacking against the marble floor, I pick up the handout and leave the sanctuary, and Ms. O'Connor, for good.

Later that evening, the anguish on Heather's face floats through my mind when I attempt to eat a peanut butter and jelly sandwich. After two bites, which I force down my throat, I push the plate aside and roam into the living room in search of something to distract me from today's earlier events.

At first, I consider calling Julia to update her about my decision not to return to Beijing, but numbing my mind with the latest celebrity reality show seems like the better option. I locate four TVs in front of a large window and attempt to turn each one on. When none of them do, I revert to my usual MO when stressed. Organizing.

I empty one of the oversized dollar store bags from the couch and start collecting anything that closely resembles trash off the floor, furniture, and flat surfaces. Filling that bag up in under a minute, I retrieve larger yard bags from underneath the kitchen sink and continue sorting through the various piles of books, trinkets, blankets, and old magazines my mother has held onto as if they were precious jewels.

No time like the present to start clearing up the mess. If I can't save New Hope, at least I can save my mother from being homeless.

I manage to rid two armchairs of the clutter that has consumed them for as long as I can remember when my mom stumbles into the room from running errands.

"What are you doing?" Mom drops the sacks of groceries she's carrying and rushes over to me. Snatching the half-filled bag from my hands, she pilfers through it before looking back at me. The friendliness in her eyes has frozen into a blue as cold as ice. "Why are these things in a garbage bag?"

"Mom." I rub my hands over my face. "We have to clean this place up enough to satisfy the city, and we have fewer than thirty days to do it. If we don't, they're going to throw you out and condemn your house."

"I think you could have had the courtesy to wait for me before deciding what's trash and what's not." She turns the bag upside down, freeing all the items I'd just discarded back onto the floor.

"I'm sorry, but I needed something to do, and this seemed like the most logical choice. It's not like we can put this off any longer."

She unties another one of the stuffed black bags. "I know, but we need to go through everything one by one—"

"That's not possible." I raise my voice louder than I ever have with her before. "There's too much stuff in here for us to look at everything individually." I dart over to her and gently push her away from the bag.

"You can't do this to me, Nicki." She stumbles backward. "These are my things, and you don't get to say what's trash and what isn't."

"I'm not doing anything to you, Mom. You said you want to

stay in the house because of Dad. The only way to do that is to get rid of some things."

She plants her hands on her hips. "This is my house, and I'm not leaving it."

"If that's what you want, then these things have to go." I reach for the bag in her hands.

"No." She pulls it back behind her.

"What are you going to do when the city comes here and sees you haven't done what they've asked. Then what, Mom? Where will you live?"

"I don't plan on leaving. Somehow, I'll find a way to stay *and* keep my things." Her face turns red and beads of sweat line her upper lip. "Everybody, including you, thinks they know what's best for me, but they don't."

Heat scalds my lungs as I lift my head to the ceiling and blow out a huge puff of air. While I knew this would be difficult, I didn't think she'd be this way right from the get-go. Earlier she'd seemed happy to have me stay and help her. Now she was like a momma bear whose cubs had been taken from her. Downright scary.

"We'll discuss this later. You're too worked up right now to talk about this." I do my best to stay as calm as possible.

She ignores me and continues to empty contents from their captivity.

"Mom." I grab her arm. "Listen to me."

She snaps her head at me and gives me a death stare. "No, I don't want to talk to you right now. Leave me alone."

I hold my hands up in surrender. "Fine, I'll give you some time to think about everything, but we're not done here."

As I retreat to my room, the doorbell rings. With nothing else to do, and knowing my mom is in no condition to greet anyone, I walk around front to see who's at the door.

"Nicki Mayfield?" A uniformed teenager stands in front of me, a large manila envelope in his right hand.

"Yes."

"Heather Campbell asked that we deliver this to you." He holds out an iPad. "Can you sign here please acknowledging your acceptance?"

Once I've done as requested, he slips me the package.

"Have a good evening," he says.

Back inside I head straight to my room with the thick package. Plopping down on my bed, I remove the contents and read the handwritten note that's paper clipped to pages of typed documents.

Nicki,

I understand the choice you've made not to return to China. Please know that there are no hard feelings, and if there's anything I can do to help you with your family issues, I'm here for you.

Enclosed you'll find the documents you requested from me earlier. I wasn't sure if you'd still want them or not, so I sent them over anyway. Whenever you're ready, we can discuss our next steps and who might replace you.

I'm also sending a letter Katherine asked me to give you after her funeral. With everything going on today, I forgot to pass it on. Please forgive me.

Wishing you and your family all the best,

Heather

I set aside the business documents and look for the letter from Ms. O'Connor. A smaller red envelope, which reminds me of the *hóngbāo* from Chinese New Year that the children received, has my name written on it. Tears well in my eyes at the sight of Ms. O'Connor's familiar script.

139

Taking a deep breath, I open the envelope, unfold the personalized cream stationery, and begin reading.

Dearest Nicki,

If you're reading this letter, then you know that I'm gone. I wasn't certain if you would be able to make it to my funeral or not, so I hope this letter reaches you in a timely manner.

I want to say thank you for being not only a faithful employee but also a good friend. We were an unlikely pair, but we made a strong team that accomplished much. Except for Princess and Heather, I don't have many close friends or family. Not only am I honored to count you as a dear friend, but part of my family as well.

I also want to extend my deepest gratitude to you for all you are doing at New Hope. As an only child who never married or had kids of my own, my only legacy in this world will be the work and support I offered to worthy causes. I'd like to think of these as my children and that the effort I put into them will have an impact on multiple generations. Your help in making my legacy a worthwhile and positive one means more than you know.

Finally, it's my deepest desire that you continue the work my father started and that I pledged to carry on. While there are others who could fill this position, there is no one else who understands and cares about it like you do. That is why I've entrusted you with getting things in order at New Hope and am asking that you personally present the submission to the O'Connor Foundation for continued funding when the time arrives.

As of now, there is enough money in their trust account for all necessary surgeries and general expenses for the remainder of this year and next. However, without the Foundation's commitment to financially support this program, I worry that it will be more difficult to help these children in the future. Please, I beg you, do all you can to ensure these children receive the care and nurturing they need for years to come.

Continue the wonderful work you've been called to, Nicki. Though it may prove more difficult than you believed, in the end, it will have been worth it.

Your friend,
Katherine O'Connor

I read the letter two more times—the first to hear Ms. O'Connor's voice again and the second to fully process everything she said and asked of me. When I finish, I drop the letter onto the comforter and collapse back on my bed.

My mind whirrs from the day's events and my boss's final words to me. There would have been no way she could have known about the situation with my mom, so her heartfelt request adds another layer of complexity to my decision. She counted me as her family too.

Staring at the popcorn ceiling, I debate what to do. No matter what I decide—to stay or go—I'm going to disappoint one of the women I care about most. Something I never like doing.

My mother's wails shatter the quiet of my internal wrestling match. Listening to her replace the clutter I had removed back to its original home, I question if I can be the one to truly help her. There's no doubt I can do the job, but at what cost? As much as I admired my late boss, I don't want my relationship with my mother to resemble the one Ms. O'Connor had with her father. If I stay, that just might happen.

But that doesn't mean I can't get her the help she needs.

I have several former organizing colleagues who are specifically trained to deal with people who suffer from this illness. If I'm being honest with myself, they're a better choice than me. Not only are they more skilled to handle the magnitude of my mother's messy house, but they'd also be less emotionally invested as well. If I reached out to one of them, I'm certain they'd be happy to assist her if available.

It might just be the best thing I can do for my mom right now. And our relationship in the future.

With a lightness in my spirit that wasn't there before, I focus on Ms. O'Connor's request, as well as something she mentioned in her letter. I reach for the paper lying next to me and search for the sentence that's nagging at me. Once I find it, I read it again, slowly digesting the truth it reveals:

As of now, there is enough money in their trust account for all necessary surgeries and general expenses for the remainder of this year and next.

I jump up off my bed. If Ms. O'Connor is to be believed, which she is, why did AD Chang say there was no money for Lei Ming's surgery? There must be a discrepancy. Is that why the monthly reports hadn't been turned in to the CMM? Is there more going on than unsubmitted paperwork and missing employee contracts?

Curious, I sift through the financial documents Heather supplied with an eagle eye. It doesn't take long for me to grasp the gravity of the situation. And that going back to China is a must.

With Ms. O'Connor's picture from the funeral still fresh on my mind, I grab my phone off the nightstand. Before making the call I pray will finally solve my mom's issues and keep our relationship intact, I send Heather a text message.

Change of plans. Can we talk?

12

A fish not caught by a hook may be caught by a net.
~ *Chinese Proverb*

With my mother in capable hands and on her way to more suitable living conditions, I return to Beijing the first week of March. This time, however, I don't intend just to get things in order. I want clear answers as to how things got so bad in the first place, and I want them right away. The clock hasn't stopped ticking and my deadline is looming with a week of March already gone.

The hunt starts with AD Chang.

"Miss Mayfield," she says when I march through the open door of her dimly lit office. "I wasn't sure if we'd ever see you again."

I park myself in the chair directly in front of her. "Wishful thinking on your part." I plaster a smile on my face. "There's a lot of work for me to do around here, so until it's complete, plan on me sticking around."

"What are you doing in my office then?" she scoffs. "As you can see, it's not in need of your services."

"Sometimes my clients look like they have everything

organized but when I start searching behind closed doors, I find all kinds of chaos." I glance over at her filing cabinet. "Maybe you're hiding something in your files or in your drawers that you don't want anyone to see?" Remembering her earlier directive to not go through her things without her permission, I lean forward in my seat just enough to make her think I might get up and start working.

"That won't be necessary. I keep everything in perfect order, both inside and out." She smiles wanly. "I appreciate your willingness to help me, but I don't need it. Plus, I believe you said you had work to do elsewhere?"

"I do, but first, I have a few questions I'd like to ask you." I fall back in the chair.

"Make it quick." She shuffles the papers on her desk. "I'm busy."

I roll my eyes. "First things first. How's Lei Ming, and when can I see her?"

Reluctantly, the AD stops fidgeting and addresses me. "She's doing remarkably well, considering her perilous condition a while back." She grins. "Her new family will be here in a few weeks to take her home."

With her subtle reminder that this little girl can't be mine and that my time with her is limited, my heart constricts. "Yes, I'm aware. That's why I'm anxious to see her and submitting my request to visit the Recovery Unit today."

"I'll check with the staff about a good time for you to visit, but I must insist you keep it short. She doesn't need to get worn out." The AD lets out a heavy sigh. "If that's all, then ..."

"Thank you. There's just one more thing." I pull a stack of papers from my bag. "These are the last three financial reports submitted to the CMM from New Hope." I slide them across her desk.

She reaches for her reading glasses and places them on the tip of her turned-up nose before collecting the documents. "What about them?" She rifles through the stapled sheets.

"According to these documents, there should still be more than four hundred thousand yuan in the bank for surgeries." I pause and allow her to absorb that information. "However, you told me at the hospital that there were no funds available for Lei Ming's operation. Why the discrepancy?"

Her eyes stay glued to the reports. "As I told you then, there have been other surgeries, so the numbers don't properly reflect our current balance since this was submitted."

"So, you're saying since August, the last time a report was provided, that twelve or more children had surgeries? Seems like a lot of procedures in a small amount of time when there might be two or three operations in one month and then none the next."

She flips through the documents again. "I don't make the rules about who needs medical attention and when, Miss Mayfield. When a need arises, we meet it."

"Okay, then could I have a list of those children who've had surgeries in the last six months?"

The AD's head pops up. "I don't see why that is necessary or what right you have to request that information. You're just an organizer after all."

I stiffen my back. "I am Ms. O'Connor's liaison, and since her family donated the funds, I'm asking you to provide the details to me on her behalf."

"Her behalf?" She smirks. "Considering Ms. O'Connor's untimely demise, I'm not sure you hold that position any longer, and as such, I don't feel that I should be divulging that kind of information to you."

Hearing the AD mention Ms. O'Connor's death in such a harsh manner, I suck in my breath as if I'd been punched in the stomach. "You're wrong about that, but if you won't tell me what I want to know, then I can ask someone else. Someone who will not only affirm that I'm the one who needs to be given this information but who will also tell you that without it, the orphanage's funding will cease."

"Good luck with that." She snorts. "I'm in charge at New Hope, and I can make it quite clear that no one is to speak with you about our finances or the recent surgeries we've paid for."

"I don't believe in luck," I say without blinking.

"Oh, that's right," she says dryly. "You go to church. A Christian, I suspect?"

I furrow my eyebrows. How did she know that? Even though I'm not the best at sharing my faith, nor am I ashamed of it, I don't shout it from the rooftops either.

"I'm not here to talk about my church-going activities. I want to know why you claim there was no money available for Lei Ming's operation when ample funds are available." My voice rises a notch. "And if there aren't any left, like you claim, then I would like evidence showing how the funds were used."

Standing, the AD presses her palms against the top of her desk. "I don't like the accusations you're making, and I refuse to answer any more of your questions. This is China. We have our own way of doing things. It's likely just a different accounting procedure which is frankly none of your concern nor part of your job description." She flings the documents back to me. "I'm done talking."

I rise from my seat. From her reddened face, I can tell I hit a sore spot, which only confirms my suspicions. "Whether you like it or not, part of my job is to determine why these reports aren't matching." I loop my bag over my shoulder. "Without those answers, I can't submit the proper documents needed for the O'Connor Foundation to continue their support. So, for the sake of the kids, I'll get to the bottom of this. With or without your help."

The vein in her forehead bulges. "We'll see about that." She collapses into her chair. "Now if you'll excuse me, I have an orphanage to run."

"I'll happily leave you to your work, but I have one last question."

No response.

"Who's responsible for submitting the reports to the CMM?" I ask despite her refusal to acknowledge me.

The AD cocks her head, her eyes shooting arrows at me. "Director Wu is the last person to handle them before they are submitted, so you'd need to ask her."

I purse my lips. "Maybe I will." Inching toward the exit, I halt and look back over my shoulder. "Don't forget to alert the Recovery Unit of my visit to Lei Ming later today," I say before stepping back into the sunny hallway. A shiver courses through me when her office door slams and a loud thump resonates throughout the building.

"What was that noise?" Julia asks when I meet her at the threshold of Director Wu's office.

I glance back down the hall toward the AD's office. "I think the boss lady is a tiny bit upset." My eyes take in the progress Julia made while I was gone. Although the room looks better than it did a few weeks ago, a lot of work still needs to be done.

"What did you do or say that made her so mad?"

"How do you know *I* did anything?" I step inside the office.

"Because this is your first day back and it's been quiet while you were gone." She trails after me. "It doesn't take much to make the connection."

"Yeah, she wasn't too happy to see me. But at least you are, right?"

"Of course!" Her eyes light up. "I've been lonely working here by myself."

"Sorry about that." I shimmy out of my coat. "I tried to get back as soon as possible, but I had some things I had to take care of before I could leave."

"Everything okay?" Julia's eyes convey the sweetest concern.

"It will be." Or at least that's what I'm praying. Based on the updates I've received from my mom and the hoarding specialist working with her, things are proceeding as well as can be expected when there's ten years of stuff to go through.

"So," I steer the conversation away from myself and my mother, "how are things going with the paperwork?"

Julia surveys the room. As she does, her silky black hair flies over her shoulder, allowing her bubble gum-scented shampoo to cut momentarily through the room's ever-lingering musty odor. "I've managed to go through a lot of it, but I still haven't come across any of the missing documents we've been anxious to find." Her usual cheeriness dissipates when she finishes her scan. "We're about seventy-five percent done, Nicki, and if I'm being honest, I think we're running out of options."

"It's okay." I place my hand on Julia's shoulder. "I appreciate all the hard work you've put into this, but I think we need to try something else."

"You mean all of this was for nothing?" The slightest bit of anger tinges her words.

"No, of course not! We still need to finish sorting through these papers so we can organize and digitize them, but in terms of worrying about finding the missing contracts and reports, I've decided to take a different approach."

Julia's brows knit in puzzlement.

"You're going to have to trust me on this." I offer her a sly smile.

My friend studies my face as if trying to discern if I've gone crazy or not. I haven't. In fact, I'm thinking more clearly than ever.

"You know I do, but I don't understand why you've changed your mind. You do remember that if we don't find those employee contracts, New Hope could be in serious trouble," she reminds me. Again.

"I haven't forgotten, but while I was home, I came across some new information, and I think the only way we can get to the bottom of all of this is to stop searching and start talking."

"I don't understand." Julia scratches her head.

I screen the hallway for any signs of people, then shut the heavy wooden door. Once I feel it's safe enough to share my information, I quickly update Julia on what I discovered in the documents Heather supplied to me, how things weren't adding up, and my tense conversation with AD Chang.

"Then I came here and found you." I lean back against the Director's cleared-off desk and admire the beauty of the grain that had been hidden underneath the stacks of paper and clutter.

I rub my hands together like a mad scientist on the verge of discovery. "I think it's time we spoke to Li Na and the other two recent hires and ask if they remember signing their contracts."

"But didn't the AD say she wouldn't let anyone talk to you? How do you think we'll get any answers from them if they follow her directive? And wouldn't that signal to the new hires that there's an issue with their contracts?"

"I'm willing to take that risk. Besides, AD Chang said she'd tell people not to talk to me, but she didn't say they couldn't talk to you." I wink. "Are you willing to chat with the newest employees of New Hope Orphanage?"

"Smart thinking." She taps her head. "Sure, I can do that."

"Good, but I don't want you to think I'm being deceptive. I'm simply trying to get to the bottom of this whole mess. Something's going on, and I can't think of any other way to uncover the truth and get the funding requests completed."

Julia sets down the stack of papers she's been holding against her chest since I arrived. "Should I go now?"

"Not yet. When I go see Lei Ming later, you can take a break and ask around. That way, it won't look so obvious."

Julia nods in confirmation. "So what do we do until then?"

"We'll just keep working in here. Between the two of us, we should make good headway. Maybe we'll finally find what we've been looking for and won't have to start an inquisition."

We quickly get to work and manage to sort through another box when a knock at the door interrupts us.

It creaks open before either one of us can answer it.

One of the receptionists from the front desk pokes her head

in the room and rattles off some information in rapid Chinese to Julia.

"What did she want?" I wipe sweat from my brow.

"She was passing on a message from the AD." A grin flashes across her face. "You can visit Lei Ming between two and three this afternoon after she's finished with her follow-up doctor appointment."

My spirits brighten by the good news. "Wonderful!"

"Also, she said there's a package for you at the receptionist desk."

"Me?" Prickles of unease nip at the backs of my knees. Who would mail me a package here at the orphanage?

"Yes, were you expecting a parcel, or do you have a secret admirer I don't know about?" She giggles.

"Ha, ha." I swat at her. "No, it's probably just something from Heather. She's the only one who would have this address." I ease my way to the door. "I'll go get it and be right back."

I slip out the door and head toward the entrance. When I get there, a large bouquet of flowers that weren't there earlier sits atop the desk. Their sweet scent fills the lobby, and their bright colors bring a breath of fresh air to the otherwise drab room.

"These are for me?" I point at the vase overflowing with unfamiliar flora.

The receptionist nods and smiles.

Pulling the large envelope with my name written on it from the arrangement, I remove the letter inside and start reading:

Dear Nicki,

Longchen told me about Ms. O'Connor's death. I know how much she meant to you and I'm sorry for your loss. I've been praying for you over these past few weeks and if there's anything I can do to help you during this time, please let me know.

The last time we were together, I felt like things were a little off between us when we parted ways. I'm not sure if it's because of what I told you about Katie or my less-than-supportive attitude about you wanting to adopt Lei Ming, but I hope these flowers will restore our friendship and remind you of how much it means to me. Even if we don't see eye to eye on some things!

Since that night, I've thought about you often, and I'd love to spend more time together. However, I remember what you said about not wanting a knight in shining armor to sweep you off your feet. Would you be interested in a court jester for a friend instead? I'm open and available for the job if you're willing.

Give Lei Ming a hug and a kiss for me. I'll be waiting to hear from you.

> *All my best,*
> *Ben*

Smiling, I read Ben's words again before tucking the letter back in the envelope. While I had been disappointed he didn't think pursuing adoption was a good idea, I'm not upset with him in the least. He was right when he said I'm uninterested in romance right now; I have too many plates spinning in the air to add that to my life. But friendship I can do.

Once I've figured out what's going on here at the orphanage, maybe Ben and I could have fun exploring Beijing. Until then, my first priority is spending time with Lei Ming and ensuring the place that has been her home won't go under.

When I return to the director's office, Julia isn't there. I type out a text to Ben to thank him for the flowers, apprise him of my work situation, and promise I'll be in touch soon.

As the swoosh sound of my phone confirms my message has sent, Julia scrambles into the room.

"There you are. I was wondering what happened to you." I

open the box we need to sort through next. "Ready to get to work?"

She scampers over to me and shuts the box closed. "We need to talk."

I jerk back my head at her unusually serious tone. "Is something wrong?"

"I'm not sure."

"Well, don't keep me in suspense."

Julia takes one long look over her shoulder before turning back to me. "I was too anxious—okay, curious—to wait until you went to the Recovery Unit, so I started looking for the new hires while you were in the lobby." She eyes the flowers on the desk. "Are those yours? Who are they from?"

"I'll tell you about it later." My heart pounds faster. "Right now, I want to know what you found out. Do they remember signing any contracts?"

"That's the strange thing. All three must be off today because I couldn't find any of them." She frowns. "Since we're short on time, I decided to ask some of the other staff members about them instead. But everyone I asked had no clue what I was talking about. They just kept saying *bù zhīdào*."

"What?" I wrinkle my forehead and make sure I heard her correctly. "You mean no one knows who these women are even in a tight community like this?"

"It's like they don't exist." Julia throws her hands up toward the ceiling. "Not one person I spoke to knew anything about them."

"That is odd." I pace the room, grateful for the floor space to do so without fear of tripping and falling over random piles like Director Wu had. "Do you think they quit before the contracts were finalized, and that's why we can't locate their paperwork? Since they didn't sign off on them, they simply got destroyed?"

"Possibly, but what about everyone not knowing who they are?" She twists her mouth. "And why would every person I spoke with answer the same way when I asked?"

"I don't know, unless ..." I halt as a light bulb goes off in my head. "Unless Chang already told people not to talk to either one of us, so no one is willing to answer your questions for fear of getting in trouble with her."

"Could she do that so quickly?"

"I wouldn't put anything past that woman." I massage my temples and try to think of what else I can do to get information. To get the truth once and for all.

"So now what?" Julia's voice pulls me out of my thoughts.

"If AD Chang refuses to offer any insights and no one here will talk to us, then I think it's time I speak with someone who might be able to give me the answers we're looking for."

Julia huffs. "Who are you going to talk to, Nicki? If they won't talk to me, they certainly won't talk to you."

I glance at my watch—eleven o'clock. If I hurry, I can get the information I need and be back in plenty of time to see Lei Ming.

"I think it's time I go see Director Wu." I march back to my belongings. No time like the present to stop by and check on her. And ask a few simple questions. "Maybe she can enlighten us about this mystery and tell me what's really going on around here."

13

Patience is a tree with bitter roots that bears sweet fruit.
~ Chinese Proverb

Surrounded by mountains on three sides and a small reservoir on the fourth, Director Wu's quaint village is nestled in the valley, a mere fifteen minutes from the orphanage. A stark contrast to the more modern and flashier Beijing, it's truly a hidden gem.

I stare out the window and take in the storefront shops and eateries as the Buick rolls down the main street. Unlike the capital city, which is a constant rush of people and noise, this town is serene. I can see why the director likes it here. The car turns into a narrow alley filled with identical bungalow-style houses, then stops at the third one on the left.

"Here." My driver points to a simple brick house.

I exit the car and step through an arched passageway and into a tiny courtyard. On each side of the entryway are large rectangular flower beds, which currently lie empty. I imagine Director Wu fills them with lush flora that give off radiant colors and tantalizing aromas during the spring and summer months.

In the distance, the squawk of geese, chickens, and a lone

rooster captures my attention. Does the director have animals as well? I tread lightly through the courtyard in case one of them decides to make a sudden appearance.

Because of the cold weather and my need to get in and out as soon as possible to have my time with Lei Ming, I knock rapidly on her front door. A series of locks are unfastened a few minutes later and the door opens. Through a small gap, a younger version of Director Wu peeks out at me.

"Can I help you?" she asks in perfect English, much to my surprise.

"Hi, I'm Nicki Mayfield. I'm here to see Director Wu." I thrust my glove-covered hand in her direction.

She studies me carefully before opening the door wider and placing her hand in mine. "Nice to meet you, Nicki. My mother's told me a lot about you." Letting go of my hand, she wraps herself with her arms to shield against the cold. "I'm Xu Xuan, but you can call me Victoria."

"It's lovely to meet you as well." I crane my neck to get a glimpse inside. "Would it be okay if I visited with your mother for a few minutes?"

"I don't think that's a good idea." She straddles the doorway.

"I understand why you'd be hesitant to let me in," I argue, unwilling to give up without a fight. "But I wouldn't be here if it weren't important. New Hope, and the children for that matter, could be in jeopardy, so it's critical that I speak with her." I gulp. "Today."

"What's so urgent it can't wait?" she snips. "Mother isn't in any condition to be bothered with problems right now. She needs to rest."

I bounce on my toes. The chill is working its way through my bones, and I'm not sure exactly how to answer her. How much should I tell her to gain entry?

"I really don't have time for this." She eases the door shut.

To keep it from hitting me in the face, I stick my foot between the door and the frame. "There are some paperwork issues only she can answer. Without her input I'm worried that the orphanage's funding could be in trouble. Serious trouble." I clasp my hands together. "Please. I just need to ask her a few questions. Nothing taxing, and I promise it won't take long. Fifteen minutes max." I pause. "For the children."

Gripping the door with her hands, she taps her fingers against the metal. "Fifteen minutes," she says through clenched teeth. "And not one minute more." Reluctantly, she swings the door back open so I can enter.

I expect the director's house to be a carbon copy of her office and cluttered with junk, but it's surprisingly clean and tidy.

"This way." Victoria leads me down a narrow hallway to a small bedroom.

The only light filtering through the space is the morning sunshine, but it's enough to help me see the director's still, sleeping frame buried under layers of blankets on her bed. The only signs of life are the rhythmic movements of the thick coverings as she breathes.

Victoria strides over to the bed and whispers in her mother's ear. Director Wu's eyes flutter slightly but stay sealed.

"I'm sorry," Victoria turns back to me. "She was awake when I left to answer the door." She looks down at her mother. "The pain medicine makes her drowsy."

I stand at the foot of the bed and stare at the elderly woman. Her face is pale, and without her glasses on she looks even older. And more fragile. Is this how Ms. O'Connor looked at the end? I take a deep breath and shove the question aside. I can't afford to get sidetracked by my grief right now.

"Is she in a lot of pain?" I ask.

"It's hard to say." Victoria strokes her mother's thinning gray hair. "She doesn't complain, but I can see it in her face. Even though it's been a few weeks, healing comes slowly at her age."

My eyes stay locked on the director, but my heart fills with sorrow that this sweet woman is in so much agony.

"Could you come back tomorrow or the day after? If we

schedule a time, I can make sure she's awake for your visit," Victoria says.

"No, I can't come back." I peel my gaze from the mother to the daughter. "It's urgent I speak to her today."

Victoria's eyes bounce between her mom and me. "I'm sorry, but she's sleeping, and I'm not going to wake her."

"I understand that." I search the sparsely furnished room for a chair and locate one next to a tall chest of drawers. I amble over to an oversized and well-loved rocking chair. "I can wait here quietly until she wakes, if that's okay." I plead with my eyes. "It's important."

"Fine." A muscle in her jaw twitches. "But just know it could be an hour or so before she wakes."

"That's okay." I fall onto the worn, camel brown fabric. "I can be patient." I check my watch. 11:30. I could wait to talk to the director and still have plenty of time to return to New Hope for my appointment with Lei Ming.

Without saying another word, Victoria spins and scurries back out the door.

I settle into the chair and search for a comfortable position for my vigil. Thanks to all my fidgeting, the ancient rocker emits a loud squeak that echoes throughout the quiet room. I freeze and watch the director for any movement but she's unfazed by the noise.

As I continue my efforts to find a cozy spot to hunker down in, a large leather-bound book wedged between the chair and the chest of drawers catches my attention. A crucifix dangles from its top edges.

I glance around the room before reaching out and lifting the heavy tome onto my lap. Anxious to see if it's what I believe it is, I flip it open at the bookmarked section near the back. There's nothing but symbols on the onionskin paper, but the text format and red font leave no doubt as to what I'm holding.

A Bible.

Is Director Wu a Christian? We've never discussed faith, but she made comments before that led me to think she might be. That would explain much about her and her love and devotion for the children at New Hope.

I shut the book. Though it's not a secret government attaché, unease engulfs me. Nosiness has its limits, and I'm clearly crossing them. With tiny, careful movements, I place the Bible back in its original home. As I study the spot to make sure it is back in its proper home, a voice startles me.

"Something interesting down there?" Victoria stands in front of me, holding a tray of drinks.

"No." I lean back against the chair and steady my breathing.

She sets the tray down on the small footstool in front of the rocker then plops down on the tile floor cross-legged, seemingly unperturbed by its coolness.

"Tea?" She holds up an ornate blue and white teapot, then proceeds to pour the dark green liquid into two cups.

"Yes, please." I perch closer to the edge of my seat.

"Mother only has green tea. I hope that's okay." She passes me one.

"Thanks." I remove the steaming cup from her hand. "Actually, that's the only tea I like. I have funny tastebuds when it comes to beverages."

Victoria blinks but doesn't comment.

Did I really admit that to a woman I just met? I take a long sip of the tasty elixir and pray it will calm my nerves.

"So," Victoria says, "Mother told me over the holidays that you'd be returning to China to ensure that the orphanage continued receiving money from the O'Connor Family Foundation." She sips on her tea.

"Yes, but now that Ms. O'Connor is gone, I'm not sure what will happen. I'm doing my best to make certain the kids have what they need for years to come. If I can solve all the problems, that is."

"We were sorry to hear about Ms. O'Connor." Her gentle tone whispers with sincerity.

"Thank you." Another soft squeak escapes from the chair as I shift my position. "How did you find out?"

Victoria places her cup up on the floor next to her. "Someone from the CMM called and informed her of Ms. O'Connor's passing."

"Oh, yes, of course."

"*Māmā* was upset when she found out. She said she'd hoped Ms. O'Connor would have had more time to see all the work her father had set up on her behalf."

Me too.

Since she won't be able to, it's my job to ensure that both their legacies continue there for many years to come. And I would, if I could untangle this financial debacle.

My eyes shift over to the bed where the elderly woman is resting, hoping she'll sense my gaze on her and wake up. But her closed eyes and measured breathing only remind me that I'm not a Marvel superhero and will just have to wait until the time is right.

"Nicki."

Victoria's call pulls my attention away from the director and back to her daughter.

"Yes?"

"Are you certain the issues you need to discuss with my mother won't be too upsetting for her? From everything you've told me so far, it seems quite serious."

A pang of jealousy hits me as I listen to Victoria's concern for her mother. Unlike me, she's present when her mother needs her most. Even though I had my mother's blessing and permission to return to China, guilt about abandoning her weighs on my conscience.

I clear my throat. "Well, it's kind of a long story, but I've been going through the papers in her office trying to sort and organize them—"

"You're cleaning out her office?" Victoria's eyes bulge. "You're either a saint or a glutton for punishment. Does she know you're doing this?"

"It was her suggestion, actually."

"Really? I can't believe it." Her black lacquer hair shakes back and forth. "She's fanatical about people going through her stuff. Whatever you're doing in her office must be extremely important if she's willing to let you have a stab at her clutter." She chuckles. "I know the kids mean a lot to her, but I never dreamed they'd be the key for her to let go."

"She doesn't seem to have an issue at home." I scan the sparsely decorated room. "With holding on to things, I mean."

Her mouth lifts in a sly smile. "I've been cleaning up around here for the last few weeks while I've been caring for her."

I gasp. "You've been throwing her stuff away?" While I admire her chutzpah, I know firsthand how dangerous that can be.

"Not all of it, just what looked like trash. The rest I stored in boxes for us to sort through once she's feeling better." Her voice drips with familiar irritation. "My mother grew up poor and thinks she needs to keep everything. In her mind, nothing should go to waste because it might be useful later. She doesn't understand the problems that causes, so I've taken it upon myself to clean things up around since she won't."

A familiar pang pierces my heart. Better than anyone, I can relate to Victoria's struggle.

"I've learned from experience we can't always make sense of why people cling so tightly to their possessions." A heavy sigh escapes my lips. "One person I've tried to help time and time again refuses to let go because of the sudden death of her husband. She doesn't want to lose anything else, so she hoards everything. But then some, like your mother, do it because of their unfortunate upbringing."

"She lived under Mao's regime as a young girl." Victoria picks at her fingernail. "Times were hard for families out in the villages back then. They still are, but despite her improved living conditions, she clings to the same old mentality."

Listening to Victoria describe Director Wu's personal issues, I ache for this mother-daughter duo. I'm fortunate to have access to help for my mom so we can keep our relationship intact, but I doubt that's an option for them. There probably aren't many professional organizers or hoarding specialists in China. I wonder if I could get Marie Kondo to visit them?

"But enough of that." Victoria props her elbows on her knees. "We were talking about why it was so urgent that you speak with Mother. What is going on at the orphanage?"

I sigh. "There are a few financial issues I can't figure out. I was hoping she could fill in some of the missing information for me."

Victoria tilts her head and furrows her eyebrows. "What kind of financial problems?"

"It seems there's a discrepancy with the surgery funds, some questions about employee contracts, and about six months of missing reports to the CMM."

A flicker of panic flits across Victoria's face. "That's a lot of problems."

"Yes, and I'm worried that if we can't resolve them in a timely and positive manner, New Hope's future could be in jeopardy."

"Mother never mentioned anything was wrong before." She looks over her shoulder and then back to me. "Why do you think these issues are coming up now?"

"I don't know." I grab the armrests of the rocking chair. "I've been trying to figure it all out myself and even have someone helping go through the papers to see if we can trace the issues. So far, we've come up empty-handed. Even AD Chang—"

"What about her?" The friendliness in her eyes is replaced by something much darker.

"Well, she claims that there's been a lot of surgeries, and that's why there isn't any money available. She said your mom was the last person to sign off on the reports."

"Ugh." She pops up off the floor. "I should have known Chang would try to pin this on my mother. She can't wait to have her position and take over at New Hope." Her cheeks grow a deep shade of red. "Every time I visit the orphanage, I get a strange feeling around her. I've never liked her, and I certainly don't trust her. What else did she say?"

"Honestly, not much. She says I'm not entitled to that information since I'm only an organizer." I wrap that last word in air quotations. "That may have been my original role, but now it's my job to present the proper documents to The O'Connor Foundation. If I can't have what I need by the deadline, then the orphanage is in jeopardy of being defunded."

At Victoria's growl, I squirm in my seat. The rocker emits another squeak, only louder and higher-pitched this time. I freeze at the noise, but it's unfortunately too late as Director Wu's eyes begin to crack open.

"Xuan?" The director's whisper is almost inaudible.

Victoria rushes to her side and the two converse in their native tongue.

For the first time in thirty minutes, I stand. Although my legs are numb, I quickly jiggle them and then amble over to the bed.

"Director Wu?" I ask in a hushed voice so as not to startle her.

When our eyes meet, she smiles.

"Nicki, it's good to see you." Her throat is scratchy, her words slurred.

Victoria pours her a glass of water from the pitcher on the nightstand. The director sits up and takes the drink from her daughter, then quickly gulps it down.

"Much better." Her voice, which had been thick with sleepiness, sharpens immediately. "I'm surprised to see you here." She pats the white hospital blanket draped atop the mountain of them.

I take her gesture as an invitation to join her and situate

myself at the foot of the bed. Even from this distance, I can smell the minty medicinal ointment used to ease her pain.

"I'm sorry it's taken me so long to visit," I say as my cheeks heat in shame. "How are you?"

"Managing, although I'm sure my appearance contradicts that." She raises her hand to her hair.

"You're beautiful no matter what, *Māmā*," Victoria chimes in.

"Thank you, dear." The director beams at her daughter before returning her attention to me.

"It's lovely to see you, Nicki, but I'm guessing something's wrong. You should be busy at New Hope. There's not much time left before the imposed deadline."

"Well, there have been a few problems."

"What kind of problems?" The lines in her forehead crease.

I glance at Victoria for permission to speak. Although the director seems capable of handling my questions, I don't want to make any assumptions.

Victoria's eyes bounce between her mother and me. Finally, she nods.

With her stamp of approval, I scoot closer to the director. "The finances are a little bit off. Lei Ming needed surgery, but there weren't enough funds."

"What?" She bolts up off her pillow. "How is that—" Her voice falters as a twinge of pain clouds her face.

"*Māmā*," Victoria reprimands her. "Sit back, or else I'll have to ask Nicki to leave."

"*Hǎo de, hǎo de.*" She reclines back onto the pillow before closing her eyes for a moment. "I don't understand." Her eyes snap open. "There are plenty of reserves for operations. Several of them."

"There wasn't, but fortunately, AD Chang was able to secure the money for the hospital to operate on Lei Ming by asking potential adopters to pay for it."

Relief washes over the director's ashen face. "I'm glad to hear that, but what happened to all the other money?"

"AD Chang refuses to discuss orphanage operations with me, so I can't tell you that. Did she ever talk to you about it?"

"Not that I'm aware of, but then again, these pain medications make groggy." She gives a sideways glance at Victoria. "Has she called or come by here and you forgot to tell me?"

"No." Her eyes burn with rage. "And she'd better not."

Before things can escalate and get too off track, I jump back in. "Director, can you recall how much money was earmarked for surgeries on the last report you signed off on six months ago? Maybe if you could remember, that would help me get to the bottom of this."

Director Wu bends forward. From her scrunched-up forehead and pursed lips, I can tell she's trying hard to recall anything she can. I lean back and give her some space.

After a few agonizing minutes, she looks up at me. "No, I—I can't. But I do remember that the last report I signed off on was January, not August."

"That's odd. The CMM hasn't received any reports since August."

Her face ripples with anguish.

"Don't worry about that, though." I pat her leg in reassurance. "I'll look into it."

Victoria levels a stern glance in my direction. A warning sign to tread carefully.

"Director, I only have one more question for you before I leave and let you rest." I lower my voice. "Did you hire a woman named Li Na recently? Or any other employees in the last few months?"

As if overwhelmed by the questions, the director sits back and closes her eyes.

"That's enough questions for today," Victoria states matter-of-factly. "Perhaps you can visit Mother again later."

"Of course." I take that as my cue and rise from the lumpy bed. "I'll come back another time."

LIANA GEORGE

Deep down, I'm disappointed she couldn't handle more questions. While I would love to stay and get the answers I so desperately need, I don't want to jeopardize the director's health.

"It's been great seeing you, Director Wu," I raise my voice a notch to make sure she hears me. "I can't wait for you to return to New Hope soon."

When she doesn't respond, I lean in closer and make sure she's okay. The steady movement of her chest assures me she is.

A gentle tap on the shoulder from her daughter tells me it's time to go, with or without a proper sendoff.

Before retreating to the rocker to grab my things, I take one last look at the woman who has commanded New Hope for the last thirty years. A lump forms in my throat at the realization that the director will likely not return to the helm at the orphanage she loves so dearly. Or to the children under her care. There's no doubt her absence will leave a large void in their lives, and her dedication to them will be hard to replace.

Between that and the financial troubles it faces, I pray New Hope will survive.

I have one foot in the hallway when the director cries out, "Who is Li Na?"

At the sound of the familiar but mysterious name, I spin around and race back into the room. "What did you say?"

"Li Na." She looks up at me, determination filling her eyes. "There's something about that name tickling my brain, but I don't know why." Her eyes plead with me to help her.

"I found a folder in your office for a woman by that name who was hired to work at New Hope, but no one seems to know who she is, and her file is empty."

Tapping her lips with her finger, the director stays lost in her thoughts.

"Did you hire Li Na, or do you remember meeting her?" I ask, shattering the heavy silence that's descended upon the room.

166

"I don't know who she is." She shakes her head. "I never met her."

"So you didn't hire her?"

"No," she says, her voice firm.

"Did AD Chang?"

"Yes!" The director lights up, seemingly connecting the dots. "Right before the holidays, the head of accounting asked me about Li Na. I had no idea who she was talking about since there hadn't been any money in the budget for staff in quite some time. She said Chang had hired the woman as a caretaker for one of the children's rooms, so I asked her to bring me the paperwork."

My heart pounds like a jackhammer in anticipation. After weeks of combing through boxes and coming up empty-handed, a ray of hope flashes in front of me that I might finally have a piece of the puzzle. Li Na does exist.

"Was there documentation for other new hires or just hers?"

"No, just Li Na's."

"Do you recall if there was a signed contract with her paperwork?" I don't want to alarm the director, but I need to know.

"I'm sorry, I can't."

Her words cause a mix of fear and dread to shoot through me. The director was my last chance to figure this entire mess out.

"But the paperwork was all in Chang's handwriting, which I thought was unusual," she adds.

"Why is that unusual?" I dash to her bedside.

"Perhaps Li Na can't read or write, *Māmā*. You know that's not uncommon for many of your workers," Victoria interjects after remaining quiet by the door. "Did you ask Chang about it?"

"I couldn't," the director's voice softens. "She had already left for the holidays. I was going to talk with her about it after the new year, but then I fell."

I chew on the inside of my cheek, trying to make sense of

the director's words. Like everything else I can't figure out, I have no answers to this situation.

"I did bring the paperwork home with me, though, so I could do some research, but with all the New Year preparations, I got busy and forgot."

"The papers are here?" My spirits soar at this information.

"Yes, in the kitchen." She looks at Victoria. "Can you locate them and bring them here to me? Nicki can take them and see what she can find out."

My eyes shift from the director to her daughter leaning against the door. Victoria looks as white as the snow on the mountaintops outside.

At first, I worry something's wrong with her physically, but then it hits me. She said earlier she'd been cleaning up and getting rid of her mother's things. *No!*

When Victoria doesn't move, her mother calls out to her in Chinese. The two women exchange words, but I don't need to be fluent in Mandarin to understand what's transpiring between them.

Li Na's paperwork is gone. Deflated, I drop my head to my chest.

"Nicki," the director calls out to me.

"Yes?" When I look back up, I notice Victoria is no longer in the room.

The director must sense my wonder at her daughter's sudden disappearance. "She's looking for the papers."

"She didn't throw them away?"

"She admitted that she discarded some things, but the rest she stored in boxes for us to go through together when I was better. She thinks they might be in one of these and went to check." She shakes her head. "There's no telling how many boxes there are, though."

"Should I go help her?" I look over my shoulder toward the hallway, where I hear the screech of tape pulling away from cardboard.

"No, she works for a lawyer, so she's used to spending hours digging through papers to find what she needs." She repositions herself in the bed. "I'd like you to fill me in on what else has been happening since I've been gone."

I look at my watch. One o'clock. Not much time to bring the director up to speed and return to the orphanage to visit Lei Ming at my appointed time. I'll reschedule until tomorrow to check on her.

"Of course. Let me call my translator, Julia, and let her know I won't be back for a while."

"Take your time. It's not like I'm going anywhere." Seemingly more alert, she chuckles at herself before fiddling with her hair.

I unearth my phone from my bag on the floor and open it. As it was on silent, I notice one missed phone call and two text messages from Julia.

That can't be good.

I open the first message.

Lei Ming has been taken to the hospital again. Call me!

The second one is similar in nature.

I need to talk to you about Lei Ming. ASAP.

I click off my phone and tap it against my chin. The tug-of-war on my heart threatens to tear me apart. While I want to be with Lei Ming, I'm so close to finally getting the answers I've been looking for from the director. I don't want to leave until I have those papers firmly in my grip. Not just for my sake but for the kids and New Hope too.

"Nicki, is something wrong?"

I jolt my head at the director's question.

"Yes, I mean, no." My chest squeezes with indecision.

The director pats the spot next to her. "Sit down and tell me what's wrong."

169

Touched by her grandmotherly concern, I fall on the bed next to her and tell her about Lei Ming's touch-and-go condition. When I'm done, my nose is as runny as a leaky faucet.

"I don't think there's any need to debate this," she says. "You should go be with Lei Ming."

"But, but—" My thoughts swirl in a chaotic mess. "What about the paperwork? I've been searching for them for weeks and to be this close ..."

"*Gè rén zì sǎo mén qián xuě , mò guǎn tā jiā wǎ shàng shuāng.*" The director reaches for my hands. "It's an ancient proverb which means your own problems are enough to handle without worrying about other people's affairs. When Xuan finds the documents, I'll have her call you. Don't worry, I'll make sure New Hope is taken care of. I've been doing it for thirty years." She rests her head back on her pillow. "You just go make sure Lei Ming knows someone who cares is with her."

I swallow. While I know she's right, a small part of me worries that even though the director's heart is in the right place, can her body withstand the effort in its current condition?

"Go, Nicki. I promise I'll be fine and so will New Hope."

Buoyed by her words, I spring from the bed, kiss her messy silver hair, and dash out the door.

As desperate as I am to solve the financial mystery at New Hope, I can't leave Lei Ming on her own again at the hospital. Until she has a family who can be there for her, I will fill in for them however I can.

My only hope is that she'll make it to meet them.

14

If you don't eat fish, your mouth won't smell fishy.
~ *Chinese Proverb*

"What are you doing here?" AD Chang asks when I walk into the hospital lobby an hour later.

Her eyes, which burned with anger during our earlier encounter at the orphanage, are still aflame, as if infused with heat straight from hell.

Regardless, I refuse to be rattled. Her beef with me will have to wait. Lei Ming is my priority.

"I heard Lei Ming was brought back here." I withhold telling her how or where I was when I heard the news. When the time is right, I'll divulge that information. "Is she okay? What happened? Is it serious? What do the doctors say?"

"Miss Mayfield," the AD snaps. "If you'd like me to answer your questions, perhaps you should give me a chance to speak."

"Fine." I narrow my eyes. "Let's start with what happened."

She grabs my arm and leads me down a hallway away from the crowded lobby. When we're a good distance from everyone else, she finally fills me in. "One of the nurses alerted me this morning that her incisions were oozing. That's usually a sign of an infection, so I had the Recovery Unit doctor look at her. After his examination, he felt it was best to bring her back for further observation." Deep lines of concern etch across her forehead.

"So, what do the doctors here say? Have you spoken with Dr. Wong yet?" I ask, hopeful this was being overly cautious.

"I've requested to speak with him, but—" She pauses until a young patient in a wheelchair has been pushed past us before continuing. "I haven't heard anything yet."

"Well, no news is good news, right?" I'm unsure whether I'm trying to convince myself or her with my optimism.

The AD smirks.

"Is this reaction normal for patients who've had a surgery like hers?"

"Every patient is different," she says, her voice flat.

I tap my foot and try to think of a question that will assure me everything will be all right and reduce my heart rate to its normal level of beating. Right now, it's about to burst out of my chest.

Like a detective trying to solve a crime, I continue my intense line of questioning. "How did Lei Ming look the last time you saw her? Did she seem good to you?"

"I checked on her a few days ago, and she seemed to be recovering nicely." She lets out a heavy sigh. "But in all my years of doing this job, I've learned that things can change in an instant. There are never any guarantees."

Not exactly the answer I needed to quell my fears.

But this isn't about me. It's about Lei Ming. "What do we do now?"

"For now, Miss Mayfield, we wait." She leans her shoulder against the wall. "Since you're a Christian, you believe in prayer, don't you?"

"I do." I square my shoulders.

"Then I suggest you toss up one or two of your prayers ... unless that's only something you do at church."

"That's the beauty of prayer," I say, delighted by the opportunity to share a bit of my faith with a woman who seems to know little about it. "You can do it anytime. I can talk with God when I'm at church on Wednesday evenings or Sunday mornings, in my bed when I first wake up, or standing here in the hospital."

She rolls her eyes and then pulls her phone from her pocket. If her quick fingers typing away are any indication, she's uninterested in my faith or my prayer routines.

Although, if I'm being honest, I haven't been praying much these past few weeks. It was something I'd practiced regularly on my first trip here. Even when I was back home and deciding about returning to work at New Hope, I'd journaled my prayers faithfully.

But lately not so much. With everything going on and stacked up against me, it felt like God had forgotten about me. So I drifted away from Him and fell out of the habit of praying regularly.

Maybe this was a wake-up call from the unlikeliest of sources to draw me back into the sacred ceremony of communion with God. Feeling a strong tug on my heart, I bow my head and begin to intervene for the little girl who means so much to me.

For her full and speedy recovery.

For the doctors to have wisdom for her treatment.

For nothing more serious to be wrong.

For her family to not be anxious during this time away from her.

At the thought of her new family, my eyes pop open and I raise my head. "Lei Ming's adoptive family."

"What about them?" The AD's voice is laced with irritation.

"Did you let them know she'd been brought back to the hospital?"

"Of course, but—"

A loudspeaker dings and spits out an announcement in Chinese.

The AD lifts her head to the ceiling. "They're paging me. The doctor must be ready to discuss Lei Ming's condition."

Sidestepping orderlies and patients, we race back down the hallway to the information desk. When we arrive, Doctor Wong, dressed in the same scrubs and cap I saw him in last time, waits for us.

At his forlorn expression, the blood in my veins goes cold. That can't be a good sign.

"Doctor." The director and I speak at the same time.

His eyes dart between the two of us.

When the AD shoots me the evil eye, I concede and let her do the talking.

"Doctor, how is Lei Ming? What's her prognosis?" AD Chang asks in English.

I'm touched by her concern. Even though she's rough around the edges most of the time, she's a mother herself, and deep down I think she wants what's best for the children.

"She's resting at the moment and receiving antibiotics for the infection." He rubs the back of his neck. "However, we're going to have to operate to clean out the site. I'm hoping that once we open her back up, we'll have a better idea of what's wrong."

"Does that mean there's a bigger problem?" I blurt out.

The doctor shifts his attention to me. "Anytime a patient develops a post-operative infection, it's a problem, Miss ..."

"Mayfield," I remind him.

"Ah, yes." He clasps his hands together in front of him. "I'm hoping this procedure will go smoothly, but regardless of the outcome, her condition will always be an issue that she and her family will have to monitor."

"You mean the original surgery didn't fully heal her?" Now I'm perplexed. "Wasn't that the point of doing it in the first place?"

"With most heart patients like Lei Ming we see a complete recovery; however, some of the children continue to need further care."

My heart sinks. I'd assumed Lei Ming was one-and-done with the procedure performed a few weeks ago. It seems the battle isn't over for this child. At least not yet.

"Doctor, when will you operate?" The AD takes charge again.

"Did you speak with the family?" he asks.

At his question, my ears perk.

"I spoke with them and told them about her admittance but that I was waiting to speak with you before providing them any more details." She holds up her phone. "They're awaiting my call."

"I'd like to give her another round of antibiotics before taking her into the OR." He glances at his watch. "You can let them know I hope to proceed sometime tomorrow."

"I will. Thank you, doctor." The AD punches a number into her phone, dismissing him.

I quickly chase after him.

"Doctor Wang!"

He halts and looks back at me. "Yes, Miss Mayfield?"

Not wanting the director to hear, I step closer to him. He's a mixture of smells—breath mints, cologne, and anti-septic—rolled into one. I scrunch my nose and try to ignore the aroma wafting between us.

"I was wondering if I could see Lei Ming. Just for a few minutes to let her know I'm here and that she's not alone."

His eyes soften. "That's kind of you, and I don't see why that—" His gaze flicks past me momentarily. It takes a few moments before he looks back at me. "I mean, I'm sorry. I don't think that will be a good idea right now." Sweat beads along the top of his lip. "Please excuse me. I really must be going."

Watching him speed off, it doesn't take me long to put two and two together concerning his sudden change of mind. He was simply following orders.

I spin around and march back towards the AD. "Why? Why did you tell him not to let me see her?"

"I'm not sure what you're talking about." The director feigns innocence and places her hand over her chest.

"Really?" I harrumph. "I think you're lying. For whatever reason you instructed him not to let me see her."

"I don't appreciate you calling me a liar."

Tired of her games, I call her out. About everything. "Then how do you explain the fact that Director Wu confirmed to me a short while ago there was money in the reserves for surgeries when you said there were none?" I draw closer to her. "Or that there wasn't any money in the budget, yet you hired Li Na anyway?" My voice escalates to a booming level inappropriate for the setting, but I don't care.

Her nostrils flare. "How dare you speak to Director Wu about these matters," she howls. "First of all, she is recovering. Secondly, that's none of your business."

"When it's clear something shady is going on that affects the future of New Hope and the lives of the children there, I make it my business." I stiffen my back. "Don't forget my employer funds the majority of this orphanage!"

Narrowing her beady eyes, she gives me a death stare.

Like a gunfight at the OK Corral, we stare each other down until the shrill ring of her phone interrupts us.

She pulls her steely gaze from me and looks at her screen. "I have to take this. It's Lei Ming's family." She walks away and answers the call.

Although her words are a heart-wrenching reminder that this sweet little girl has already been matched to someone else, I don't allow them to paralyze me. Instead, I wander into the waiting room and search for a chair where I can gather my emotions. They're going up and down like a roller coaster at Disney World right now.

But there's not a single seat available.

Out of the corner of my eye, I see a small store open just down the hall. A gift store. Maybe a cold drink will help temper my boiling blood.

I grab a bottle of water from the cooler at the back of the shop and then slither through the aisles and other customers to pay upfront. There, I find a familiar face.

Tao, the orderly who snuck Ben and me into the ICU a few weeks ago, is now manning the cash register. When it's my turn to pay, he instantly recognizes me.

"Nicki, yes?"

"Hi, Tao, how are you?" I place my water down and retrieve my wallet. "How's your English coming along?"

"Much better, thanks to Mr. Ben's help. We meet every other Wednesday morning in the cafeteria. Can you tell?"

"I can." I smile and hand him twenty yuan. "He was going to tutor you in English in exchange for you helping us." Me, actually. Goosebumps form on my arms knowing Ben had kept his word on my behalf.

"I have learned so much from Mr. Ben's teaching." Tao leans over the counter. "He is so kind and patient. You are lucky to have him as your boyfriend."

"Oh, no"—I shake my head emphatically—"we're not dating."

"Really?" He scratches his temple. "He talks about you all the time, and when he does, his face turns on like a light bulb."

I'm caught off guard by Tao's words. I thought Ben and I were just friends. Does he want more than that? Worried I misinterpreted Ben's intentions, I extend a trembling hand to the orderly.

Handing me my change, he asks, "Do you want to get one of the bears for your little girl?" He points to a tan, fluffy Build-a-Bear imitation propped next to the register. "On sale today. Very cheap. Your little girl will love it."

Daggers plunge into my heart. She's not my little girl. She never will be.

Yet I could give her something that might remind her of our time together.

A parting gift that she can carry with her wherever she goes even though I have to let her go. The idea offers me a slight sense of comfort. Not much, but some.

"Is this the only one you have?" I ask, excited by the prospect of giving her a present.

"No." Tao pulls out three others from under the counter. "We also have these."

I survey my options and pick the one with the sparkly pink bow and matching corduroy dress. Like Lei Ming, she's perfect.

Without asking about the price, I pass Tao a wad of bills, tuck the stuffed animal under my arm, and grab my drink. "Great seeing you, Tao." I head for the exit.

"Nicki, wait. You forgot your change."

I look back at him from the hallway. "Keep it for yourself."

"Thanks. If you need any more secret visits, you know where to find me." He winks and diverts his gaze back to the next person in line.

I squirm. Not at his gesture but the implication behind it.

While I'm grateful for his help and the time it allowed me to spend with Lei Ming, I won't be needing his services again. It was desperation alone that caused me to break the rules that night and ignore the AD's directives. But one way or another, I'll find a way to see Lei Ming and comfort her myself. No exceptions.

When I return from the gift shop, the waiting room is less crowded. I scan the small space and spot AD Chang hunched over in a chair in the corner, her face as white as the wall behind her.

"What's wrong?" I rush over to her and brace myself for the worst. "Has something happened to Lei Ming?"

"The family in California changed their minds." She flips her phone over in her hands. "They don't feel they can handle a child with continuing medical issues."

Flabbergasted, I drop into the empty seat next to her. "Why would they do that? Don't they understand what a precious gift she is?"

"They're nice people but feel inadequate to handle her fragile condition." She raises her head. "But that's not the only problem."

"What?" I brace myself for more bad news.

"Since the family has changed their minds, they will no longer be funding her medical costs. They'd like to be placed with another child and prefer the money be applied to that. Without their help, there's no way we can pay for any additional surgeries Lei Ming may need."

I grip the armrests. How was this happening again? Director Wu confirmed to me there was plenty of money available. For multiple operations. Even in her groggy, medicated state, I'd believed her.

If AD Chang is this distraught, though, there really must not be any funds available.

Which only leaves one option.

"How much is the surgery?" I ask.

"About twelve thousand yuan." The AD doesn't flinch. "And if additional surgery is needed, well ..."

Two thousand dollars. While it's almost all I have in savings, I could cover the hospital bill. Beyond that, I'm not sure how I would manage. Now that Ms. O'Connor is gone, I have no idea what my future earning and employment options might be, if any. Or my housing situation. But that doesn't matter. For Lei Ming's sake, I'll find a way.

"I'll pay for the surgery," I say without hesitation.

AD Chang's head whips around. "You?"

"Yes." Then without skipping a beat, or even really thinking for that matter, I blurt out, "And now that the other family is no longer adopting her, I plan to."

"Do you have the funds for any additional surgeries?" She asks, conveniently ignoring my other declaration.

While I want to cower back, knowing that I don't have the money for anything beyond today's procedure, I push my shoulders back. "I'll find a way to pay for them if needed." A loan from Heather, working two jobs, or, or ... my mind races for any other viable options.

She scrutinizes me as if debating whether I can be believed.

Ignoring her doubting expression, I continue thinking out loud. "Or maybe Director Wu can help. I just came back from her house where I informed her about the money discrepancies. Perhaps the three of us working together can find some additional funds to cover the cost or clear up the clerical errors and discover that the money has been there all along."

Despite the heavy claims I've just made, a lightness overtakes my limbs. It's as if my body knows I'm doing and saying the right things.

But when I lock eyes with the AD Chang, her agitated expression belies my optimism.

"I don't know how many times I have to tell you, there is no money!" She leaps from the chair, spit flying from her mouth. "I'm tired of listening to you talk about the financials, which are none of your concern. Not only that, but your constant nosiness is wearing on my nerves."

"But the finances are my concern because I work for the people funding you." Not one to be bullied, I stand and meet her gaze. "It's not like you can fire me."

"Maybe not." The vein in her neck bulges. "However, as Acting Director and one who gets a say in the adoption process, I'll do whatever's necessary and within my power to make sure you aren't matched with Lei Ming." She crams her purse under her arm. "And even though I will let you pay for her surgery tomorrow, I assure you we won't be needing your American money for anything else."

She storms out of the waiting area without giving me a chance to respond, a trail of dust following behind her.

The room grows quiet as twenty pairs of eyes focus on me.

"*Bàoqiàn.*" I apologize to them as best as I can with my limited language skills, then dash out of the room.

But instead of chasing after the AD or heading for the

hospital exit, I hustle back to the gift shop.

Since I'm not allowed to see Lei Ming, and even more so after that argument with the AD, I find myself in need of Tao's services. Again.

Once I'm certain the shop is empty of any curious customers, I approach the counter.

He flashes a wide grin at me. "You're back."

"Tao, I need your help," I say point-blank.

"Of course." He leans over the barrier between us and lowers his voice. "Do you want me to sneak you in to see your little girl?"

I swallow as my words form a logjam in my throat. Every fiber of my being wants to answer yes. To have him take me to Lei Ming's room so I can hold her hand, stroke her hair, and let her know I'm doing everything I can to fight for her.

But I can't.

If I'm serious about pursuing adoption, I must walk the straight and narrow from now on. Regardless of how hard the dueling emotions of frustration and yearning are tearing at my heart, I have to do what's right. I can't afford to take any risks that might cost me a future with Lei Ming. Chang will be watching my every move from this point forward.

"Could you take this to Lei Ming for me and tell her that everything's going to be okay?" I hold the stuffed animal out to him. If I can't be with her right now, maybe this bear can be my replacement. My temporary replacement.

Scrunching his eyebrows together, he takes the flattened bear from my quivering hands. "O ... okay, if you're sure that's all you want me to do."

"It is," I whisper before bolting out the door towards the exit and the safety of my car.

Back in the hallway, I lean against the wall and make a silent vow to myself. And to Lei Ming. Never again will anyone watch over, take care of, or shower love on that child on my behalf.

I'll make sure of it.

15

Enjoy together the happy times and face together times of trouble.
~ Chinese Proverb

I meet Julia later that evening at a dim sum restaurant just a few blocks away from Mother's Love. As I slip through the front doors of the hole-in-the-wall eatery, the different aromas of China assault me. Hints of jasmine rice, meats, garlic, soy sauce, and ginger linger in the air and cause my stomach to grumble.

"Nicki, over here," Julia calls out to me from the back corner of the room.

At the sound of English, all eyes swivel in my direction. I can only hope those dining at the restaurant don't want their picture taken with the only curly-haired Westerner in the establishment. A repeat of my experience with Julia at the Great Wall is not on my agenda for the evening.

I slink to the table and quickly join my friend. "I'm surprised you beat me here considering how far you had to come from New Hope."

"Thanks to all the excitement, I left earlier than I expected."

"Why? What happened?" I unwrap my winter layers and place them next to me.

"You have no idea."

Pushing her glasses up on her nose, Julia leans across the table and details the AD's unhappy return to the orphanage. From her vivid description, I imagine the tiny-statured woman stomping through the halls of New Hope like Godzilla, destroying everyone in her path with either her fire-breathed words or the sharp daggers shooting from her eyes.

"I think I even saw the receptionist crying," Julia says, bringing the story to a climactic end.

I cringe at her words. There's no doubt in my mind that our shouting match at the hospital was the genesis of her rage.

Contemplation settles in Julia's expression as she studies me. "Did you do something to make her mad?" Her eyes widen. "Did something happen between the two of you that I don't know about?"

I dig my fingernails into the edge of the wooden table. "It's possible."

"Do I have to ask, or are you just going to tell me?"

"Let's order first, then I'll spill the beans. I'm starving."

The waiter arrives with some hot water, the customary drink during winter months in China, and takes our order from Julia.

Once he's gone, she pushes her chopsticks aside and leans across the table. "Okay, I'm listening."

After a cursory glance around the restaurant to make sure we're not catching anyone's interest, I spread my elbows on the table and recap the afternoon's events.

I start with my time at the director's house, including my talk with her daughter, Victoria, Director Wu's own admission about having the paperwork we'd been looking for, and how Victoria might have accidentally thrown it out during one of her cleaning frenzies. "I'm hoping Li Na's application will be the first thread to unravel the mystery of New Hope's finances."

"I'm sorry to hear that her daughter misplaced them, but I'm so glad to know they actually exist. I was beginning to think we were never going to find them." Julia fiddles with her chopsticks.

"I wasn't sure how to tell you this, but I don't know how much longer I'll be able to help you at the orphanage."

"What? Why?"

"After you left, I got a call from Mother's Love about Mingyu. She's been acting out lately, and I'm pretty sure it's because I've been gone so much."

My shoulders sag. "I'm sorry, Julia. I didn't intend to cause you, or her, any distress."

"I know that." She gives her chopsticks one more twirl and then sets them down on their tiny wooden rest. "But I'm the only family she has, which means she is my responsibility. Not only do I provide for her, but I must give her the attention she needs." Her mouth lifts in a smile. "However, now that we have a lead on the paperwork, maybe I won't have to be away as much."

"Yes, but if Victoria doesn't find them, we're back to square one." I shudder to think that could even be an option. I don't want to intrude on Julia's life any more than I already have. I'm not sure I have the guts to ask for her continued assistance considering what she's told me, let alone tell her the rest of my news.

"I guess we'll just have to pray otherwise," she says as if it wasn't up for debate.

Oh, to have faith like hers. Just the mention of prayer sends my heart fluttering. That's twice in one day. Was God trying to tell me something? If so, I might want to start listening.

"So, what happened when you left Director Wu's and met with the AD at the hospital?"

My face grows as heated as the bottle of Chinese hot sauce next to me. While I know I was right in what I said to the AD earlier, my actions weren't the best example of Christian behavior.

"Well, I'm not proud of how I handled things at the hospital, but maybe once I tell you, you'll understand."

"Okay," she says, unfazed by my confession.

Free to speak without worry of judgment or condemnation, I continue the saga.

As I'm about to tell her that the opportunity for me to adopt Lei Ming is back on the table, the waiter returns with our food.

"One moment." Julia holds up her finger to put me on pause. "I want to make sure they got our order right." She takes each dish from the waiter's hands and studies the plates before setting them on the table.

While she monitors the dishes, I peek at my phone to see if Director Wu had tried to reach me. Nothing. Still hopeful, I turn my attention back to the table and all the food being unloaded.

Once everything is in proper order, Julia unmutes me. "Okay, so what happened after you got back from the gift shop?"

"Nope. No more story until you tell me what I'm eating."

She sets down her chopsticks. "Sorry, I probably should have thought about that."

Working from right to left, Julia begins to recite the name and ingredients of each plate. According to her, the spread laid out in front of us includes *Char Siu Bao*, steamed buns stuffed with barbecue pork, *Cheung Fun*, rice noodle sheets filled with shrimp, *Ham Sui Gok*, deep-fried crescent dumplings, *Jin Dui*, sesame seed balls, *Lo Mai Gai,* sticky rice and meat wrapped in lotus leaves, and *Chun Juan*, spring rolls.

"These are my favorites, though." She simultaneously raises the lid on two steaming bamboo trays. "*Fung Jeow* and *Lo Bak Goh*."

I crane my neck to get a better view inside the baskets. One holds a small cake sliced into pieces, the other deep-fried chicken toes.

"Hmm ... are those what I think they are?" I point a single chopstick in the direction of the three-pronged meat dish.

"Chicken feet, you mean?"

"Yes, chicken feet." I try not to let my voice drip with horror.

"Oh, they're a delicacy here in China." She beams with pride. "You should at least try one."

"Thanks, but I think I'll pass," I say before we both burst out laughing.

After we've made a dent in the food, Julia wipes her mouth with her napkin and then pushes her plate aside. "Now will you finish telling me what happened at the hospital?"

I toss my napkin on my plate, then pick up where I left off earlier.

"They changed their minds?" Julia's face swells in astonishment. "Why?"

"They felt her condition was more than they could handle, especially if more surgery was needed."

"Wow!" She sits back against the booth cushion with shock covering her face. "So now what?"

"Well, someone has to cover the cost of her surgery tomorrow." Worried she might think I've gone crazy at what I'm about to admit, I fidget in my seat. "Although Director Wu claimed there should be money, from the AD's behavior, I knew there wasn't. So ..."

Julia's mouth falls open as my words hang in the air.

"So, I said I'd pay for it myself."

"Nicki! Do you have the money to pay for it?"

I nod. "She said the follow-up operation would be about twelve thousand yuan. I have it in savings."

"That's generous of you, but what if she needs more operations?" Julia stabs at a foot. "The doctor said that may be a possibility."

"He did." I take another swig of water to hide my excitement at finally being able to share my big news. "If it's necessary, her new potential adopter said she'd figure it out."

"She? As in you?"

"Yes!" Excitement bubbles inside of me.

Julia reaches across the table and takes both my hands in hers. "I know how much you've wanted this." Sincerity fills her eyes. "If you can make it through the adoption process, I have no doubt you'll be a great mom."

I choke up at her words. Me, a great mother? I can barely take care of myself, so I'm not sure how well I'll be able to parent Lei Ming, but I'm going to do my best. No matter how ugly I may look doing it.

"Thanks," I squeeze her hands, then ease mine out. "I'm aware of how difficult this may be, but I'm also hoping you'll be able to guide me through the process. If you do, then I think I can manage it." I tuck a strand of hair behind my ear. "I don't want to ask AD Chang for anything."

"Why not? That's her job."

I lift my eyebrows as high as they will go. "Do I really have to explain it?"

"Just because the two of you have personal issues, doesn't mean she shouldn't help you navigate the paperwork or stand in your way."

"I'm not so sure about that. She's made it clear that she'll do everything in her power to make sure I won't be matched with Lei Ming." I take a deep breath. "Can she do that?"

"She can definitely provide input to the decision-making board, but they have the final say." Julia bites on her thumbnail. "But she might not be the only hurdle standing in your way."

"What do you mean?" Blood rushes in my ears.

"Have you done any research on Chinese adoptions?"

I shrug. "No, other than what you and Ben have told me."

"Who's Ben?" Julia's face scrunches up.

"Just a friend from church," I say cooly. "We were talking about it a while back."

Satisfied with my response, she continues, "It's not impossible for foreigners to adopt, but the government hasn't made it easy for them, either. That's why I tried to discourage you before."

"I appreciate your concern, but nothing will change my mind or keep me from trying. Nothing." My voice is firm.

"Okay, then you should probably know a few things before we start on the paperwork."

"You're going to help me, then?"

"Of course." She grins. "But as I said, you need to know the odds are stacked against you."

"I don't care. Lei Ming is too important." I gulp. "What do I need to know?"

Julia taps her fingers on the table. "Well, it's good you have money in savings. They'll want that plus proof of your worth. Basically, they want to know you have the means to support her."

My stomach churns, and I wince.

"You do have more money in savings, right?"

Closing my eyes, I push down my dinner, which is about to make a second appearance.

"Nicki?"

I crack open my eyes. "I do, but paying for her surgery tomorrow will basically drain it."

"Hmm, that might be an issue." Her tapping resumes, only this time harder. "You'll just have to assure them that your job with Ms. O'Connor will be enough to cover not only the adoption fees in addition to her continued medical needs and overall well-being."

Deflated, I shrink back in my seat even more.

"Now what?" Julia asks, noting my body language.

"I don't know what my job prospects are once I'm finished here. Heather and I didn't discuss it after Ms. O'Connor's funeral. I thought my opportunity to adopt was a shut door, so I assumed she and I would figure out my future job options before I headed back home. I never thought ..."

"Nicki." Julia covers her face with her hands. "That's not going to go over well or have them look on you positively."

As she rattles off the additional hurdles I'll need to be concerned about, such as my family medical history, intense home visits, and the long amount of time it may take for everything to be processed, my heart sinks to my stomach. From the sound of it, adoption will be the battle of my life—financially, emotionally, physically, and spiritually. Do I have the stamina to overcome all the obstacles?

My mind drifts back to Lei Ming's tiny frame in the hospital bed. She looked so fragile. Almost helpless. A love so fierce only a mother could know it swells within me. So yes, if facing difficult challenges meant a future with Lei Ming, I'd pick up my sword and fight with all I had.

"Rather than focus on what's against me, can we discuss the things I do have going for me?" I ask to steer things in a more positive direction. "There are some, right?"

The waiter returns with the bill and the final plate of the evening. Watermelon slices. A Chinese tradition. I quickly pick one up and savor the sweet fruit as I wait for my friend's response.

She blows out a puff of air. "Well, they do allow single people to adopt, so that isn't against you."

Red juice runs down my chin. I wipe it away and perk up at her words.

"It also helps that you don't have a criminal record. If you had any mix-up with the law, either here or abroad, that would automatically take you out of the running."

Check. I've never even received a speeding ticket. My record is squeaky clean.

"Oh." She bounces in her seat. "You have an established relationship with her, and you're personally covering the cost for her surgery, so that is a plus."

As my earlier despair wanes a flicker of joy jolts through me. Maybe things aren't as dismal as I'd thought. However, I can't allow myself to get too far ahead. It's good to be positive but I have to be realistic.

I look my friend squarely in the eyes. "But are those things enough to outweigh the other issues you mentioned?" I choke back tears. "And AD Chang?"

"Honestly, I don't know," she whispers.

I nod. Julia would never lie to me.

"But," she says in an optimistic tone, "I'll talk to some of the people at Mother's Love who work directly with potential adoptees and see what they say. Maybe there's a loophole we don't know about that could change things for you."

"That would be great. Thank you!" I smile at her. "I don't know how I will ever pay you back for all the help you've given me these past few months!"

"I'll think of something." She winks.

"Oh, wait! I forgot I do have a little something for you." I reach into my bag, pull out a stack of *People* magazine issues, and place them in the center of the table. "For you."

"These are for me?" Her face lights up as she draws the pile closer to her.

"All of them." I take a drink, delighted I could do something besides pay for this meal in return for all she's done for me.

"Where did you get these?" She flips through the magazines as if they were ancient artifacts. "Some of these are really old."

I sputter. "My mom had a few lying around the house so I asked her if I could bring them to you." I point to the one on top. "That one is the most recent edition. I picked it up at the airport."

"Why did your mom have all of these old copies in her house?" She tilts her head. "Some of these are from a few years ago."

I strum my fingers against my glass. I've kept my mother's hoarding a secret from just about everyone—Julia included. But now is not the time to unlock the vault and share my most intimate secrets. There are bigger issues that need to be addressed. Plus, I'm hoping that with the specialist's help my mother will no longer have a problem I have to hide from those closest to me. At least that's what I keep telling myself.

"She loves them almost as much as you do, so she holds on to them." And almost everything else.

"Well, please thank her for me."

"I will." I glance at the bill and then pull the required amount from my bag.

Laying the yuan on the shiny black tray, an idea pops into my head. "Hey, why don't I take a picture of you with the magazines that I can send to my mom? She'd love that." I grab my phone.

While I get my camera ready, Julia sorts through the magazines and picks a few to pose with. Then she holds up her fingers in a peace sign and grins from ear to ear.

Once I've finished taking the picture and forwarded it to my mom, my phone rings.

Director Wu's name flashes on my screen.

"It's Director Wu." I lower my phone and look over at Julia. "She must be calling about the paperwork."

"Answer it." Julia's face shifts from a playful demeanor to a more serious one.

I push the answer button and raise the phone to my ear. "Director Wu?"

"Nicki, it's Victoria. I'm calling from my mother's phone," she says.

"Is she okay?"

"She's resting," she assures me. "I thought it would be better to call you from a number you recognized."

I let out a huge sigh of relief. "Then you're calling about the paperwork, I assume?"

"Yes, I found Li Na's application." Her voice remains neutral, offering me no hint of what was written on it. "I apologize, it took longer than I thought it would, but I'm holding it in my hands right now."

"And?"

"Mother reviewed it carefully, but other than Chang's handwriting, there doesn't seem to be anything to cause concern ... except why Chang hired her in the first place."

Like a spent balloon, my joy shrivels and deflates.

"I was hoping for better news," I say in all honesty. "Something that would connect the dots to the financial issues going on at the orphanage. Now I have no clue what to do next."

"I'm sorry I couldn't be of more help. Would you like me to scan what I have and text it over to you?"

"Sure." I try to keep my voice light and not let my disappointment seep through. "I'll take it back to New Hope and see what I can figure out from there."

"No problem. I'll send them over now." A pregnant pause crosses the line. "Nicki, just one more thing."

I push my ear closer to the phone. "Yes?"

"New Hope means everything to my mother. I'm not sure what her future is there exactly but if you need any help sorting out the depleted funds, Li Na's application, or the missing reports you told me about, please let me know. I'll do anything I can to assist you."

"I appreciate that." I'm doubtful she could but grateful for the offer anyway.

"I'll text my contact info over when I send the paperwork, so you'll have it. Don't hesitate to call if the need arises."

"I won't." I end the call and drop my phone into my lap.

"Let me guess." Julia interrupts my pity party. "Bad news?"

I nod as my mind whirrs with the possibilities of what this all means. "I thought we were on to something. Now this means that we must find those signed contracts, locate the missing reports, and figure out what happened to the surgery funds in less than six weeks so I can organize all the submissions in time for the Foundation's deadline. Or else New Hope's financial issues could be their demise."

"Well, look on the bright side." Julia's tone echoes optimism.

"There is one?"

"Yes, there is." She grins.

"What is it?" I shake my head. "Because for the life of me, I'm not seeing it."

"Since we know the paperwork exists, it means Li Na is not a ghost. Now we just have to wait until she comes back to work and ask her whether or not she signed a contract. If she did, that might mean the other two recent hires did as well, and that would be one less financial concern for New Hope."

"True, but why wait?" My voice lilts higher.

"What do you mean?" Julia looks at me like I've lost my mind.

Maybe I have.

Giddy with excitement, I pick my phone up and tap on Victoria's text messages. I hold up one of the images to her. "If this is Li Na's application, then it would list her home address, right?"

Julia rushes over to my side of the table and scoots in next to me. "Let me see." She plucks the phone from my hand and starts flipping through the images. "Yes, it says she lives here in Beijing. Do you want to go and talk to her?"

"Why not? If she remembers signing the contracts, then we don't have to worry about paying any fines, and it's one less hurdle for me to have to overcome before I make my presentation to the board." I swipe my bag off the cushion and push Julia out of the booth. "The car is outside. We can be there in no time."

Frowning, Julia doesn't speak.

"What's wrong?" I ask, confused that she's simply standing there like a statue.

"Well, for one, it's late and I need to get back to Mother's Love and check on my sister."

I glance around the restaurant which had been overflowing with people when I first arrived. Now it only has a few tables occupied. How long have we been talking?

"Second," she says, handing me back my phone. "It would be rude to show up at her house at this hour and start asking questions."

I shift from side to side. She has a point.

"And finally, there is no *we* going to visit her." Her tone turns all lawyer-like.

"What do you mean?" I balk. "You know I can't talk to her myself."

"I do, but I don't think you should go to her house. If anyone goes it should be me. Alone."

"Why?" My blood begins to boil.

"Don't take this the wrong way, but you're a Westerner, which might be off-putting and keep her from speaking freely."

I open my mouth but don't deny her statement.

"And." She holds up her finger as if making an indisputable point. "If AD Chang found out you had gone to Li Na's house to talk with her, that would only give her more reason to block your adoption. She's already said she doesn't want you being nosy." She arches her perfectly shaped eyebrow. "This is definitely nosy."

I exhale and emit a tiny growl. Not because I'm mad at Julia, but because she's right. Chang would be livid if Li Na told her some Westerner showed up at her door to discuss her job at New Hope. There would be no doubt in the AD's mind exactly who the Westerner in question was.

This was too important not to go. But so was Lei Ming. For her sake, I'm willing to walk the straight and narrow. Again.

And I'm grateful Julia's willing to go along with my crazy idea, especially after what she said earlier about Mingyu's recent behavior. She could have left me on my own. I wouldn't blame her if she had. This may be my strangest request of her so far in our short relationship.

"All right, you win." I hold my hands up in surrender. "I won't go to Li Na's."

"Good choice." She gathers her stuff from the table, clutching the heaping stack of People magazines close to her chest.

We exit the restaurant in silence, lost in our thoughts.

"Do you want a ride to Mother's Love?" I ask when we reach the car.

"No thanks, I can take the subway. It's just a few stops away."

I open the car door and lay my hands on top of it. "Do you know when you'll go to Li Na's?" I bite my lip.

"As soon as I get back from Mingyu's follow-up doctor appointment tomorrow morning, I can head over there."

Out of habit, my brain always flocks to the worst-case scenarios. "And what if she's not there?"

Julia shrugs. "I'll either wait until she is home or talk to whoever happens to be at the house." She hikes up the magazines in her arms. "Chinese people love to talk. Don't worry, I'm not walking away from there empty-handed."

"You're the best." I release my white-knuckled grip on the car door and rush to hug Julia.

"So you keep telling me," she mutters from beneath my embrace.

I step back and chuckle at her words. "You'll call me as soon as you know something, won't you?"

"I will." She starts walking backward, letting me know our time together this evening is over. "Text me the paperwork, then get some rest." She spins around and continues down the sidewalk.

Once her petite frame has disappeared into the darkness, I slide into the warm, waiting car. As promised, I quickly forward all of Victoria's messages to my trusty sidekick then lean back against the headrest and close my eyes. I'll sleep easier knowing that at least one aspect of this financial fiasco is about to be solved. Hopefully, the other two won't be that much more difficult or time-consuming to figure out.

If that's the case, I'll have more time to spend with the one person who has captured my heart. A lot more.

16

A spear openly thrust at you is easy to dodge; an arrow shot from hiding is hard to defend against.

~ Chinese Proverb

When I crack open my eyes the next morning, bright rays of sunshine poke through the bedroom window, sending streaks of yellow dancing across the carpet. That doesn't happen often. Because of the thick smog and heavy pollution in China, sunny days like today are meant to be cherished.

Embracing the radiant light as a good sign, I scramble out of bed, pull back the curtains and bask in the warmth. Between Lei Ming's surgery and Julia's secret expedition, I could use some positivity today. Prayer probably wouldn't hurt either.

After yesterday's two unmistakable nudges hitting me in the face, a sudden urge to talk with God one on one tugs at my heart.

I grab my journal and Bible from my suitcase and then plop down onto the floor next to the window. As the glorious sun rays wrap themselves around me, I open to the next blank page and begin pouring out my heart to the One who always listens.

For Julia.

Help her balance her responsibilities and give her wisdom as she speaks with Li Na today. I pray that whatever she discovers will be the missing piece of the puzzle we've been needing. When she knows something, don't let her delay in telling me, please!

For Ben.

Thank you for his friendship and the support he's given me. I'm not sure why you placed him in my life, but I'm so grateful you did. He's been a lifesaver.

For my mom.

That she is finally able to let go of her clutter and find healing. Let her efforts be just enough to satisfy the city's demands, so eviction is no longer an option.

For New Hope, Director Wu, and yes, even AD Chang.

Whatever is going on at the orphanage, I pray it can be resolved quickly and without too much collateral damage to the kids and the hope that place offers them.

And finally, for Lei Ming.

Guide the doctor's hands today. Let there not be any major issues with the surgery or my upcoming application to adopt her. If there was ever a time I needed You to move mountains, now would be it.

I close my journal and clutch it against my chest. While they aren't eloquent or lengthy, I hope my prayers are enough. They have to be. So much is counting on them.

After reading my Bible, I set everything aside and head out the door. It's time for me to start my vigil at the hospital while I wait to hear back from Julia.

Thankfully the waiting area is empty when I arrive. My only company is a low-humming vending machine and a flickering overhead light. Settling into a cold metal chair in the back corner of the room, I empty a banana, a bag of chips, two bottles of water, and a stack of organizing magazines from my bag, then check the time. Nine forty-five.

Lei Ming's surgery is scheduled to start in fifteen minutes. With shaky hands, I open the bag of cucumber-flavored chips and browse through the magazines. After twenty minutes, I've only managed to force down two less-than-tasty pieces and learned all there is to know about the latest organizing trends and products in the industry. Unable to sit any longer, I abandon my distractions and pace the room instead.

I memorize every scuff mark and stain on the white tiled floors, but even that doesn't put my mind at ease. No, I need something else. Instinctively I begin picking up trash, straightening chairs, and corralling all the magazines from around the space and placing them into one pile.

When there's nothing left for me to clean or organize, I take a step back and admire my efforts. Although the room is in better shape than when I arrived, my insides are as jiggly as my grandmother's jello mold. No, there's only one thing that will make me feel better right now.

I glance at the wall clock. Ten twenty-five. I sprint to the information desk.

There, two elderly women chatter away in their native tongue.

"*Dǎrǎo yīxià.*" I excuse myself, leaning against the desk and smiling.

Both ladies stop their discussion and glare at me. Clearly, they don't want to be interrupted.

"Can you help me?" I ask in the best Chinese I can muster.

They look at one another and start their conversation again. This time, however, their voices ring with agitation as they occasionally point and look in my direction.

I don't need a translator or a Ph.D. in Chinese linguistics to know they're arguing over which one of them is going to get stuck dealing with me.

While they continue their sparring, I whip out my phone and type my question into Google translate. Once it's worked its magic, I hold it out to the dynamic duo.

As if connected at the hip, they rise from their seats and squint at my screen. Then, like synchronized swimmers, they shake their heads fiercely before rattling off a slew of words that mean nothing to me.

Of course, this wasn't going to be easy. Before taking more drastic measures, I try a different approach. The one I've had to resort to every time I've needed to connect with Lei Ming at the hospital.

Tao.

"Can I speak with Tao, the orderly?" I type on the keyboard as fast as I can then push translate.

When I hold up the converted text, only one of the women tries to assist me.

She pulls up her glasses from the chain dangling at her chest and reads my question.

"*Bù zhīdào.*" She doesn't know. Of course she doesn't. There are probably a hundred Tao's working in this place. I might as well have been asking for John Smith.

"*Xièxiè.*"

Downtrodden, I return to the waiting area and resume my vigil. The once-empty space is now overflowing with people, shattering my hopes of being alone to ponder what else I can do to glean information on Lei Ming's progress.

I grab the bottle of water I brought with me, twist it open, and take a swig. As soon as the water droplets tickle my tongue, I instantly spit it back into the bottle. "Yuck!"

Every head in the room spins in my direction.

Sliding down in my chair, I place my hand over my mouth and do my best to apologize with my eyes for my outburst. I hate being the center of attention.

When I'm no longer a circus spectacle, I study the bottle of water. The tiny bubbles floating to the top instantly clue me in to my mistake. It's sparkling water, not regular.

I let out a heavy sigh. Nothing's going my way today. At all.

With more force than I intend, I stuff my uneaten snacks and dog-eared magazines into my bag and then tromp out of the waiting room in search of the cafeteria and something more pleasing to drink.

A few steps into the space that transports me back to middle school lunch hour, I spot a familiar smile, soft green eyes, and wavy blond hair across the room. Ben. My legs wobble at the sight of him next to Tao, the two of them hunched over a book. They were the last people I expected to see, yet here they are. *Thank you, Lord!*

As if sensing my gaze, Ben looks up and locks eyes with me. "Nicki, over here," he says, his thick Southern accent on full display.

Tao swivels around as well. His face lights up when he recognizes me.

Buoyed by their excitement at seeing me, I snake through the tables and join them.

"What are you guys doing here?" I ask, trying to play it cool. Yeah, middle school all over again.

"We are having our English class." Tao's smile grows even larger.

I turn to Ben. "That's right, you guys meet here on Wednesdays for your lessons. Am I interrupting? I can come back."

"Not at all." His eyes flicker towards Tao. "We were just about finished, right?"

Tao's brows knit together. "Ah, yes, we are done." He pushes out a chair for me. "Please sit down, Nicki."

I fall into the seat offered to me, grateful for their kindness and God's perfect timing.

"Good lesson, Tao?" I ask.

"Very good." Tao puffs out his chest.

"It's great to see you, Nicki, but what are you doing at the hospital?" The color in Ben's face drains. "Wait, are you here for Lei Ming? Is something wrong?"

I choke back tears, knowing what her little body must be enduring at this moment. "She developed an infection, so the doctors had to go back into the operating room and clean it up."

"Is that all?" There's a gentleness to his voice and deep concern.

"No. They said if they see any other issues, they may need to do additional surgery."

"I'm sorry, Nicki. I know how worried you must be." He places his hand on mine.

"I am," I say, trying to sound strong despite the trepidation wrapping around my heart like a spidery web. "I've been trying to get information, but there's a language barrier as usual."

Tao leaps from his seat. "I will go and see what I can find out. I'll be right back."

Before he can race off like the Flash, I catch his arm. "Please don't tell anyone you're asking on my behalf."

"Don't worry," he whispers. "I'll be a Chinese James Bond." He winks at me before sprinting for the exit.

Ben leans back in his chair and folds his arms across his chest. "Well, if worst comes to worst, we can always sneak you back in to see her once she's out of recovery."

At his suggestion, I cringe. While I would give anything to see her and know firsthand that she's okay, I can't settle for short-term gratification in this situation. No matter how badly I may want it, I must stay focused on the long-term goal of adoption and a life with this little girl.

"I appreciate your offer and willingness to do that for me, but I can't take that risk."

"Why not?" He cocks his head and studies me intently.

I fidget in my seat and debate telling him about my recent decision. It didn't go over well the first time I brought it up with him a few weeks ago, and I worry he'll react similarly this time around. However, I'm not in the mood to defend my choice to him, or anyone really, right now. But he's been a good friend to me. Maybe he'll appreciate my honesty and not try to deter me again.

"Things have changed with Lei Ming's family," I tell him. "Because of her continuing medical issues, they decided not to proceed with the adoption." Joy springs anew in my heart. I'm getting a second chance with this child.

"Oh." His breath hitches.

"I'm going to pursue adoption again." I push my shoulders back. "Since AD Chang's opinion carries a lot of weight with the decision-making board during the matching process, I don't want to do anything that will make her dislike me more than she already does. Including sneaking in to see Lei Ming. If she were to find out, my chances at being matched would be ruined."

"Gotcha." He clicks his tongue. "Then no, you shouldn't take the risk."

"As much as I'd like to, I can't." I glance back at the cafeteria doors, watching for any sign of Tao. "Hopefully our Chinese James Bond will return with some good news."

"I'm sure he will."

"From your lips to God's ears," I chuckle.

His mouth curves upward. "I do believe in the power of prayer." He scoots forward in his seat closer to me. "I'll keep you, Lei Ming, and the whole situation with the adoption in my prayers. Just remember, nothing is impossible with God."

"I think I've heard that somewhere before." I tilt my head and smile at the reference to his sermon. "I will need all the help I can get, so I'll gladly take you up on that prayer covering."

"You got it." He leans in closer to me. "Would it be okay with you if I mention this at the special prayer meeting at church tonight?"

"There's a prayer meeting ... tonight?" My words come out more stuttered than clear. "Can anyone attend?"

"Of course. Are you interested in coming?"

Honestly, I've never been to a meeting like that before. Usually, it's church services only for me. But these are unusual circumstances. Plus, my mother loves to remind me that in these situations, prayer can make all the difference. Even against the impossible. Which is definitely what I'm facing right now.

"Will I have to pray out loud?" I wince at the thought of vocalizing my prayers in front of people. I'm best at connecting with God through pen and paper.

"Not if you don't feel comfortable."

"Okay, good. What time does it start?"

"At six and lasts about an hour." His phone alarm goes off. "That's my timer reminding me to head out for my class." He stands and collects his things. "Text me and keep me updated on Lei Ming, okay?"

"I will."

He grins and throws his backpack over his shoulder. "See you later?"

"I'll be there." Even though the thought of such a meeting makes my skin crawl, it's exactly what I need in light of today's events.

Before I can finish a regular bottle of water, Tao returns to the cafeteria red-faced and sweaty.

"Is everything okay?" I leap from the chair at the sight of him.

"Everything's ... good." He bends over to catch his breath. "I ran back here to tell you that Lei Ming is out of surgery, and there were no problems."

Without asking, I wrap Tao in a big hug. "Oh, thank you!"

Despite his perspiration seeping onto my shirt and the slight smell of body odor, I squeeze him tighter. "That's wonderful!" I hold him at arm's length. "What did they say about future surgeries?"

"They couldn't make any promises. Even with a repaired heart, she will always be at risk." He encloses my hands in his. "But for today, she is well."

With Tao's words, peace washes over me. "Yes, she is."

"I need to go back to work, but here is my number." Tao passes me a business card and then tucks his English book under his arm. "Call or text me if you need any more help. I will keep an eye on Lei Ming, so do not worry, Nicki."

"Thanks, Tao."

He speeds out of the cafeteria again as I stuff his card into my pant pocket. I sit down and say a silent prayer of thanks for everything. Once I utter amen, fatigue hits me like a wrecking ball. Now that I have a way to keep tabs on Lei Ming, I throw the water bottle into my bag and head back to the hotel for a much-needed nap.

And to await Julia's call.

When I wake up a little after four o'clock, I check my phone. There are a few message updates from Tao letting me know that Lei Ming is doing well, but nothing yet from Julia.

My insides coil in a pretzel again at her lack of communication. Should I take that as a bad sign? Then I remember that she had to attend to Mingyu this morning, which might have taken longer than she expected. If she said she'd go to Li Na's house, she will. I just have to trust that when the time is right, she'll reach out to me. Isn't that what I asked for in my quiet time earlier? If I want to see answers, I need to put some faith behind those prayers.

Refusing to let doubts and worries overtake me, I get ready for the prayer meeting instead. After a quick shower and change of clothes, I head out the door.

The shrill tone of my phone resonates throughout the empty corridor while I wait for the elevators.

I dig my phone out of my purse, look at the caller ID, then push the green button. "Julia?"

"Nicki, where are you?"

"At the hotel. Where are you?" My heart thumps wildly.

"I just got back from visiting Li Na's. I came to New Hope looking for you, but no one had seen you all day."

"I figured there was no point in going there today, so I camped out at the hospital instead."

"How's Lei Ming?"

"She's great and should be back at the orphanage soon." I smile, happy to share the good news even though the hairs on the back of my neck stand up as I anticipate what's coming next over this call. "So, what happened at Li Na's? Did you talk to her? What did she say?"

"Nicki, slow down." She stops talking and yells out something in Chinese. "Look, we need to talk."

"I've got time. Go ahead."

"No, I don't want to talk over the phone. I don't trust saying anything that could be overheard here. Stay where you are. I'll come to you." She shoots off more rapid Chinese to someone.

My stomach lurches. I'm desperate to know what she talked about with Li Na. Was she able to resolve the paperwork issues? From the tone of her voice, something serious is going on.

Yet I need to get to the prayer meeting as well. Although I'm not the best at prayer, I want to change that. This time at church may be the jumpstart that will set me on the path toward a more prayer-filled life. Plus, I promised Ben I'd be there, and I don't want to let him down.

Perhaps I can have both.

"Julia, I was just about to leave the hotel. There's something going on at the church tonight I was anxious to attend. Can you meet me there? I think there will be enough time for you to fill me in about your visit with Li Na before anything starts."

"Okay, send me the address of your church. I'll catch a taxi and meet you out front. Chinese locals aren't allowed inside."

While I'm curious about her statement, there's no time for a lesson in Chinese culture or religious protocols.

Instead, I give her the exact location, which she repeats back to me before hanging up.

Forty minutes later, I'm standing outside the church building, shivering. I scour the hordes of people, street vendors and bicyclists all fighting for their claim of the concrete for any sign of my friend but come up empty. My hair whips my face as the glorious weather from this morning turns nasty. Dark, looming clouds hover over the city and threaten to wreak havoc on everyone below.

Not only does the storm leave me with an unsettled feeling in the pit of my stomach, but the prayer meeting is about to start. I can't stand being late to anything, especially church, but I don't want to go inside until I've talked to Julia and learned all there is to know about the mysterious Li Na.

"Nicki!" Julia's voice rings out from down the street.

A rush of adrenaline races through me. Finally, the answers I've been waiting for.

Julia weaves through the masses to reach me. "Sorry, traffic was crazy," she says, struggling for breath. "The taxi driver refused to bring me all the way, so I had to run two blocks to get here."

"I have some water in my bag." I hold out my Bible and my phone to her. "Let me look."

"No, we don't have time." She pushes my things away. "I need to tell you what I discovered at Li Na's house."

Before I can dig anything out or question her about her findings, the sound of rushing feet overtakes us.

I look up in time to see three police officers hurtling toward us.

"Stop!" One of them yells while the other two push Julia back on the sidewalk.

Like vultures, they circle me as if I were dead prey. Then the oldest of the group pulls a pair of handcuffs from his belt and dangles them in front of me. "Drop everything," he hollers. "You're under arrest."

17

A peony in bloom is a lovely thing, but it still needs the green leaves
to support it.

~ Chinese Proverb

"Nicole Mayfield!" A female police officer calls my name
then removes me from the paltry mix of drunks,
shoplifters, and white-collar criminals, both Chinese national
and foreign.

She leads me down a narrow hallway. I'm hopeful this
excursion is leading to the exit and the admission that this was
nothing more than a blunder on their part. However, our arrival
at a small meeting room dashes any chances I might have had of
being let go.

The space is a ten-by-ten concrete block reeking of body
odor and yielding little light. The officer pushes me down into
one of the two plastic chairs situated on either side of a card
table and places a water bottle on the table's vinyl top. Then she
scurries out of the room, leaving me alone with nothing more
than my thoughts and some lukewarm liquid.

After breaking the seal, I down half the bottle then prop my
head against the table and wonder how I landed here in the first

place. I've replayed the events surrounding my arrest over and over but can't pinpoint anything I did wrong. The only logical conclusion I can come up with is that this is a case of mistaken identity.

It has to be. If it's not, and I'm being held for an actual crime, any possibility I have of making Lei Ming my daughter is greatly diminished. A conviction would mean my chances of adopting would be null and void.

I close my eyes. *Please, Lord, don't let that happen!*

The sound of a loud buzzer and the click of the door handle causes me to jerk up my head and blink. A Westerner stands in the doorway.

"Nicole Mayfield?" The man makes his way towards me.

"I ... I'm Nicki."

A smile tugs at his lips and he sets his leather briefcase on the desk. "I'm Mitch Gordon with the US Embassy." He holds out his hand.

"Nice to meet you." I place my sweaty palm in his and cling to it for dear life.

He removes his hand from my death grip, drops into the seat across from me, pulls out a manila folder from his briefcase and begins studying its contents.

My chest squeezes. They already have a file on me. That can't be good.

Anxious to know why I've been detained for hours and what I need to do to get out of here tonight, I clear my throat. "Excuse me, but do you know why I was arrested?"

Ignoring me, he keeps reading.

"I think there's been a misunderstanding." I scoot closer to the table. "I didn't do anything wrong, and I need to get out of here. Now."

He holds up a finger and continues scrutinizing my file for a few more minutes. Finally, he puts down the folder and looks me squarely in the eyes. "I'm afraid that's not going to be possible, Miss Mayfield."

I blanch. "Why not? I just told you I didn't do anything wrong. They can't keep me here when I haven't committed a crime." I gulp. "Can they?"

"Yes." He pushes his large frame back against the chair. "Someone tipped off the police that you were proselytizing to a Chinese National in front of the International Fellowship Church. That's why they arrested you."

"Proselytizing?" My mind whirrs through my limited vocabulary. "Doesn't that mean trying to convert someone to a religious belief?"

"It does, and it's illegal here in China."

Realizing the mix-up, I break into a smile for the first time in hours. "Mr. Gordon, I wasn't trying to convert anyone. I was simply visiting with my friend, who happens to be Chinese national, in front of my church building, that's all. This is a mistake. You need to explain that to them so I can get out of here."

"I'm sorry, but I can't help you with that." He crosses his arms over his broad chest.

"I thought that's why you came ... to get me out."

"No, I'm here to inform you of your rights as a US citizen and to help you obtain legal counsel."

I spring from my seat. No, no, no, no, no! This is not what I thought his presence meant. I was certain he was here to set me free. I pace the room, which now feels even smaller than when I first entered it.

"Miss Mayfield." His voice is stern. "Please have a seat so we can discuss a few things. My time here is limited."

I interrupt my nonstop back and forth and do as he asks. Maybe some of the information he has to share will shine a ray of light into my otherwise dark and dismal situation.

"Now," he says once I'm seated across from him again. "The first thing you're going to need is a lawyer." He reaches back into his briefcase and pulls out a sheet of paper. "This is a list of

English-speaking lawyers we recommend you use." He slides the paper across the table.

In the dim light, I quickly scan the names provided. "Do I have to use one of these?"

"You don't, but if you have one, it's best if he's local. Overseas attorneys don't fare well in Chinese courts."

Not exactly a boost of confidence. "I've been thinking about this since I arrived here, and I know someone who works for a local lawyer. I'd like to reach out to her first."

"A criminal lawyer, I presume?"

Director Wu hadn't mentioned what type of lawyer Victoria worked for, but at the moment, I don't care. I need someone I can trust. "I'm not certain, but if not, I'm sure they'll be able to get me in touch with someone who knows what needs to be done."

"That's fine." He removes a small notepad from his jacket pocket. "Since you can't have visitors, I'll need your friend's name as well as any family or other friends you'd like me to contact on your behalf and apprise them of the situation."

"I can't have visitors?" I stiffen my back.

"The only people you're allowed to see are me, your attorney, and a clergy of your choosing."

"But back home—"

"Miss Mayfield, you're not back home. You're in the People's Republic of China and as such you are bound to their laws and procedures."

"Even as a US citizen?" My voice lilts higher.

"Yes. And it's my job to make sure you are treated fairly and to be your liaison to the outside world." He removes a pen from the spiral rings of his notebook and clicks it on. "Now, who should I contact and let them know of your arrest? Any family members stateside you'd like me to call?"

I lower my gaze and tap my fingernails on the table. While I know I should contact my mom, I don't want to worry her. Once my name has been cleared and I can laugh about the mix-up far off in the future, I'll let her know what happened. But not until then.

"I'd prefer not to burden my family with this."

"Your choice." He shrugs. "Any friends or associates here in China you'd like me to notify then?"

I let out a huge sigh. "Julia."

Opening the notebook, he scribbles down her name. "Surname and phone number?"

I balk. Other than her given Chinese first name, which I can't recall at the moment, and the English name she goes by, I don't know anything about Julia's personal identification— including her last name or if she even has one as an orphan. "I ... I don't know. I just call her Julia."

He arches his thick, hairy eyebrow. "Phone number or address?"

"I dropped my phone when I was arrested, so I don't know it off the top of my head. She lives at Mother's Love Orphanage, but they probably won't know who Julia is if you asked for her by that name."

Blowing out a puff of air, he sets down the pen. "Do you have any local names or numbers you can give me?"

Fear courses through my body. I don't. Everyone's information—Julia's, Ben's, Longchen's, and even Director Wu's and Victoria's—are all on my phone. I had Tao's business card in my pocket, but that was confiscated when I arrived at the detention center. I have nothing to offer. And now, even less hope.

"Miss Mayfield," he says in a gentle tone. "I know this is overwhelming, but I need you to take a few deep breaths and relax."

Closing my eyes, I follow his suggestion. Inhale, exhale. Inhale, exhale. After a few more repetitions and a silent plea to God for help, I open my eyes and look at him. While my fear hasn't completely subsided, I am much calmer.

"Good." He picks up his pen. "Your paperwork says you're

here on a work visa. Maybe I can contact your employer instead. Where do you work in China?"

My pulse, which had slowed to a normal rate, ramps back up at his question. The last thing I want to do is alert anyone at New Hope about my detainment. Chang can never know I'm in jail. That would only hurt my chances with Lei Ming.

No, not hurt. Destroy.

"I work at New Hope Orphanage here in Beijing, but my boss is Heather Campbell in the States."

"And the name of the company?"

"The O'Connor Foundation," I say, relieved to finally have a solid response for him. "In Bridgeport, Connecticut."

He jots down the information. "I'll see what I can find out and contact Ms. Campbell for you."

I nod. I'm glad there's someone he can reach out to, but knowing that he's informing her of my arrest doesn't give me cause for joy. It makes me want to crawl into a hole. The last people I ever want to disappoint are my mother, my employer, and Lei Ming. Fortunately, only one of the three will have to learn of my disgrace.

"Well, that's all the questions I have for you right now." Mr. Gordon clicks off his pen and slides it back inside the notebook coils. "Let me see what I can do, and I'll come back tomorrow with any updates." He snaps his briefcase shut. "Do you have anything you want to ask me before I go?"

"What about bail options?" I swallow. "Are they available in China?"

"They are, but it varies depending on the crime." He scratches the stubble on his chin. "I would imagine yours would be about twenty-five thousand yuan or roughly four thousand dollars. Do you have access to that much money?"

Tears pool in my eyes. After paying for Lei Ming's surgery, I'm basically broke. "Heather, my boss, might be willing to post bail for me. Otherwise, no."

"Then I'm afraid you'll have to stay here until you're cleared or convicted."

"How long can that take?" I'm not a hundred percent sure I want to hear the answer.

"They can hold you up to thirty-seven days while they investigate and make their formal charges." He pushes back from the table and rises.

"Thirty-seven days? And I can't have any visitors at all during that time? No phone calls? Nothing?" My fear is replaced with panic as I quickly calculate my timeline. Although isolation from the few friends I have here isn't ideal, it's not my primary concern. It will be nearly impossible for me to finish the paperwork and submit it to the O'Connor Foundation by May 1 if I'm forced to stay here another month. By then, I'd only have fifteen days left to get everything perfectly organized.

Even worse, Lei Ming could be matched to another family during that time.

That would be a tragedy. For me, for New Hope, and for the children.

"Those are the rules. But if you want me to set up a fund so your friends can raise the bond money, I can assist you with that." He shuts his briefcase and lifts it off the table. "I'll be back tomorrow to see if we can make any progress with your lawyer and what, if anything, your employer has to say." Without another word, he turns and heads to the door.

I'm lost in my thoughts as he traipses across the room, busy reviewing the list of people he said could visit me. As strange as it seemed, clergy was on his list. It was also a lifeline.

"Mr. Gordon, wait." I leap from my chair.

He swivels back in my direction.

"When you said clergy, did you mean a pastor or a preacher?"

"That's what clergy is, Miss Mayfield."

For the first time since my arrest, something is going my way. My heart pounds as I contemplate my option.

While Ben works in China as a teacher, he's also a fill-in

preacher at the church. Would that qualify him as clergy who could visit me? If so, then there might be hope for me yet. But could it cause him trouble in the process?

Like it or not, it was a risk I had to take.

"Mr. Gordon, I need you to contact my pastor and have him come see me as soon as possible."

MORNING COMES EARLY IN PRISON. Not that I ever went to sleep last night. Between the rock-hard mattress I was given, my cellmate's constant wails, and the scratching noises of unwanted guests scurrying beneath me on the concrete floor, the sweet lull of slumber was not a possibility.

I was too preoccupied replaying yesterday's events, searching for anything that would shed some light of how this could have happened to me. Who put it into motion? If Mr. Gordon's information was correct about someone tipping off the police, then this was no longer a case of mistaken identity. This was intentional.

When the breakfast trays slide across the floor, I'm still no closer to figuring out who is responsible for all of this. I rise from the bunk bed, sore and weary, and try to take care of personal business before attempting to eat. I may not feel like a normal human being right now, but at least I can resemble one.

Once I've finished making myself presentable and taken a cursory glance at the fried rice and egg option made available to me, I fall back onto the bed and close my eyes. *Lord, I have no idea why You've allowed me to be stuck in here, but I need to get out. Immediately.*

I check the slow-moving clock on the wall again. How much longer until Ben arrives? Since Mr. Gordon hasn't let me know if he's contacted Heather or not, Ben is my only hope. For bail and for possibly contacting the lawyer. But if he doesn't come, then what?

As the exhaustion and emotions of the last twenty-four hours take their toll, I slip from prayer mode to sleep mode.

The rattle of keys jars me from my nap sometime later.

"Mayfield," the guard calls out.

The door swings open, and I run to it. Maybe my prayers have been answered after all!

Wearing my fragile hopes on my sleeve, I quickly fall in step with the guard. There's no doubt in my mind she's leading me to freedom this time.

But any dreams I carried of leaving this place crash to the ground and shatter into tiny pieces when we arrive back at the same meeting room.

Heavy-hearted, I amble into the room. That's when I see a familiar face waiting for me at the table.

Ben.

"You're here!" I race toward him and collapse into his open arms.

"How are you holding up?" He keeps me at arm's length and gives me a quick once over.

The tenderness I see in his eyes pierces the depths of my soul. "I'm hanging in there." I brush the tears from my cheek. "Sorry for my less-than-stellar appearance."

"Except for the dark circles under your eyes and your knotted hair, you look great."

"I appreciate the compliments, I think." I swat at him, then quickly rake my fingers through my hair.

He chuckles and pulls out a chair for me. "Have a seat. I only have thirty minutes, so we have to talk fast." He takes a seat across from me.

I perch on the edge of my chair. "First, thanks for being here. I was worried you might not come if it compromised you or your position in any way."

"Don't worry about me. I'm just glad you thought to ask for me as your clergy. Smart move."

"It was all God." I cut my eyes toward the door to make sure it's safe to talk. "I need to tell you what happened."

"Nicki, I already know."

"You do?" My eyes bulge. "How?"

"Julia told me."

"Julia?" I jerk my head back. "How did she even know who you were or how to find you?"

"After the police carted you off, she came inside the building. Since Chinese nationals aren't allowed inside because it would put them in jeopardy with the police, I knew something had to be wrong if she was willing to take that risk."

I put my hand over my heart at the lengths that girl would go to help me.

"She told me who she was and how she knew you, then we went to a nearby restaurant and she filled me in on what happened."

"Oh, thank goodness," I say, relieved. "One of the reasons I wanted to see you was to ask you to get in contact with her. I'm hoping she reached out to Director Wu and her daughter, Victoria, for me." I force myself to slow down a bit. "Victoria works for a lawyer, and it looks like I'll be needing one if I have any chance of getting out of here soon."

"Is it really that bad in here?" He scrunches his nose.

"Other than the one-star accommodations, it's fine," I joke. "But we both know from watching TV that I need to be careful in here. I'm not gang material."

Ben's head drops and his shoulders shake. "You certainly haven't lost your sense of humor, have you?"

"I can't make any promises if I'm forced to be here much longer. That's why I need someone to contact Director Wu for me. Her daughter works for a lawyer, and I'm hoping he can get me out of here. Today."

He raises his head, looking grave. That can only mean more bad news.

"What is it?" I search his face for clues.

"Julia contacted Director Wu to let her know of your arrest, Victoria made some calls, but she couldn't get the lawyer to look at your case until tomorrow." He lowers his voice. "I'm sorry, Nicki, but you're going to have to stay here another night."

I suck in my breath. "Tomorrow?"

"It was late last night when she reached him, and that was the earliest he could get here."

A lump forms in my stomach, weighing me down. While I'm grateful for all they'd done on my behalf, I was certain I'd be released by now. That belief was the only thing keeping me from losing my mind inside this dark, dank place. If I had to stay much longer, what would become of me?

"Then I have to get out on bond. Today," I say with steely determination.

"You have that option?"

"Sort of." I squirm in my seat. "The Embassy liaison said I could get out if I could come up with bail, which is about four thousand US dollars."

"Do you have that kind of money?"

"Not anymore. I used everything I had in savings to cover Lei Ming's surgery."

"Could you ask your mom for the money then?"

"No." I keep my answer simple on purpose. I don't want to delve into my mother's issues and her bleak financial status because of it. Nor can I tell him of her inability to assist me because she's unaware of my current predicament. He'd think I was crazy. Maybe I am.

"Hmm." Ben rubs his temple. "Nicki, I would be happy to pay the bond fee myself and get you out of here right now, but—"

"You would?" My heart swells with affection at his offer. "That would be amazing. I promise once I've cleared my name so my chances with Lei Ming aren't hindered and I can finish the job I came here to do, I'll pay you back."

"I know you would, but that's not the problem." Darkness

clouds his eyes. "I only have that kind of cash in my savings, which isn't liquid. I would have to sell some stock and then have the money transferred over here. It's doable, but since it's almost the weekend, it would take a while before I could do anything for you."

My hope withers at his words. "I appreciate that you'd even consider doing something like that for me."

"Of course." He offers me a weak smile. "Is there something else we could do or someone else we could ask?"

"I don't know anyone who would have access to that kind of cash other than my boss, Heather, back in the States. Mr. Gordon is reaching out to her, but even if she agreed to cover the cost for me, I'm not sure it would get here as quickly as I'd like."

"What other choice do you have then?" His voice is laced with worry.

"Mr. Gordon suggested I could set up a fund where people here could contribute to my bail. It wouldn't matter the amount. A little can still go a long way."

"It's a good idea, and I'm sure I could round up some people from the church to give, but even then, it would take me a while."

"Right." I drop my head to my chest.

"Nicki, I know this is not an ideal situation, but you may have to be patient and let God handle the details."

I clench my hands into fists. Easy for him to say. He gets to walk out of here in a few minutes. And he's not trying to save an orphanage or adopt a little girl.

"I hear what you're saying, Ben, and I'm trying hard to lean on God right now. But it seems like the enemy has the upper hand."

"How so?"

"If I don't make bail and must stay the full thirty-seven—no, thirty-six days now—that will only leave me two weeks to get the documents in order to keep the orphanage operating. Not only that, but I won't get Lei Ming. I can't let either of those happen. And that all balances on me being found innocent."

Ben cocks his head. "You mentioned an enemy. Do you have any idea who might have orchestrated all of this?"

I ponder his question. Is he expecting a spiritual answer or the one that's been forming in my mind after my sleepless night?

"I don't have any proof, but the only person in China I'm at odds with is AD Chang."

"Interesting," Ben says, not the least bit surprised by my accusation.

"Why do you say that?"

"Because Julia said the same thing last night."

"She did?" My heart beats faster. "Did she say why?"

"Well, for one, Julia said when you spoke with her about the location to meet you at, she was at New Hope. She thinks either Chang or one of her loyal employees must have overheard the conversation and used it to tip off the police."

Any claim I made that the AD was somehow behind all of this was pure speculation, an outlet to blame someone for my misery. But hearing Julia's suspicions changes things. Could it be true?

"Secondly." He holds up two fingers, shaping them into a peace sign. "She was anxious to tell you what she discovered yesterday at the address she visited."

I gasp. "Did she find Li Na?"

"No. The house belongs to one of Chang's cousins. After talking to him for a bit, Julia thinks Li Na doesn't exist."

"What?" My voice trails off as all the puzzle pieces start to move around in my head. No one knew of Li Na at New Hope. Not only that, but Li Na's application was written in Chang's handwriting, and the address listed on it belongs to one of her relatives. And of course, the surgery funds, money that should be readily available, are also missing. Are all these financial issues related? Is Chang behind them?

Just as I'm about to get a clear picture of everything and its meaning, a tap on the door keeps the pieces from falling perfectly into place.

"That's my cue to go." Ben rises from his chair. "I'll see what I can do to get you out of here as soon as possible. I promise." He walks around the table and folds me into his arms.

"Thanks, I appreciate it." I squeeze his torso and inhale his familiar woodsy cologne. "I know you'll do everything in your power to help me."

"I will." He kisses my forehead before stepping back and lifting my chin. "And in the meantime, maybe this is the situation to show you that you can trust God. He won't forsake you."

The door opens and the same female guard snaps at Ben in Chinese. He acknowledges her with a slight nod then heads for the exit.

"I'll be back as soon as I can." He winks at me before leaving the room.

My heart constricts as I watch him go. Although I'm sad to see him leave, I'm grateful he came and offered me more than just hope. He provided me with the final piece of the puzzle.

Chang. All along, my instincts were right. Not only does she have it out for me, but she's up to no good. Knowing that, it's even more important that I get out of here as soon as possible. I need to find out exactly what mischief she's guilty of and why.

Then I have to stop her.

18

A blind cat bumping into a dead rat.
~ Chinese Proverb

As I wait for my attorney to arrive the next day, I run through the information Ben provided yesterday and all the possible scenarios of what Chang has possibly been doing at New Hope. While I have a few ideas of how she might be siphoning funds from the orphanage, I don't have anything solid. Yet.

If all goes well with my lawyer, we can clear up this entire misunderstanding, and I'll be free to gather the evidence I need to reveal her deceptions. I watch the clock and wait patiently for the guard to escort me back to the room that's quickly becoming a second home.

Two hours later, my heart pounds like a jackhammer when I step into the space assigned for our meeting. I blink rapidly to adjust my eyes to the different lighting. Once they have, I see Victoria waiting for me at the table.

"What are you doing here?" I rush toward her.

"I'm assisting your legal counsel, Mr. Jiu, as a translator." She rises and embraces me. "Are you okay? Mother and I have been so worried about you." Her thick, black hair is rolled in a tight bun, and she's dressed in more formal attire than the first time I met her.

"I'm ... managing. I'm so glad you're here." My eyes scan the surroundings. "Where's Mr. Jiu? I'm anxious to talk with him."

"He's presenting your case to the authorities now." She points to the chairs, indicating we should sit.

"I don't get to talk with him first?" I slump into the chair. This is not how it played out on TV or in the movies.

"Not yet. He's providing them with the witness details and seeing what evidence they have. He'll be in shortly to discuss everything with you."

While it's not as I imagined it going, I'm glad to know something's happening on my behalf. Plus, it gives me a chance to test my theory about the AD with Victoria. "I think I've figured out what's going on with the finances at New Hope."

"You have?" Her voice carries a thread of alarm.

"Thanks to some information from a friend, I spent all last night going through everything that seemed off, as well as formulating how Chang might be embezzling money."

"What? How?"

I cast a sideways glance at the door before saying more. "Ms. O'Connor knew something was unusual with the finances when she sent me to China in the first place. However, we just assumed it might be an oversight with your mom's age and disorganization."

She doesn't bat an eye. "I probably would have assumed the same."

"Okay, good." I nod and continue. "While we were looking for the reports that hadn't been submitted and trying to get things organized, Julia discovered three new employee files buried in old paperwork. When she went through them, they were empty."

"You're referring to Li Na's application, right? The one I found at Mother's?"

"Yes, as well as two others. Because the files didn't have signed contracts in them as they should've, Julia was worried New Hope would have to pay restitution to the employees, money the orphanage might not have since the financials were already in disarray."

"Correct. That's Chinese law."

I lick my lips. "Yes, but I remembered your mom telling me and Ms. O'Connor there hadn't been any money for new staff in quite some time, so it seemed odd that three new caretakers had been recently hired. We looked high and low for those contracts but couldn't find them. Finally, I decided we needed to take a chance and ask the employees themselves."

"What did they say when you confronted them?"

"Oddly enough, we couldn't find them. When Julia asked the other staff members about those new hires, everyone she spoke to said they didn't know anyone by those names."

Victoria sits back in her chair. "That's strange. It's a small staff. Everybody knows everyone there."

"Exactly," I say, delighted she sees things as I do. "It was as if they didn't exist. That's why I needed Li Na's application. I wanted to see if there was anything that might help us solve the problems we were facing."

"But there wasn't." The corners of her mouth dip. "We went over it repeatedly, and mother said other than Chang's handwriting, everything was in order."

"Yes, that was disappointing and seemed like a dead end, so I had to look at the one other issue that was staring me in the face."

"Which was?" Victoria asks with bated breath.

"The depleted surgery funds." Just saying the words causes me to shudder. That anyone could steal from that type of fund, knowing that sick children were in desperate need of the money, makes my empty stomach roil.

"I remember that conversation." Victoria's eyes light up. "Mother said there should have been plenty of money to cover

Lei Ming's surgery and a few more." She rubs her fingers over her mouth. "I know my mother is old and growing forgetful, but that's her life's work. If she says there's money, there's money."

"Right." I smile at Victoria's confidence in her mother. Maybe one day I'll have that with mine. "And I had access to some older reports that showed sufficient money. However, when I asked Chang for the names of the most recent surgical patients, the ones she claimed used up all the funds, she told me that wasn't my business and refused to give me the information."

"Of course she did."

"Well, I wouldn't drop the subject. When Lei Ming was readmitted to the hospital, I brought up the topic with her again. This time, however, I mentioned that I had spoken with your mom about the discrepancies." I pause. "I don't need to tell you how she reacted to that."

"I can only imagine." Victoria suppresses a laugh. "I would have given anything to see that."

"That's the night when you sent over the application. Julia and I decided we'd go to Li Na's house and see her in person. But it was late, and Julia was afraid that Li Na wouldn't talk if I went along, so she went by herself the next day."

Deep lines of worry are etched in Victoria's forehead. "And what did she find out?"

I rub my hands together. "I'll get to that, but first, you need to know that when Julia returned to New Hope after her visit to Li Na's, I wasn't there. I was on my way to church. When Julia called me, I suggested she meet me there. I gave her the address, she repeated the information, then left to join me. Someone at the orphanage, either Chang or one of her loyal employees, must have overheard our conversation and tipped off the police."

"That's how they knew the two of you would be in front of the church so they could make the arrest," Victoria says, putting the pieces together.

"Exactly. I think she was getting concerned about what Julia and I were discovering, so when an opportunity to stop our work was handed to her, she took it."

"What did Julia learn that was such a threat Chang would do something so vile and have you arrested?"

"Li Na doesn't exist." I pause and let the power of those words resonate in her mind a moment. "According to Julia, the person who lives at the address on Li Na's application is some distant cousin of Chang's. I suspect she used her relative's address on the application and created ghost employees to take their paychecks."

"That's terrible!" Horror sweeps across Victoria's face.

"That's not all. I'm willing to bet she made up patients to siphon the money from the surgery funds. Then she never submitted the reports to the CMM even though she let your mother think she was. Both would then be related as financial crimes. She's skimming or embezzling, or both."

Victoria slams her fists down on the table, causing it to tremble. "I knew there was something about her I didn't like."

"The only problem is I don't have any hard evidence." I blow out a puff of air. "There's nothing tying her to the ghost employees that I can think of, and we still haven't found the missing reports that show the discrepancy in the surgery funds."

"There has to be something or someone at New Hope who must sense the financials are a bit off. Did you talk to any of the accountants there?"

"No, I never had the chance. But now that I've been able to put all the pieces together of what I suspect Chang's been up to, it should be easier to get the proof we need. That is, if I can get out of here and get back to New Hope sometime soon."

"We can't quit looking, Nicki. That orphanage and those kids mean everything to my mother. To know her life's work had been destroyed and those kids left with nothing would devastate her."

"We will, I promise." I steady my voice. "That's why—"

Before I can finish, the door flies open and a middle-aged Chinese man in a three-piece suit strides in.

When he addresses Victoria sharply, she promptly switches back into professional mode. "Miss Mayfield, this is Mr. Jiu, your lawyer."

He bends his head slightly in acknowledgment and places his briefcase on the table. Ignoring me, he talks to Victoria in rapid Chinese.

The two converse for a few minutes before she turns back to me. "He wants you to know that he has spoken with the police and explained the situation."

As if on cue, he nods again.

"He provided them Julia's sworn testimony that you were not proselytizing," Victoria continues. "Once the detectives matched that up against what you told them when you were arrested, they agreed to drop the charges and let you go," she says.

I leap from my seat and wrap the stiff-necked attorney in my arms. "Thank you!"

"Uh-hum." Victoria clears her throat, letting me know I've crossed the lines.

My ears burn as I release Mr. Jiu from my tight embrace. "Sorry, I was just excited."

The lawyer offers a small smile then brushes his hands over his wool suit, de-wrinkling any evidence of my overzealous affection.

"That's not all, Miss Mayfield," Victoria says.

Bouncing on my toes, I look back and forth between the two of them. "What else is there?"

"They're letting you go, but they're going to void your work visa and insist you leave the country within ten days."

"Why so soon?" I stumble backward.

"To ensure you don't try to convert more people." Her eyes gloss over. "Although they agreed to release you upon hearing Julia's testimony, you were found outside a church. With a Bible."

Panic takes hold of my lungs, making it hard for me to breathe. I drop back into my seat. This can't be happening. I'm innocent!

The joy that had bubbled up within me only moments ago swiftly fizzles as my mind whirrs at the implications of the police's decision.

I can't leave China now. If I do, I won't be able to finish what I've been tasked to do. Returning home is not an option for me.

"What if I don't take the deal?" My voice cracks.

Victoria stares at me for a moment as if questioning my mental state before shifting back toward Mr. Jiu and translating what I've asked.

Instantly, the muscles in Mr. Jiu's jaw twitch, and his face turns crimson red. The longer they talk, the more vigorously he shakes his head. As his nostrils flare and the veins in his neck bulge to twice their normal size, I'm afraid I've caused him to lose face. I don't mean to disrespect him or his efforts to help me, but I can't leave the country yet. Not when Chang's wrongdoings need to be uncovered. And righted.

When Victoria finally looks back at me, her face is ashen. "Mr. Jiu says you'd be foolish not to take their offer. According to him, ninety-nine percent of those charged with a crime in this country are convicted and sent to labor camps." She leans against the table in an effort to gain composure. "That would most likely be your fate."

I pull my knees to my chest, burying my head between them. If the statistics Mr. Jiu quoted are true, then my hands are tied. I have no choice but to leave China as they demanded.

Maybe I could do what needed to be done for New Hope from afar. "Fine." I pull my head up. "I'll do it as long as it not only gets me out of jail but also keeps my records clean."

Victoria's voice quivers as she conveys my decision to my lawyer.

After a few minutes of tense back and forth, Victoria's eyes meet mine. "Yes, you get to leave here, and nothing goes on your record."

Fresh tears sting my eyes. "Okay."

"First, you need to complete this." She sets a piece of paper and a pen in front of me.

"What is it?"

"Mr. Jiu's retainer agreement saying you'll pay his fee for brokering the deal with the authorities."

A jolt of adrenaline shoots through me. I have a little bit of money, but not a lot. If I can't pay the fee for his services, then what happens?

"How—how much will that be?"

"Twenty-three hundred yuan, or roughly three hundred and fifty dollars," she says.

"I can manage that."

Relieved, I pick up the pen and read over the paperwork. Written in both English and Chinese, it's something I can do without anyone's help.

My hands trembles as I jot down all my information. When I get to the payment section, I freeze. For the money to be transferred from one bank to another and for Mr. Jiu to get paid, I need to provide both my bank account and routing numbers and his. Common procedure for any type of financial transaction.

That's when the lightbulb turns on in my head.

"I know how we can prove Chang's guilty." I drop the pen onto the table and look up at Victoria, who is staring at me, dumbfounded.

"How?" She steps closer to me.

Out of the corner of my eye, I spot Mr. Jiu's disapproving frown at my delay in signing the papers. "Can you ask him to give us a moment?"

Upon hearing my request, he lifts his chin and glares at me. His eyes bore into me for a few minutes before he peels his briefcase off the vinyl tabletop and stomps out of the room.

When the door slams shut with a loud thud, Victoria and I huddle around the table. "Please, tell me what you think we can do to catch Chang," she says.

I push the retainer form, my source of inspiration, towards her. "This." I tap the section earmarked for payment information.

"What about it?" She studies the paper. "I'm not following you."

I force my brain to slow down so I can convey my rapid-fire thoughts in a coherent way. "I know she's been taking money from the orphanage, but for the life of me, I couldn't figure out how she was doing it." My pulse skyrockets. "Thanks to this piece of paper, I think I might have a clue."

"You do?" Her eyes bulge in anticipation.

"I do, and if I'm right, it should be the thread that unravels her malicious doing." My shirt clings damply to my back. "But first I need to ask, do you still have Li Na's application on your phone? I need you to look for something on it."

She takes her phone out of her purse then searches for the document. "Yes, but what am I looking for?"

"Can you see if Chang wrote down a bank account number where Li Na's paycheck should be deposited?"

Recognition dawns in Victoria's eyes, and she draws the screen closer to her face.

"She did." She shouts, pointing to her device and the proof we need.

"Perfect. This account information should belong to the AD or someone related to her. If we can somehow trace it back to her, we'll have the evidence we need."

"And what about the surgery funds?" Victoria pulls her phone back. "How will we prove that she was stealing from those funds as well?"

"There should also be an account number and routing number to take funds from the surgical account," I say. "If it went to the hospital, she's innocent. And if it went to Chang ..."

"Then we would have all we need to have her arrested!" She looks up at me, a twinkle in her eyes.

"Exactly. We just need someone at the orphanage to track down this bank information for us and see if it belongs to the AD." I tamp down my excitement. "But it needs to be done discreetly. We don't want to tip off Chang that we're on to her. Could your mother help us with this?"

Victoria's earlier joy wanes. "I'd like to keep her out of this, if possible. She's improving but still fragile."

"I understand you want to protect her." I place my hand on top of hers and squeeze it. "I don't want to do her any harm, but she's the only one who might be able to get that information without setting off any alarms."

Wrinkles crowd her forehead. "No, you're right, and knowing my mother the way I do, she'll want to get to the bottom of this as well."

"If I could do it myself I would, but I'm afraid this is our only option."

"I'll ask her to speak with one of the accountants." Victoria shifts her weight from side to side. "Now what?"

"I'm going to sign this retainer, get my belongings back and get out of here." I pick up the pen and slide the paper toward me. "Then we're going to right this wrong."

19

Heaven's net is vast; it's cast far and wide but lets nothing through.

~ Chinese Proverb

After a long hot bath, some tasty food, and five hours of sleep, I relish my newfound freedom and the promising opportunity to put Chang behind bars. But I must act quickly. Ten days may not be enough time for me to sort out the mess at New Hope and reconnect with Lei Ming, but I'm going to do everything in my power to make it all happen.

Before I race out of my hotel room in search of the evidence I need, I spend a few moments with God in prayer. I settle onto the couch, open my journal, and pour out my gratitude to Him not only for getting me out of that precarious situation but for using it to help me discover what Chang likely is up to and how to solve this mystery as well. There's no doubt in my mind He used what was intended for harm to bring about good.

When I'm finished asking for guidance and wisdom for the days I have left in China, I check my phone messages, anxious to see if Victoria or Julia responded to my earlier texts. They did.

I open Victoria's first.

Still haven't heard back from bookkeeper at New Hope about bank information, but we are pursuing it. Will keep you updated.

Dismayed but not discouraged, I move on to Julia's reply to my request to meet so I could fill her in on my revelations about the conniving AD.

Can't leave Mother's Love right now. Can you come here?

My breath hitches at her text. Had Mingyu's behavior gotten worse? If so, Julia will blame herself. If anyone is guilty, however, it's me. The one crime I've actually committed was keeping Julia from her sister. I'm not sure an apology will be enough for the trouble I've caused them, but I can try.

When I arrive at the orphanage an hour later, my trusty sidekick is waiting for me in the lobby. The flannel button-up she's wearing looks like it's been wadded up in a drawer for days before she put it on, and her slick black hair is messier than usual. Not only that, but her normal vibrancy is replaced with a forlorn and tired look. Definitely not the Julia I'm used to seeing.

"Is everything okay with Mingyu?" I ask when we sit down on a bench next to a large set of windows.

She rubs her bloodshot eyes. "Somewhat. Her asthma is giving her problems again."

I plop down beside her on a bench next to a large set of windows. The March sun warms our backs. "You look exhausted. Are you getting any rest?"

"Not really." She yawns and her hair swishes back and forth. "All I do is watch her sleep and make sure she's breathing."

"I'm sorry. This can't be easy for you." I pat her back like my dad used to do when I wasn't feeling well.

"It's not, but she's my responsibility, so what else can I do?" She looks back at me. "It does help to see you out of jail, though."

"I'm glad to be out of there, even if I only have a little more than a week before I have to leave."

She pushes up her glasses. "I can't believe the officials want you gone so quickly. I wish my testimony with the police would have made a bigger difference."

"What?" I crane my neck back. "Julia, if it weren't for you, I'd still be in jail. You risked a lot for me. That's one of many reasons why I wanted to see you. To say thank you."

"There isn't anything I wouldn't do for you." Her shoulders sag. "But do you have enough time to finish all the work at New Hope and figure out what shady things the AD is up to?"

"Leave all that to me. I've got a plan."

"You do?" Her voice lifts with hopeful uncertainty.

"Of course, I do. I am an organizer, remember?" I wink. "Can you spare a few minutes for me to catch you up and fill you in on my next steps?"

"Yes. One of the caretakers is watching Mingyu." She swivels her body and pulls her legs up onto the bench. "I'm listening."

Delighted to see the old Julia again, I dive into all the details of my detainment. It takes me almost an hour to tell her about my visit with Ben and how the information he shared, as well as signing the retainer paperwork, paved a way to prove Chang's guilt.

"So now what?" Julia asks when I bring the story to a close.

"We're just in waiting mode until we hear back from the bookkeeper where that paycheck is deposited." I wring my hands together. "I think it's the key to figuring out all these problems."

"And what about the surgery funds?"

"We're researching that too. But until we have the proof in hand, I need to keep looking for those missing documents and uncover the patients Chang claims sucked up all the money. If they even exist."

"That's a lot to do in a short time."

"Tell me about it, but don't worry, I'll handle it." I take her hand in mine. "That's not the only reason I came to see you."

She furrows her eyebrows together. "It isn't?"

"No, I need to apologize to you." I gulp. "I took you away from your sister when she needed you most, and I'm sorry. You're so kind and helpful and would never deny me anything, but I became more dependent on you than God. It took unusual circumstances for me to understand that, but I do. I should have been relying on Him the whole time."

"I wanted to be there for you, though." Her eyes glisten.

"And you were." I squeeze her arm in reassurance. "But now I see that it caused you to juggle a lot, and I didn't recognize the heavy burden I was placing on you. For that, I'm truly sorry. Can you forgive me?"

"Of course." Julia places her hand atop mine. "I appreciate your words, but you forget, I needed the money. Plus, you know orphanages hold a special place in my heart. There isn't anything I wouldn't do for them or the kids they care for. I just have to be better at balancing things, that's all."

"And saying no." I chuckle.

"Yes." She throws her head back. "I mean no."

We laugh for a few minutes more before I rise from the bench. "All right, I'm off to New Hope to do the work I was sent here to do."

"How will you translate the papers?" She stands and jiggles out her legs.

"Didn't I tell you? I have a new friend called Google translate." My mouth curves into a sly smile. "I'll get one of the receptionists to help me, and we'll communicate that way."

"You know that will take much longer, right?" She cocks her head. "And time isn't on your side."

"No, but God is, and that's all I need."

"True, but I can think of one other person who would probably be willing to assist you."

"You can?" For the life of me, I can't imagine who she might have in mind. "Who?"

"Ben," she says with a glint in her eye. "He speaks excellent Mandarin, and from the way he smiles when he talks about you, I'm sure he'd be happy to help you. He's smitten with you."

"Sorry to disappoint you, Julia, but we're just friends." I waggle my finger at her and any ideas she may have about me and Texas guy. "Not only that but he told me a long time ago his Chinese reading and writing skills weren't up to the task."

"If you say so, but I still think you should call him." She wraps me in a warm embrace before letting me go. "You never know. He might be the very thing you need to solve your problems."

Before I can explain how friendship works between a girl and a guy like me and Ben, my phone chimes.

"I should probably get this." I dig my device out of my purse. "I've been waiting to hear from Victoria about that bank trace."

"I need to get back upstairs anyway." She walks backward toward the elevator. "Let me know what you find out, okay?"

"I will, I promise." I wave goodbye and dash out the door.

Once I'm outside, I tap the green button. "Victoria?"

"No, it's Director Wu." Her voice is all business. "I wanted to call you myself."

"Oh?" I clench my teeth. "Is everything okay? Did you hear back from the bookkeeper?"

She clears her throat. "I need you to meet me at New Hope right away."

"Sure, but can you tell me what she said first?"

"I'd prefer to wait until I see you in person. How soon can you be there?"

"I'm on my way."

The moment I step foot in the orphanage, I sprint toward Director Wu's office.

But when I open the door, I crash to a halt. The room is spotless.

There's not a single sign of books, files, or boxes to be found. And the musty odor of old papers that had lingered in the room has been replaced with a fresh-smelling aroma. I sniff the air. The slightest scent of lemon tickles my nose. Am I in the right room? I lean back and read the plaque on the wall, which confirms that I am.

I stagger inside and set my belongings down on the barren desk. The space seems much larger now without all the mess. But where is everything? What happened to all the papers Julia and I had already organized and prepped to be digitized for the O'Connor Foundation? More importantly, where is Director Wu?

"Isn't it wonderful?" the AD calls out from the doorway.

The sound of her shrill voice causes my chest to tighten. I spin around to face her. "What did you do?"

"I had a few of the workers finish up in here." She traipses into the room. "I'm really not sure why it was taking you so long."

"This room was off-limits to you."

"The door was unlocked so I thought I'd help you out." She cocks her head. "As you were detained."

I take a deep breath and clench my fists.

"Such an unfortunate thing to have happen to you," she clucks, circling the room. "But I'm glad you were able to get out. If I recall, there isn't much time left until you are supposed to submit the papers to The O'Connor Foundation, so in your absence, I had the staff finish sorting through everything. Then they organized and digitized it all. Once that was taken care of, we disposed of what was no longer needed then gave the room the deep cleaning it desperately required."

"You got rid of it? As in you threw it all away?" My stomach churns.

"What would be the point in keeping it?" She reaches inside her blazer pocket and pulls out a small flash drive. "It's all stored on here now."

I grab the silver drive dangling from her fingers. "Everything

I need to submit to the Foundation is on here, including the files from your cabinet, the new hire applications, and the missing CMM reports?"

"Miss Mayfield, I'm not sure what you're implying, but I can assure you that all the paperwork and important documents you'll need to convince the Foundation to continue funding New Hope can be found on there." She smirks. "And now that you have everything you need, you can leave. Both New Hope and China. You've got what you came for. And nothing—and no one —else."

Chills ice my spine. Does she really expect me to believe her innocent act? Every ounce of my being wants to tell her I know what she's up to, but I can't. To do so would jeopardize any chance we have of collecting the information we need to have her arrested. Otherwise, she might run.

"Oh," she says, pulling me from my thoughts. "If you had plans to see Lei Ming, don't bother. I've given the hospital clear instructions not to let you in." She pauses. "For safety reasons, of course."

"You just love this power trip you're on, don't you?" I sneer. "Sadly, it's not going to last."

"We'll see about that. From what I understand, Director Wu is not in any condition to return to New Hope anytime soon, so for the foreseeable future, I'm in charge."

"Actually, I am doing quite well," Director Wu says from the open doorway, her daughter next to her. "And though I'm not all that organized, I believe it's time I got things back in order around here." She steps inside the room with Victoria's help.

Although she's leaning heavily on a cane, her presence is formidable.

"Speaking of order, where is everything?" Director Wu scans her office. "Did you do this, Nicki?"

"No." My heart squeezes at the anguish in the director's eyes of what's become of her beloved space. "AD Chang thought she'd help me out since I was detained."

"You should sit down, *Māmā*," Victoria suggests.

"I'm fine." She dismisses her daughter with a wave of her hand. "Why don't you wait outside while I talk with Nicki and AD Chang? You can watch for our guest."

Victoria shoots me a warning glare and then heads out of the room, shutting the door behind her.

When it's just the three of us, AD Chang begins conversing with her boss in Chinese.

"English, please." Director Wu leans against her desk. "We don't want to be rude."

"Of course." A muscle in the AD's jaw flinches. "Are you certain you're ready to return to work so quickly or meet with visitors? You probably shouldn't overexert yourself."

"I'm only here to check on things and to see if you've had any troubles while I've been gone."

"Just one." The AD casts a sideways glance in my direction. "But I think I've gotten rid of it."

"That's good to hear." The director ignores AD Chang's jab at me. "With the extra staff Nicki told me you hired, your job must be much easier."

"I'm not sure who you're referring to." Chang's top lip beads with sweat.

Director Wu furrows her eyebrows. "Nicki, what was the name of the new employee you mentioned to me the other day?"

"Li Na," I say.

"Doesn't ring a bell." AD Chang's voice quivers. "Should I know something about her?"

"You filled out her application, so I would think the name should be familiar." Director Wu keeps a steady gaze.

"Hmm." AD Chang grimaces. "I do remember several years ago helping a young girl by that name complete her application, but I believe she left shortly after signing her contract."

"It must be all these medicines I'm on, or it could just be my old age causing me to mix things up." Director Wu scratches her forehead. "Perhaps she was one of the children to recently have surgery, then." She looks pointedly at Chang. "You are aware that we've had quite a few of those lately, aren't you? So much so that our funds are depleted."

"Yes, I'm not sure how it happened, though," AD Chang grumbles. "I told Miss Mayfield we'd have to ask you about it once you were better." She shakes her head. "Such a shame, really."

"That's a lie, and you know it." The frustration in my tone matches the angry heat burning my cheeks.

"You should be careful believing anything she says, Director." Chang nods her head in my direction. "I don't need to remind you that she just got out of jail."

Director Wu taps her cane against the tile floor, which echoes loudly through the empty room, reprimanding us like schoolchildren. "So, you're saying you have no idea how the surgery funds disappeared?"

"I don't, but it is worrisome. If you'd show me the most recent financial reports you submitted to the CMM, I'd be happy to search around and see if I can come up with anything."

"That's not possible, as you took over that job in August." Director Wu offers her a fake smile. "Why don't *you* show *me* the reports?"

"My friend, I'm concerned about you." AD Chang's voice softens with compassion. "If you recall, I asked you several months ago to let me help you with that task, but you insisted you were capable of doing it yourself."

I stare in astonishment at AD Chang. How does she lie so easily?

"That's not quite how I remember it." Director Wu glowers at her subordinate before sitting down in one of the chairs across from her desk.

"Are you okay, Director?" I study her face for any signs of discomfort. Although she looks a little pale, she seems to be quite alert and aware of what she's doing.

"Yes," she assures me.

"Director Wu, I don't think you should be here in your condition." AD Chang inches toward her. "And I'm slightly concerned that with your age and diminishing memory, it would be better if I take over the orphanage."

"You're right," the elderly woman affirms. "I do think it might be time for me to step down. I'm not as young as I used to be."

"I'm glad you see things my way. I'd be happy to draw up the paperwork and name myself as your replacement."

"That's kind of you, but won't be necessary," the director says.

"Why not?" AD Chang jerks her head back.

"We'll get to that in a moment." Director Wu shifts her gaze toward me. "Nicki, could you please see if my guest has arrived?"

While I have no idea who she's expecting, I dash to the door as she asks.

I find Victoria waiting in the hallway with an older woman who's clutching a large ledger against her chest.

"The Director will see you now." I wave her into the office.

"This is the New Hope bookkeeper, Gui Ping." Director Wu introduces her to me as I escort the portly woman into the office and seat her next to the director.

AD Chang smiles smugly. "Hello, Gui Ping, nice to see you again." She turns back to the director. "What is this all about?"

"Well, there were so many questions swirling about concerning New Hope's funds," the director says, "I thought I'd have her check on a few things for me."

"Like what?" Rage flits across the AD's face.

"Li Na, for one." She takes a paper from the bookkeeper's hands. "According to the records here, Li Na has been receiving a paycheck for the past few months."

"I've told you already, I don't know anyone by that name."

"Interesting, because her paychecks have been deposited into your personal bank account." She peruses the document. "As well as the paychecks of Bao Zhang and Dong Ying, neither of whom actually work here."

I tingle inside. I was right about the ghost employees and the banking information. What other evidence does the director have against her?

"A clerical error, I'm sure." The AD balks.

"Possible," Director Wu says. "But then there's the issue of these recent surgery checks to the hospital."

"Again, I don't know what you're referring to." Her expression remains locked in neutral.

The bookkeeper hands the Director a stack of checks.

"Well, it looks like someone has been writing checks to the hospital for surgeries on children who don't exist at New Hope and diverting those funds." She fans the checks out. "To a personal bank account."

"Miss Mayfield has had access to your office as of recent. Perhaps she found some blank checks and had her friend forge your signature while working here and stole the money from us for her own benefit."

"Me?" I blurt out. "I would never do something like that."

"So you say." The AD narrows her eyes. "But as I've mentioned several times already, you were arrested and thrown into jail. Why should anyone trust you?"

"I would be careful about casting stones, AD Chang." Director Wu rises from her seat. "These checks are in your handwriting. The same as Li Na's applications."

"I wouldn't be surprised if Miss Mayfield forged my signature on those to set me up."

My mouth drops open. How would that even be possible? I can't read or write Chinese.

Before I can muster a complete sentence to contradict her accusation, Director Wu continues. "You can deny everything, but I'm fully aware of your schemes to embezzle money from New Hope into your bank account. And I have the proof that could put you away in prison for a very long time." She nods in the direction of Gui Ping, who holds up a large envelope.

"This is all speculation." AD Chang skirts toward the door. "We'll just see what happens when I speak to your supervisors and tell them how your dementia and lack of oversight has run this place into the ground." She marches out of the room, slamming the door behind her.

"You aren't going to let her just go, are you?" I ask the director point-blank.

"Don't worry, dear, I have it all under control. She won't get far."

My eyes bounce between the door and Director Wu. I'm not sure she understands who she's dealing with. AD Chang is ruthless. She won't go down without a fight.

Without saying a word, I race out the door to the AD's office. Although I'm uncertain what I will do when I track her down, I can't let her get away with this. She must pay for what she's done. To me, to the director, and most of all to these children.

Arriving at her doorway, however, my fear diminishes when I see Chang handcuffed and surrounded by police officers. Maybe they were the anticipated guests. I grin. This is why Director Wu was so confident she wouldn't escape.

"You!" Chang yells at me. "This is your fault."

I catch my breath before addressing her. "No, this is on you." I take a few steps toward her. "And Director Wu has the proof that will keep you locked up for a long time."

"None of this would have happened if you hadn't shown up here." Chang thrashes about, words spewing out of her mouth like venom. "You and your obsession with getting things in order."

I ignore her snide quip. "Before they haul you off, I just want to know why you would do something like this. Those kids need that money."

"Yeah, well, so does my kid. Paying for university may not be a big deal for you Westerners, but I refuse to let my son waste his talents and future here in China. He has the opportunity for a better life, and I was willing to do anything, anything, to make sure he gets it."

"You didn't have to go about it this way, though."

"What kind of mother would I be if I saved these children's lives but not my own flesh and blood? I may not earn enough to help him, but the orphanage's donors do."

"That's not true. I know firsthand how hard it is to pay for college." The anger brewing in my heart simmers a bit. "You could have looked into financial aid or scholarships. If he's as smart and talented as you say, he would have received enough money to go to college anywhere he wanted."

"What do you know about being a parent?" She shoots me an evil eye. "Wait until you're a mother one day, then talk to me."

The officer in charge barks out a few words in Chinese and then drags AD Chang into the lobby and out the front doors.

I follow behind, and while I watch them place her in the police car, I can't help but sympathize with the woman. Seeing how AD Chang risked her own job and freedom for her kid, it's apparent there isn't much a mother won't do for her offspring. Even though she was in the wrong, I don't completely blame her. There isn't anything I wouldn't do for Lei Ming right now and she isn't even my daughter—yet.

"Did they get her?" Victoria asks when she and her mother join me in the lobby once the commotion has died down.

"Yes, she confessed." Joy that this nightmare is finally over bubbles up inside of me. "Are you going to the police station?"

"*Māmā* would like to stay while they clear out the AD's office and search for any more evidence, but I'm taking her home," Victoria's firm tone leaves no room for argument. "She's had a full day."

I glance at the director. Other than some dark circles under her eyes, she looks as if she could fight a few more rounds. "Don't worry, Director, I'll stay here while the police finish searching her office. Once they're done, I'll come to your house."

"Good, we need to discuss what's next for the orphanage as soon as possible."

Watching the director and her daughter leave, my heart skips a beat. What exactly is next for New Hope?

20

Unless there is opposing wind, a kite cannot rise.
~ Chinese Proverb

Streaks of purple, pink, and orange paint the sky when I arrive at Director Wu's house a few hours later. While I'd love to crawl into bed right now and sleep for days, I can't rest until the aftershocks of AD Chang's selfish acts have tempered. Based on what the police told me, that won't be anytime soon.

New Hope is standing on shaky ground. Now, more than ever, it's imperative Director Wu and I calculate a plan that will ensure the orphanage prevails. For both the O'Connor legacy and the well-being of the children.

"Nicki, come in." Victoria's sweet disposition warms my heart as she greets me at the door. "*Māmā* is eager to see you."

"I got here as soon as I could." I step inside the warm, cozy house. "How's she doing?"

"Tired, but she refuses to rest. Her ear has been glued to the phone since we returned home, and I'm not sure how to get her to stop working. Maybe you can persuade her to relax."

"I'll see what I can do." I place my belongings on an entry

bench just inside the doorway. "Despite her gentle spirit, she's quite formidable."

Victoria smiles. "That's because she won't stop until New Hope is restored to its proper status."

"That makes two of us."

We trek towards the back of the house to a small sitting area off the kitchen. As the director's home is not in a complete state of chaos, I assume Victoria's found ways to keep busy, as well. I hope for both their sakes it will stay tidy like this from now on. I'm all too aware of how clutter, and the chaos it creates, can drive a wedge into family relationships. I certainly don't want that for them.

"Nicki." Director Wu sits on a small plaid sofa, the only seating in the room. "I've been anxious for you to get here and tell me what the police uncovered in Chang's office." She pats the cushion next to her. "I've only been able to get bits and pieces of information on the phone."

I drop down next to her, beads of sweat forming along the back of my hairline. As I mentioned to Heather in my email updating her on the situation, this is not going to be a pleasant conversation.

"I'll make some tea and let the two of you talk," Victoria says before retreating to the kitchen.

With her daughter gone, Director Wu turns her attention back to me. "So, what did the police find?"

"They were able to confirm what we suspected about the ghost employees and her creating false patients to deposit the surgery funds into her personal accounts." I force down the bile that rises to the top of my throat as I recount the AD's actions.

"I knew she was crafty, but I had no idea she'd go to such great lengths to do this."

"That's not all." I lower my voice. "They went through her file cabinets and found the doctored CMM reports she had been presenting to you as well as the legitimate reports of the orphanage's finances."

"And?" Wu's eyebrows draw together.

"The finances are in complete disarray," I say. "New Hope is down to less than ten thousand yuan in the bank. According to Gui Ping, the orphanage needs at least triple that amount to make it through the next ten weeks until the end of the fiscal year on June first. She also said that even with the most frugal budgeting, it would still be difficult for New Hope to operate as normal."

The director turns her head and stares out the window for a few moments. When she looks back at me, there's a fierce determination in her eyes. "We can move money around to make ends meet, but I'm not sure that will be enough to carry us." She sighs. "I pray the O'Connor Foundation will renew our funding in a few weeks. Otherwise, I hate to think what might happen to New Hope." She gulps. "And to the children."

The anger which had burned within me earlier returns. "I can't believe one person could cause so much damage. Chang's self-serving antics jeopardized the lives of so many, and she didn't even care. I hope she's fully punished for what she's done."

She clicks her tongue. "Calm down, dear. She isn't entirely to blame."

"How can you say that? Who else was in the wrong here?"

"Me." Director Wu's shoulders sag. "If I had been more observant and less trusting, none of this would have happened, and we might not be in this predicament."

I freeze at the director's confession. It was bold of her to admit that to me. Unfortunately, there's a trace of truth to it and as much as I'd like to, I can't refute her. However, she's not guilty to the degree that AD Chang is.

"Well, Chang was the one stealing money, and she'll have to pay for her crimes, right? Not only with time in jail but also by returning the money she took. If she does, then New Hope won't be in such dire circumstances."

"I wish it were that simple, Nicki." The director lowers her gaze. "When I spoke to someone at the police station about getting the money back, they said AD Chang had sent it all to the Canadian university her son is attending in the fall. There's no replacing it."

A wave of nausea crests in my gut. In one fell swoop, the O'Connor's generosity has been wiped away. How would New Hope and the children survive on limited funds for the next few months? What if the Foundation decides not to renew its financial commitment now that Ms. O'Connor is gone? Or what if there is an unthinkable emergency in the immediate future? Then what?

"What if one of the children needs an operation before the O'Connor Foundation makes a decision about continuing its support?" I ask hurriedly as my mind spins with all the worst-case scenarios. "If there's no money for surgery, it might mean one of them could ..."

My voice trails off as fear wraps its spiny tendrils around my heart. Lei Ming isn't out of the woods yet, and I've emptied all my accounts to see her this far. If she had another setback that couldn't be covered, I'd be devastated. How would she get the medical help she needed? And she wasn't the only sick child there. Most of the kids at New Hope suffered from heart issues. That's the sole reason why Mr. O'Connor established the fund there in the first place.

No, there has to be a way to fix this injustice. For everyone involved.

"Nicki." The director waves her hand in front of my face.

"Sorry." I swallow to bring my heart down from my throat. "I'm just trying to think what we can do to ensure money is available in an emergency. There must be something we can do."

She pats my hand. "There are times, dear, when you can do things, and there are other times when you have to trust God to handle it, even when it doesn't seem to make sense." She pauses. "As hard as it may be to sit and wait on His provision, I think this is one of those circumstances in which we have no other choice."

No other choice? Of course, there is. My mind races with possible options, from holding a fundraiser to asking the O'Connor Foundation for an emergency grant. We just needed to get creative.

But when I glance back over at the director, her calm demeanor tells me we're not on the same wavelength. While I'm focused on results, she's anchored in relationship.

I blink and ponder what it would look like to simply trust in God's provision in such a scary predicament. In the past, I've always depended on my own resources and abilities to get me out of difficult situations rather than wait on God. Based on my recent history, however, that hadn't gotten me far.

"Director." I clear my throat. "May I ask you a personal question?"

"Certainly."

"There have been several times when we've spoken that you've mentioned God." I swallow. "Are you a Christian?"

Her eyes lock with mine. For a moment, I worry I've overstepped a boundary, but when her lips spread into a wide smile, I know I'm on safe ground.

"I am and have been for a long time." She raises her chin.

"So, you don't keep it a secret like others?"

"No, I don't. I use discretion and discernment when needed, but I'm not ashamed of my faith."

"And that's why you're not worried if an emergency should arise at the orphanage?"

The wrinkles around her eyes fan out. "Yes, because I know who Jesus is, and I believe in His promises and the plans He has. Even in the direst situations, I can rest in that truth and not be shaken."

A cold shiver lifts the hair on my arms. If I had a relationship with God like that, how would every aspect of my life—my work, my relationship with my mom, even the possibility of marriage and family—be different? While I can't fathom such a drastic change, based on Director Wu's faith, the idea appeals to me. Maybe I need to consider a new approach to my life and faith. A more Christ-centered one.

Before I can ask the director more about how to do that, Victoria pops back in with a tray of teacups and snacks. "Did you tell her, *Māmā?*" She sets the wooden tray on the coffee table in front of us.

"Not yet. We've been busy discussing other things."

"Oh, we must give her the good news." Victoria passes a cup of green tea to me.

I perch on the edge of the loveseat and take the blue and white cup and saucer from her. I'm desperate for something positive, but I'm careful not to get my hopes up too high. "I could use some good news right now."

Victoria's eyes bounce between her mother and me. "Do you want to tell her, or should I?"

"Since it was your idea, you can."

"Please don't keep me in suspense!" I blurt out.

The two ladies chuckle at my angst.

"All right, I'll tell you." She passes her mother a cup of tea. "I spoke with Mr. Jiu a short while ago."

My body heat rises at the mention of my lawyer's name. I fear their definition of good news and mine may not be the same. "Why?"

"Because in China, if someone who has been in trouble with the law helps bring another guilty person to light, the authorities are willing to overlook their prior transgressions."

I shake my head. "I'm not following you."

With nowhere else to sit, Victoria eases onto the coffee table, momentarily prolonging her explanation. "Since you unveiled Chang's schemes, I asked Mr. Jiu if there was anything that could be done on your behalf."

"But the charges against me were dropped. What else could be done?"

She grins. "They've agreed not to revoke your visa after all."

"You mean ..."

"You don't have to leave China in a few days." Victoria squeals. "You can stay as long as your work visa allows, which Mr. Jiu said is at least six more months."

"Really?" A rush of adrenaline spikes through my veins. "I—I can stay?"

"Yes."

I cast a sideways look at the Director, whose face radiates joy. Victoria is telling the truth.

"Oh, I can't believe it." I rake my fingers through my hair and let the information sink in.

"I certainly wasn't expecting this."

"Aren't you happy about the change?" Director Wu asks.

"I am." I turn back to her. "Not only can I make sure everything is running smoothly at New Hope, but I'll be able to spend more time with Lei Ming and oversee her recovery."

"You've grown quite attached to her, haven't you?" The director peers at me over her glasses.

"So much so that I want to adopt her."

The mother-daughter duo exchange solemn glances as a heavy quiet descends upon the room.

Victoria clears her throat, breaking the awkward silence. "I'll let the two of you talk in private. Just call if you need anything."

Once her daughter is gone, the Director straightens her back. "I'm not surprised to hear you say you want to adopt Lei Ming. I could see the love in your eyes for her that day in the nursery when I came looking for you."

"You did? How?"

"I've been doing this for a long time, my dear, and I know that parent-child connection when I see it. That's why I have input with the board when matching a child with a family."

"And you see that with me ... and Lei Ming?"

She winks. "I do."

A sliver of hope dangles in front of me at the director's words. If she can see that Lei Ming and I are meant to be together, then maybe she can help me convince the board to make an exception for my case. I have no doubt her words carry great influence.

"Director, I'm fully aware that the odds are not in my favor to be matched with Lei Ming."

She nods but doesn't try to contradict me.

"I—I was wondering." I gulp. "Do you know of any loopholes that could help me overcome the obstacles I'm facing, or could you speak to the board on my behalf and see if they'd make an exception in my case? It's a lot to ask, but I'm afraid otherwise my chances are slim."

With grandmotherly affection, the director takes my hands in hers. "I'm aware of the problems standing in your way. That's why I reached out to the board earlier. I wanted to let them know about all you've done for Lei Ming, as well as for New Hope, and to ask about the possibility of you adopting her despite the issues."

My heart pitter-patters against my ribcage. If the director herself was reaching out on my behalf, they certainly couldn't deny my request. Could they?

"And?" I whisper.

"I'm sorry, Nicki, but they said no." Her eyes fall to her lap.

I pull my hands from hers and rub them over my face. With only a few words, my world splinters into a tiny million pieces again. I wipe the tears trailing down my cheeks and reluctantly ask the question I need to know the answer to. "Why not?"

A heavy sigh escapes from her lips. "Because of Lei Ming's extensive medical condition and the likely need for future surgeries, they preferred she be matched with a married couple." She pauses. "They believe that two people are better able to handle the challenges of raising a child like Lei Ming. Physically, emotionally, and financially."

Sucker-punched, I gasp for air. No matter how much I'd believed Lei Ming and I were supposed to be a family, the powers-that-be had made their decision. And I had to figure out a way to live with it. There was nothing else for me to do now. I'd exhausted all my options.

"I appreciate you trying, Director." I swallow down another wave of emotions threatening to burst onto the scene. "Obviously, God placed me here to ensure New Hope's future, not Lei Ming's, and I need to accept that."

"I know you're heartbroken, and if there were anything else I could do to change the board's mind, I would." The director places her hand on my shoulder. "You know that."

"I do." I hiccup. "But you can't, so it's best if I just move on." I rise from the couch. "I'll help you get things straightened out at New Hope, then I'll head home to make sure I have everything in order for my presentation to the Foundation. Just like I was always supposed to do before I got the crazy idea I could be a mother."

"Nicki." She tilts her head. "You may not believe this, but you have been a wonderful mother to that little girl. I seriously doubt she would have survived this whole ordeal if it hadn't been for you. Don't give up hope yet. Motherhood may still be in your future."

While I don't quite have the same confidence as she does about it, I don't want to discuss the topic any longer. What's done is done, and I have to move on.

"Get some rest." I lean down and kiss the director on the cheek. "We have a lot of work ahead of us over the next few days. I'll call you tomorrow."

"You should do the same." Director Wu grabs hold of my hand before I can escape. "You've had quite the journey since you've returned to China."

I gently squeeze her hand, then release it. "The journey of a lifetime." I head for the front door.

Sitting in the backseat of the car, I attempt to formulate a plan on how New Hope can move forward since that's all I have going for me at this point. But my mind refuses to cooperate. It continues to drift back to Lei Ming.

Her infectious laugh.

Those big brown eyes that brought a smile to my face.

The warmth of her body against mine as I cradled her in my arms and read to her.

With each memory, the few pieces of my heart that hadn't shattered at the director's news slowly break until I'm certain there's nothing left of it.

Or me.

21

Red so intense it becomes purple.
~ *Chinese Proverb*

Normal visiting hours ended long ago, but I persuade the hospital staff to let me see Lei Ming for a few minutes. Once in her room, I let my eyes adjust to the darkness before tiptoeing over to her crib.

Yet when I peek into it, she's not there.

"Looking for this little one?" A familiar male voice whispers from across the room.

I spin around to see Ben's large frame crouched in a glider, Lei Ming cradled in his arms. The sight of the two of them together is more than I can handle.

"What are you doing here?" I scurry over to them.

"I've been coming here every night since you were arrested and tucking her in for you." His eyes drop down onto Lei Ming, who is draped in a thick, pink blanket. A handful of cords spider out from underneath it, as well as the bear I bought for her.

My heart melts at his words. "You did that ... for me?"

"I knew you'd want somebody looking after her since you

couldn't, so Tao made the arrangements. But even when you were out of jail, I couldn't stop myself from coming back."

I squat down next to them and brush my fingers through her soft black hair. The scent of her fruity baby shampoo wafts in the air. "Is she okay?"

He looks up at me. "They say she's doing great and should be able to go back to the Recovery Unit at New Hope in no time."

Tears pool in my eyes. Not only because Lei Ming is well on her way to a normal life, but that Ben would do something like this. I'm blessed to have him as a friend.

"That's such good news." Despite the positive report, my stomach still lurches with the knowledge this sweet child can never be mine.

Lei Ming shifts in his arms, emitting a small cry.

"Do you want to rock her for a while?" He holds her out to me.

The thought of having physical contact with her causes goosebumps to form on my arms. It seems like an eternity since I'd last held her. "Yes, that would be wonderful."

We dance around each other for a few minutes trying to carefully execute the transfer. Once she's nestled in my arms, tears spill down my cheeks. "I've missed you, little one," I whisper into her ear.

"Still planning to adopt her?"

"I'm—"

Just then, a nurse enters the room. He rushes to meet her, and the two converse for a few moments before she makes her way toward me.

"Ben?" My voice trembles.

"Sorry, Nicki, but she said we've exceeded the time limit." He stuffs his hands in his jean pockets. "We can come back first thing in the morning, though."

Reluctantly, I give in to their wishes, kissing her on both cheeks. "I'll see you again soon. Sweet dreams."

The nurse gently lifts Lei Ming's sleeping body from my

arms, making me feel empty. Both inside and out. Watching the nurse move across the room with Lei Ming, it dawns on me once more she's being taken away from me. From somewhere deep within me, the urge to have her as my own swells, even though my head reminds me that's impossible.

As if sensing my inner turmoil, Ben nudges me toward the doorway. "Let's talk outside."

Back in the hallway, I collapse into his arms. All the emotions I've been storing up for the last few hours—no, last few days and weeks—overtake me. Thankfully, he holds me and lets me release my emotions onto his sweater.

"Better?" he asks once my tears subside.

"Yes." I wipe my cheek with my sleeve. "Sorry, it's been a crazy week."

He pushes a stray curl from my forehead. "There's a nice garden next door. Why don't we go over there, and you can catch me up? Plus, the fresh air might be just what you need right now."

As we make our way down in the elevators, I begin sharing the condensed version of all the events that had unfolded since I last saw him at the detention center. I'm not sure I can handle rehashing it all in great detail again, especially the part about not being able to adopt Lei Ming, so I purposely keep it short.

"Then she confessed she needed the money for her son's college, and the police took her away." We stop in front of the entrance of the garden. I look up at the familiar Chinese gate structure looming over us. "What is this place?"

"It's the Healing Garden." Ben points to the sign hanging overhead. "The city is full of parks like this to showcase the Chinese green thumbs and for the people to enjoy, even after dark."

How strange that I haven't seen any of these before. Then again, I haven't been looking.

"Would you like to go in?" He holds out his arm to me.

"Sure." I tuck my hand through the crook of his elbow.

We wander through the garden as the moon plays hide and seek behind the clouds. The low nighttime temperatures cause the cold to settle in my bones, and I draw closer to Ben. Thankfully, he doesn't pull away.

To my surprise, Ben has extensive knowledge of the plants and trees that make up the landscape. He enlightens me on all of it as we wind down the gravel path and over a bridge.

"In Chinese culture, gardens are important. That's why there are so many around the city." He points to a small waterfall jutting out from a rock and into a pond. "And in all of them, you see the same elements: architecture, rocks, water, flowers, and trees. Each of them has some type of symbolic meaning within the garden."

"It's so serene. I can see why people would want to spend time here."

"Not only is it peaceful, but the plants in this particular garden are known for their healing capabilities."

He leads me to an area full of different greenery. Stopping at a small shrub with tiny white and yellow buds, he holds up a limb. "This one is called *Jin Yin Hua*, or what we would refer to back home as honeysuckle. It's used to treat colds and flu."

I bend down and inhale, longing for a whiff of sweet honey. "I don't smell anything."

"It will be a few more weeks before they bloom and their fragrance becomes more powerful."

I'm impressed by his ability to rattle off so much detail about the garden. "How do you know all this?"

"Well ..." His mouth lifts in a sly grin. "To be completely honest, everything I've told you tonight I learned from a pamphlet I memorized when I was visiting Lei Ming. It was the only thing to read with English translation."

"Seriously?" I swat at him.

"Hey, what else was I supposed to do to pass the time?"

"Longchen was right. You are too much." I shake my head.

"But you've got my undivided attention now, so what else did you learn?"

He takes me a short distance further to another set of plants on the other side of the pond. "Well, next month, this will bloom a bright red flower known as the *Hong Hua*, or Safflower."

I'm curious about the tiny bud and what it will do once it blooms. "What does it heal?"

"Broken hearts."

Instantly, the tears I thought had dried up once we left the hospital break free from captivity once again. I let go of Ben's arm and fall onto the closest bench, a cold, shivering mess.

"Nicki, what's wrong?" Ben rushes to my side. "Did I say something to upset you?"

"Adopting Lei Ming is not an option for me." I keep my gaze on the ground.

He gathers my shaking body into his arms. "You can't be sure, maybe the decision board will make an exception in your case, especially since you've done so much for her."

"No, that's just it." I raise my head. "After everything that happened with AD Chang, Director Wu spoke to the board without me knowing and told them all that I'd done for both New Hope and Lei Ming. Despite her influence with them, they rejected her request ... and me as Lei Ming's mother." The tears spill out faster.

Without saying a word, Ben pulls me closer to him and patiently lets me get all the emotions welling up within me—pain, grief, anger, and disbelief—out of my system. When I'm drained and have nothing left to shed, I draw back and look at him. "Sorry, I'm sure this isn't what you were expecting when you brought me out here."

"No apologies necessary." He digs a tissue out of his coat pocket and hands it to me.

"Thanks." I turn my head and blow my nose. "I was trying to be strong and hold it all together. I thought I was doing a pretty good job too, but cradling her in my arms just now did me in."

"You don't always have to be strong and independent, you know. It's okay to lean on others for help and support."

I sniffle. "That's not always easy for me." I twist the Kleenex around my finger. "But I'm grateful that you're here with me now. I don't know what I'd do if you weren't."

"Are you sure there's nothing you can do to change the board's mind?"

"The board would prefer Lei Ming be placed, matched, whatever ..." I wave my hand in the air. "With a married couple."

"But that doesn't make any sense. They allow single people to adopt. I know several who have."

"They do, but in Lei Ming's case, they want a married couple to have her because of the severity of her medical condition and the future issues it might cause. Physically, financially, and emotionally."

I wrap the tissue tighter around my pinkie and watch my skin slowly change from white to blue to purple, numbing my little finger. At least now, it matches the rest of my body.

"Nicki." Ben places his hand under my chin and turns it toward him. "I'm sorry things didn't turn out the way you wanted, but maybe it's for the best. Her medical condition could be costly, and you already said you'd drained your funds."

"I would have found a way if I'd been given a chance."

He puts his hands up in surrender. "I have no doubt about that. I know how fiercely you love that little girl." He drops his arms. "She's even done a number on me these past few nights I've been with her. Me, the guy who didn't think that would ever be possible considering my past."

"Yeah, she has a way of doing that to people. Even those with the tallest walls built up around their hearts." I recall how she even broke down Ms. O'Connor's thick barricade in just one meeting.

We fall quiet, each lost in our thoughts.

"So, what will you do now?" he asks, after what seems like a lifetime of silence.

"Finish up here and then head back home." I slowly unwrap the tissue. "There's really not much else for me to do."

"And what about Lei Ming?"

"I'd love to spend as much time with her as I possibly can, but it's probably better if I keep my distance." I exhale slowly. "It'll be easier that way. Once she's better, they'll match her with a family who can give her the forever home she deserves."

"I'm really sorry. If I could, I'd do anything in my power to make the situation better and take away your pain."

"Thanks." My mouth curves upward. "But I don't think there's much you can do ... unless you want to marry me."

The words are out of my mouth before I realize what I've said. *Did I just say that?* Fear courses down my spine at the thought that Ben might think I was serious. But when I look into his eyes, there's only tenderness in them. Not the shock or surprise I was expecting.

"Sorry, that just came out. I didn't mean—"

"Nicki, what if that's the answer?" Ben sits up straighter.

"Answer to what?" I study him intently, worried the cold may be getting to his head and messing with his brain. "What are you talking about?"

"Us. You. Me." His hands dart back and forth between us. "What if we got married? Then the board would have no reason to deny your request, right?"

"It was a joke, Ben. We're friends, remember?"

"But that's what friends do for one another, Nicki." He leans in closer to me. "If the tables were turned, wouldn't you do what you could to help me?"

"Of course, I would, but even if we were to go through with such a crazy idea—which we aren't—how would I even pay for the adoption? I'm basically broke, and I can't imagine that a teacher's salary will be enough to cover the cost." I shake my head. "Not going to work."

Ben rubs the back of his neck. "Do you remember when you

asked for me to bail you out of jail, and I said I couldn't because my money wasn't readily available?"

While I've tried to forget my time in prison, I do recall him saying something along those lines. "Vaguely. Why?"

"It's true my funds can't be easily accessed, but I have more than enough to cover the cost of adopting Lei Ming, plus whatever other amount they'd require for us to qualify."

"Wait, you're telling me you're rich?" My voice lilts higher.

"My parents are, and I happen to be the beneficiary of that wealth."

I drop my jaw, then snap it shut. My brain needs some time to process what Ben had just divulged.

After contemplating all the different aspects of why this is a terrible idea and how God could even work in such a strange way, I'm left with no other possibilities. If I truly want to make Lei Ming my daughter, I don't have any other choice but to go along with this wild scheme.

"Ben, as much as I've tried to come up with another solution, I can't think—"

He places his finger on my lips. "Okay, then. Problem solved. Now what?"

I scoot a few inches away from him. "You're serious, aren't you?"

"I am. Even though I haven't spent as much time with her as you have, that little girl means a lot to me too. Like you, I want to make sure she's properly taken care of. It would be money well spent." He crosses his arms over his chest. "Unless you have a better idea?"

"Better than a marriage of convenience to a man with money?" I chuckle. "Not right now, but maybe if I had a little more time, I could—"

"That's just it, Nicki, you don't have time. It's either do this now or possibly lose Lei Ming forever. And so could I."

While I hate to admit it, he's right. If I don't take a chance now, Lei Ming could be assigned to another family before I could even go on a single blind date back home. Then what would I do? If I believe that Lei Ming and I were meant to be together, Ben's solution may be my only option. Regardless of how crazy it sounded.

"But why would you want to do something like this?" I ask point-blank. "I mean, how does it benefit you?"

"Maybe it's my way to right a wrong from my past." His eyes bore into mine. "And to give hope to someone I care deeply about."

My breath hitches at his words. Was he still talking about Lei Ming? Or was he referring to me? Surely it was the former.

"But we'd be doing this as friends, right? No strings attached?" I ask for clarity.

"None." He flashes his palms in my direction.

My pulse races at the thought of doing something so rash, so spontaneous, so unlike me. But if these last few months have taught me anything, it's that I need to be more open and flexible in my life. Things aren't always linear, one-sided, or in perfectly arranged order. Sometimes, you have to be willing to move when opportunity knocks, because sometimes, as I was so aptly reminded when I first arrived here a few weeks ago, it only knocks once.

"If we do this, people will think we're nuts," I say, not certain that we aren't.

"I've learned not to worry about what other people think." He shrugs his shoulders. "There's only One whose opinion matters, and I truly believe this is what He wants me—us —to do."

Once more, his words pierce my heart. I hadn't even stopped long enough to consider praying about it. *But* I had prayed that God would make a way for me to adopt Lei Ming. What if this insane idea was my answer to prayer? What if God had perfectly placed Ben in my life to be the means by which I could be Lei Ming's mother?

My thoughts race back to my conversation with the director

earlier this evening. About trusting God and His ways, even when they didn't seem to make sense to our human minds. And about living a more Christ-centered life. Was this the first step in that new way of living? If so, it was up to me to take the leap of faith.

"So, you've prayed about this then?"

"Nicki, I've been praying about you since the day I got back from Texas and saw you at Longchen's. I knew then God was up to something, but I didn't know what. Now that I do, I'm willing to do what He wants." He holds out his hand to me. "Are you?"

I place my trembling hand in his. "Yes." I blurt out before I can change my mind. "Let's get married."

"Okay." He winks at me and then squeezes my hand. "But only if you ask nicely."

I scrunch up my nose. *Ask him what exactly?* It takes a minute, but I finally catch on to his request.

Assuming he wants the full drama that goes into popping *the question*, I release his hand from mine, drop to one knee, and ask, "Ben Carrington, will you marry me?"

22

Even a thousand miles apart, a couple destined for one
another are pulled together by an invisible thread.
~ Chinese Proverb

Not wanting to waste any time, Ben and I arrive at Director Wu's home just as her rooster crows.

"Nicki, what are you doing here?" Director Wu greets me dressed in a bathrobe that matches the color of her hair.

From the dazed look in her eyes, I'm not sure if she's confused or surprised—or both.

"Hello, Director," I say. "I hope this isn't a bad time."

"Not at all. Please come in." She swings the door open wider, then leads us back to the small sitting area where she and I met yesterday. Picking up her crochet work from the sofa, she drops down onto her well-worn spot.

"I wasn't expecting guests today, but they are always welcome." The director turns her gaze from me to Ben, studying him intently. "And who did you bring with you?"

"This is Ben Carrington, my ..." I flick my eyes at Ben, who resembles a giant in this small space. "He's my ... he's a friend from church." Even though I practiced saying fiancé all night, it seems too surreal to use just yet.

The director holds her hand out to him. "Any friend of Nicki's is a friend of mine."

Seemingly unmoved by my reference to him, Ben gently takes the elderly woman's hand in his. "Nicki's told me nothing but nice things about you, Director. It's a pleasure to meet you."

"Thank you." She slips her hand from Ben's and pats the cushion next to her. "So, Nicki, what brings the two of you out to see me?"

I accept her invitation and take a seat. "Ben and I have some news we'd like to share with you."

Both her eyebrows rise to her hairline.

"We've discussed, well, we decided—"

"We're getting married," Ben blurts.

The director jerks her head back. "Oh, I had no idea." Her eyes bounce between the two of us. "Nicki never mentioned she was romantically involved with anyone. I thought she was here in China solely for work."

"I was. I am." I rub my sweaty palms over my jeans.

"Nicki and I met through a mutual friend and have grown close over the last few months." Ben places his hand on my shoulder. "She introduced me to Lei Ming, and I know how much she wants to adopt her. But she also told me about the board's decision. If they insist on placing Lei Ming with a married couple, we want to be that couple. I've grown quite fond of the little girl too."

"I see." The director glances down at my ringless left finger.

I pull my hand back. "We're going to make it official right away. Tomorrow, in fact. Once we have, we were hoping you could go back to the board and convince them to change their minds."

"Money isn't an issue, either," Ben adds. "I have more than enough to cover the adoption and any future medical expenses." He reaches into his coat pocket and hands the director a sheet of paper. "These are my accounts and the balances of each. I can have the proper documentation sent over in a few days."

She takes the papers and scans them briefly. "These look fine, but that's not what concerns me."

"Is there another problem?" My pulse races. I was certain we'd jumped over the last hurdle standing in our way. What more do I have to do to give Lei Ming the home and family she deserves?

"Yes." She tilts her head. "You intended to apply as a single mother before, so how am I to explain your sudden nuptials?"

I purse my lips. Marriage of convenience probably won't go over well with the board. Or anyone, for that matter.

Ben clears his throat. "It's true Nicki and I haven't known each other long, but sometimes love hits when you least expect it."

Snapping my head around, I look up at him. Did he just say love? A shiver courses down my spine. I thought we agreed we were doing this as friends. Nothing more. Was he referring to his growing feelings for Lei Ming? Or Christian love? My heart slows down a bit at the connection between the two of them, or his profound faith, and not the inference of anything more between the two of us.

"Of course, it would have been nice for us to have a long courtship," Ben continues, "but my grandparents got married three weeks after they met and were together for sixty-two years." His eyes bore into mine. "When God perfectly places someone in your life, you can't debate Him on it. You just move when He says go."

I push down the lump in my throat and turn back toward the director. "I know it sounds crazy, but we both feel this is what we're supposed to do. For us ... and for Lei Ming."

The elderly woman winks at me. "Since we're a country known for arranged marriages, I'm sure I can make them understand the situation."

Hope expands in my chest like a balloon. "It shouldn't be an issue then?"

"I don't think so. Once you return from the States with the paperwork indicating your new marital status, I'll take it to the board and see what I can do."

"The States?" My breath hitches. "You mean, we can't get married here? Tomorrow?"

"I'm afraid not." Her lips press together in a slight grimace.

"But I have several friends, foreigners, who have gotten married in China," Ben says.

"That was possible until recently. Now it's no longer an option for non-Chinese couples. They must return to their home country to get married." She gentles her voice. "I'm sorry."

"If we have to return to the States, it means it could be a while before you're able to present our case to the board again." My chin quivers. "Who knows what could happen in that timeframe?"

"I know it's not what you want to do, but you have to trust that it will all work out as it should." The director places her hand on mine. "Perhaps if you left now to perform the ceremony, you could be back in a few weeks."

"Ben's teaching contract isn't up until July, and I need to make sure we have a solid plan for New Hope before I make my presentation to the O'Connor Foundation. I don't think we can leave before then."

"I'm sure I can find someone to take my classes for me, Nicki," Ben chimes in. "If going back to the States is what we need to do, then we should go. And you can work from there. It might even be better for you to meet with the Foundation in person."

"But I don't want to leave Lei Ming." I gulp. "If we're here, we could be part of her recovery and provide anything she might need should another medical emergency arise, which the doctors said is possible."

The director squeezes my hand. "I'll keep a close eye on her. Don't worry about that."

Although Lei Ming would be in good hands with her, I'm not certain Director Wu is in any condition to oversee her medical care. "You're going back to work?"

"I have a few more weeks of recovery, but this incident with the AD has made it clear that I should place New Hope in more capable hands and start looking for a permanent replacement. If all goes well, I will officially retire in six months, if not sooner. Until then, I will do whatever I must to take care of those precious children, including Lei Ming."

I can't imagine anyone other than Director Wu in charge of the orphanage, but it's probably for the best if she steps down. It's time for New Hope to go in a different direction. Thankfully, it won't be under Chang's lead. I just never dreamed Director Wu or Ms. O'Connor wouldn't be a part of it. Now it seems I don't have a choice.

"Feel better now?" Ben asks, pulling me from my thoughts.

"Somewhat." My leg jiggles, and I study the floor. Even though it's for the right reasons, leaving still makes me weary about the other threat. "What—what about another family?"

"I don't understand," the director says.

I lift my head. "Could the board match Lei Ming with someone else before we get back?"

"There are never any guarantees in life, Nicki. However, since one family declined to take her because of her medical condition, it's unlikely another would." The corners of her mouth dip downward. "Most people looking to adopt want children who don't have any major health issues. It takes a special couple to want a child with Lei Ming's medical history, and from the sound of it, you and Ben seem to be the right pair. It just means she'll have to stay at the orphanage a little longer, that's all."

"She's right," Ben says. "You and I may be her only chance at adoption. If we don't go home and get married, who knows how long she could be there?"

My mind whirls at their words. I was so torn about losing her to health reasons or another family I hadn't stopped to think about what would happen if she was never matched. It's sad that could be possible for any child in an orphanage, but for Lei Ming, it is heart-breaking. Given the opportunity, she would be a wonderful addition to any family.

And that's what Ben and I were. A chance for her to have a forever home.

"My head agrees with everything the two of you are saying," I whisper. "But my heart is afraid to leave her."

"Nicki." The director's voice is firm. "The unknown can be scary, but if you truly believe you, Ben, and Lei Ming are to be together, then what God has brought together, no man can destroy."

She bends down and picks up her bag of crochet yarn. Searching through the assortment of rainbow colors, she pulls out a crimson skein. "Have you heard of the Red Thread Legend?"

I cut a sideways glance at Ben to see if he's familiar with it, but his blond locks moving from side to side indicates he isn't either.

"In China, they believe an invisible red thread connects us to those we are destined to be with, regardless of time, place, or circumstance. The thread may stretch or tangle, but it will never break." The director cuts a single strand from the bunch and holds it out to me. "Whenever fear begins to wrap itself around your heart where Lei Ming is concerned, let this thread keep what God is doing at the forefront of your mind. It can be a symbolic connection between the two of you even across the globe."

I take the red yarn from her hand and rub the soft fibers between my fingers. Although it isn't a fortuitous cookie message, it's comforting to have a reminder that there's something, or should I say Someone, keeping me and Lei Ming connected. Every part of me wants to stay in China a little longer and make sure she's okay in the days to come. But if I leave now, I can ensure she's taken care of for the rest of her life.

"Thank you for this reminder, Director." I grip the yarn tightly in my palm. "It's time for me to take a leap of faith and trust that if God means for us to be together, we will be."

She grins. "I know your heart is pure and you only want what's best for Lei Ming. We all do."

Fresh tears sting my eyes. "You'll keep an eye out for her while I'm back in the States, then?"

"Of course, and if needed, I'm sure I can ask Julia or Victoria to help me." She clasps her hands together. "But don't worry about that. You just need to go and do what you can for Lei Ming and New Hope."

"I will. I promise."

"So." Ben leans down closer to me. "Should I book our flights, or do you want to?"

"Depends." I turn and meet his gaze. "Are we getting married at your place or mine?"

"You're the bride-to-be." His smile stretches from ear to ear. "You choose."

While I know my mother will be thrilled by the news that her daughter is getting married and she'll have a grandchild soon, her current situation doesn't lend itself to the wedding celebration I know she'll insist on. No, it's probably safer to go elsewhere for now.

I bite my lip. "I've never been to Texas, so let's go there. If things are truly bigger and better in the Lone Star State, as people say, why not have the ceremony there?"

"What are we waiting for then?" Ben heads for the door.

"You want us to go to the airport right this minute?" I balk.

He stops and pivots back toward me. "Is there something you need to do first?"

"Actually," I chuckle. "There is."

When Ben and I return to the hospital, a nurse is rocking Lei Ming in the glider. The tiny woman's face lights up as we cross the room, and she whispers something in Lei Ming's ear before rising to meet us. With the utmost care, she holds Lei Ming out to me, and I waste no time snuggling the little girl's frame against my chest.

"*Xièxiè*," Ben tells the nurse, who nods before dashing out of the room.

Instinctively my body starts swaying back and forth, and I can't help but smile.

"You're a natural at that, you know," Ben says.

"Really?"

"Yes, and seeing the two of you together, I know we're making the right decision."

I look down at Lei Ming and try to memorize every feature of her beautiful face. "I do too."

Sidling up next to me, he gently wraps his arm over my shoulder and kisses the crown of my head. "Save the I do for the wedding." Ben teases.

I lean back and relax in his embrace, allowing the turmoil of the past few weeks to melt away. Getting to this precious moment wasn't easy, but it was worth it.

At times I wasn't even sure I was supposed to be in China and questioned if God had made a mistake bringing me here. But as the three of us huddle together as a family, my heart swells with hope for our future.

It's as if I had been perfectly placed.

THE END

AUTHOR'S NOTE

Each book in the Hopeful Heart Series is connected to a Bible verse. *Perfectly Placed* was inspired by Acts 17:26b (NLV), *"He set the times and places where they should live."*

Where we are planted is no mistake. God sent my family to China sixteen years ago for a reason, and the purposes behind it are just now beginning to bloom through these books. It's my responsibility to share what I learned and experienced while I was there correctly and truthfully.

Having lived in China for only a short time, I don't profess to be an expert on the culture. But it's important to shine a light on issues often misconstrued in the media so that readers can gain better insights and then, with them, make proper assumptions based on knowledge rather than fear or bias.

Religion

When Westerners think of Christianity in China, they think about underground churches or government persecution. And while those things do operate or happen, foreigners can meet for worship and fellowship with other believers. However, there are specific rules a church must follow to keep its permit. The most important of these is that Chinese nationals do not attend any of the services or events held by the church. There are Chinese-sanctioned Christian churches for locals, and the material they use for study—Bibles, sermons, etc.—are strictly regulated by the government.

My family and I had a wonderful church experience while living in Nanjing. We were not prohibited from worshiping on Sunday mornings or having Bible study in our homes during the week. Despite the government's efforts to control religion, God is moving in mighty ways in China.

Chinese jail

All of us have heard stories about foreigners being arrested and imprisoned in China at one time or another. It is a serious issue and one that cannot, and should not, be taken lightly.

Often, foreigners can be detained for vague reasons and held for long periods before formal charges are made. It is a delicate matter that I carefully considered before using it as part of Nicki's story. I was even asked by one person, whose spouse had been detained in China, not to highlight it. However, I chose to write about jails because we can't ignore the truth. Visitors to another country are subject to their laws and can be arrested, even if they didn't do anything wrong. This happens more often than we realize, especially for proselytizing. I hope that I respectfully shared this topic while, at the same time, gave the reader insights they might not have otherwise had.

Heart surgeries

I touched on this briefly in my Author's Note in *Perfectly Arranged*; however, I want to bring it up again because it is a growing problem that is often overlooked.

Many children in China suffer from heart defects, but unfortunately, the cost of surgery to repair the damage is beyond the means of everyday Chinese families. As I wrote about in both books, without access to the life-saving operation, the percentage of children who have these medical conditions and die is exceptionally high. In 2003, an organization was established to prevent further tragedy for families whose children dealt with this.

Hopeful Hearts is a non-profit charity run by local Chinese and expatriate volunteers whose mission is to raise funds for life-saving heart surgeries for children of low-income families. They cooperate with local hospitals specializing in cardiac surgery for children to offset the high costs that would otherwise be impossible for most families to pay.

When I lived in China, I attended many events to raise money for Hopeful Hearts (the inspiration for the name of my series). Although I no longer have direct contact with the organization, my desire to help such a worthy cause remains strong. My goal is to donate 10% of my earnings from *Perfectly Arranged, Perfectly Placed, and Perfectly Matched* to Hopeful Hearts. I hope to fully fund at least one-life saving operation ($5,000 USD) for a child in need.

To learn more about the charity, or donate, visit the Hopeful Hearts website at http://hopefulheartsnj.org.

Just as Nicki has been perfectly placed in China for the adventures set before her, each of us is where we are for a reason. In writing, I have discovered mine. I hope you, the reader, find yours!

ABOUT THE AUTHOR

Liana George is a sought-after speaker, blogger, and author. Before pursuing a career in writing, she was a professional organizer and the former owner of By George Organizing Solutions in Houston.

Her debut novel, *Perfectly Arranged*, Book One in The Hopeful Heart Series, was released in October 2021 from Scrivenings Press. When she's not putting things in order or scribbling away, you can find her reading, traveling, or watching tennis.

ALSO BY LIANA GEORGE

Perfectly Arranged

Book One of the Hopeful Hearts series

by Liana George

Short on clients and money, professional organizer Nicki Mayfield is hanging up her label maker. That is until the eccentric socialite Katherine O'Connor offers Nicki one last job.

Working together, the pair discovers an unusual business card among Ms. O'Connor's family belongings that leads them on a journey to China. There the women embark on an adventure of faith and self-discovery as they uncover secrets, truths, and ultimately, God's perfectly arranged plans.

COMING SOON FROM LIANA GEORGE

*Coming April 4, 2023 ... **Perfectly Matched***

Book Three of the Hopeful Hearts series

by Liana George

Will beloved organizer Nicki Mayfield succeed at carving out a new career and building a most unexpected family, or will she end up in the one place she's never wanted to be–living with her mother?

Find out in the final book of the Hopeful Hearts Series, *Perfectly Matched*!

YOU MAY ALSO LIKE THESE TITLES ...

Destination: Romance

Book One of the Roadtrip Romance series

By Amy R. Anguish

It's not every day you bring a boyfriend back
as a souvenir.

Katie Wilhite is ready to settle into her new job as a librarian now that
college is through, but friends Bree and Skye want one more girls' trip,
and when Bree insists this is her bachelorette fling, Katie agrees. What
she didn't agree to was allowing fun and flighty Skye to dictate the
itinerary or for her anxiety to kick in harder than ever ... right in front
of a cute guy.

Camden Malone had no idea when he agreed to be the voice of reason on his cousin Ryan's vacation that the trip wouldn't stay in New Orleans as planned. But when Ryan plots with Skye so that the guys can tag along with the girls all week, he isn't nearly as upset as he should be. Not with Katie's fiery temper and flashing eyes intriguing him more by the minute.

Can Katie relax enough to trust Camden and a possible future, or will she continue to push him away as only a vacation fling? And can Camden move past a rocky history of his own to be able to jump into a better future? For a trip that was supposed to be all about fun, there's a lot of romance going around.

https://scrivenings.link/destinationromance

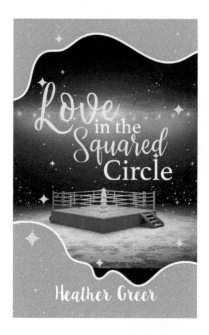

Love in the Squared Circle

By Heather Greer

Trinity Knight is not a fan of professional wrestling. But with her husband gone, it falls to her to give their son the father-son trip they daydreamed about when he was alive. After Trinity causes them to miss a meet and greet with Jay's favorite wrestler, a random act of kindness saves the trip and starts Trinity on an unexpected path.

Universal Wrestling Organization Champion Blane Sterling hears whiny children at photo ops all the time. However, overhearing a young boy comfort his mother piques his interest. Touched by their story, Blane works with the UWO Public Relations team to give Jay the experience of a lifetime.

As they learn each other's stories, Trinity and Blane are drawn to each other. But they don't just come from different states. They live in different worlds. Trinity might learn to fit into his life, but can those in her world look beyond Blane's profession to see his heart? Or will a lack of acceptance cause Trinity and Blane to lose their shot at love?

scrivenings.link/loveinthesquaredcircle

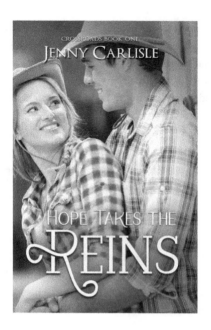

Hope Takes the Reins

By Jenny Carlisle

O.D. Billings has lived in the shadow of his brothers all his life. Even his name brings him down, so he has used only initials for years. Now, his older brother has returned home from the army, rejecting the role his family expects him to assume in their pickup truck dealership, and the younger brother is intent on risking his life on the back of a bucking bull. O.D.'s fans at the rodeo love his confident swagger during tie-down roping competitions, but every trail he heads down on his own seems to wind up going nowhere.

Hope Caldwell's world is still reeling after her mom's recent death from cancer. She thrives on keeping the family's rodeo business going. Getting back to normal seems impossible when she overhears her uncle's plans to sell out. How can she continue without the only way of life she has known for all of her nineteen years? Can she rely on the help of a big-talking cowboy? Or does he have too many problems of his own?

scrivenings.link/hopetakesthereins

Stay up-to-date on your favorite books and authors with our free e-newsletters.

ScriveningsPress.com